A Summer of Secrets on Arran

ALSO BY ELLIE HENDERSON

SCOTTISH ROMANCES
Book 1: A Summer Wedding on Arran
Book 2: A Christmas Escape to Arran
Book 3: A Summer House on Arran
Book 4: A Christmas Wish on Arran
Book 5: A Summer of Secrets on Arran

A Summer of Secrets on Arran

ELLIE HENDERSON

Choc Lit
A JOFFE BOOKS COMPANY

Choc Lit, London
A Joffe Books company
www.choc-lit.com

First published in Great Britain in 2025

© Ellie Henderson 2025

This book is a work of fiction. Names, characters, businesses, organisations, places and events are either the product of the author's imagination or are used fictitiously. Any resemblance to actual persons, living or dead, events or locales is entirely coincidental. The spelling used is British English except where fidelity to the author's rendering of accent or dialect supersedes this. The right of Ellie Henderson to be identified as author of this work has been asserted in accordance with the Copyright, Designs and Patents Act 1988.

No part of this book may be used or reproduced in any manner for the purpose of training artificial intelligence technologies or systems. In accordance with Article 4(3) of the Digital Single Market Directive 2019/790, Joffe Books expressly reserves this work from the text and data mining exception.

Cover art by Jarmila Takač

ISBN: 978-1781898819

To my Great Auntie Doris, the greatest storyteller of all

PROLOGUE

Sydney's Harbour Bridge was sparkling with lights. A huge fireworks display and party were underway, welcoming in a new year and the new millennium. Almost one million people had crowded the shores of Sydney Harbour, with hundreds more filling boats on the water, all to celebrate and usher in 2000.

Isobel had to pinch herself. She couldn't quite believe she was here in this amazing city so far from her home in Glasgow, Scotland. For the past few months she had been backpacking around Australia, with her best friend Rosie, making new friends, exploring, having the fun and adventures that a young, free and single twentysomething should have. They had seen the most beautiful beaches, with white sands and aqua waters, tried their hand at surfing on Bondi Beach, been sailing in the Whitsunday Islands, seen kangaroos, gone to open air festivals and concerts and drunk copious amounts of the local wine and beer. And they had laughed until their bellies had ached and their jaws were stiff. There had also been *plenty* of hook-ups along the way for both of them, neither keen to be tied down. Not when they were moving on the next day and the world was their oyster. They both just wanted to have fun. And they had been doing exactly that.

Until now.

As Isobel stood in the middle of what was currently the biggest celebration and party *in the world*, she realised that this was where her current adventure was going to come to a premature end. She was surrounded by thousands of delighted people, yet she also felt completely alone. Even with her best friend in the world standing next to her. She couldn't bring herself to tell Rosie what had happened. And what she had done.

'I wish Ash had stayed on with us a bit longer. What a thing to miss!' said Rosie, a huge grin stretched across her face. 'This is *immense*.'

Ash — Ashley — was their good friend from home who had jetted in to meet them a few weeks ago and was now travelling up the Gold Coast towards Brisbane and a scholarship in architecture at the university there. It was a once in a lifetime opportunity and Isobel felt a pang of envy at having that freedom to live your life exactly the way you always wanted to and do exactly what you pleased. The three of them all had a great time partying, sightseeing and hanging out together, not knowing when they would next be reunited. It might even be years before Ash returned to Scotland, if it all.

'Isn't this ace?' said Rosie in her ear now. Her breath was warm and smelt of peach cider. 'I mean, where would you rather be, Isobel? Here or dodging the pissing cold rain in George Square back home.'

Isobel forced a smile. 'I know,' she said, trying to muster up as much enthusiasm as she could. 'That's a tough one.' She forced a laugh. 'This is incredible.' But the truth was that right now she would have done *anything* to be in George Square. Even if it was cold, dark and wet. At least it was familiar, and she would feel less overwhelmed. She was desperately homesick and had spent the past few days actually being physically sick. She'd realised, in utter horror, what was going on.

She didn't quite know how she was going to break the news to Rosie, but Isobel was going to have to cut her trip short. Earlier that day she had taken a pregnancy test. It was positive. Her partying days were over. It was now time for Isobel to go home.

CHAPTER ONE

Twenty-five years later

Rosie sat on a stool at the breakfast bar listening to the sound of the rain battering against the old windows. It was pelting down with such force she was slightly worried the bullets of water might crack the glass. She pulled her cardigan tighter around her shoulders. It wasn't exactly the spring weather that anyone had hoped for. So much for the promise of pink blossom, bright, yellow daffodils and some warmth from April sunshine. Instead, the weather over the Easter break had been relentless with driving rain and a howling, Baltic wind. That was one of the disadvantages of living in Scotland — especially on an island off the west coast of Scotland — where the combination of driving rain and icy wind could cut right through you and freeze you to your core.

Coisty, Rosie's chocolate brown cockapoo, was curled up in his basket by the fire snoring. He had been affronted when she had insisted that he needed to go out earlier and had refused to budge, instead sitting down on the doorstep. She had to haul him down to the beach with the lure of treats every few steps. Then as soon as they'd got back, and she'd dried him off, he had curled himself up in a ball in his basket and immediately gone back to sleep. The rain had made his hair curlier than usual, and he looked like a perfect brown circle. She did sometimes wonder if he should have been a cat. Sighing, she took a sip of tea and opened up the travel brochure sitting in front of her.

Normally, booking their summer trip was a family tradition she and her husband would do during the Christmas holidays as it gave them motivation and focus to get through the bleak winter months. For the past few years, she and Dermot had been to Portugal and Majorca several times leaving as soon as the school term finished. Last year she even convinced him to go on holiday twice during the summer with a couple of weeks in Portugal in July and then a long weekend to Dubrovnik last August just before the schools started back. Even though they had been empty nesters for a few years — their son Ben was now twenty-four — they were still constrained by term times due to Rosie's job as a teacher. It was an issue that Dermot couldn't seem to stop grumbling about.

She glanced at a picture of Ben, on the kitchen windowsill, realising how much she missed the days when he used to join them for holidays. The photo had been taken when he was twelve and they had gone to Disney World in Florida. Ben had his arm around Mickey Mouse and was grinning at the camera. What a contrast to the selfie he had texted earlier of himself and his current girlfriend, Mabel, on a Thai beach with bright blue skies and sea in the background. *Oh, to be young again*, thought Rosie. His energy always seemed to fill the house and there was laughter and chat and *lots* of shoes in the hallway — especially when his friends came round. She used to curse falling over the many pairs of huge trainers that were always scattered around the front door. Now, she longed for the clutter to still be there. The hallway may be tidy, but it was quiet and empty.

Anyway, she had to keep reminding herself, this wasn't the house that Ben had grown up in. Although he had spent a couple of summers in the cottage during his student days, when he had worked at the outdoor centre round in Lamlash, they had moved from their home in Edinburgh two years after Ben went off to university. Rosie's parents had both died and had left their home on Arran to her. Instead of selling it, like Dermot had suggested, Rosie wanted a complete change of lifestyle. Dermot had agreed to it on the understanding that they would buy a flat in Edinburgh which he would stay in during the week for work and he would come over to Arran at the weekends.

But things hadn't quite turned out the way she had expected. Dermot seemed to be increasingly distracted with work and got so frustrated with cancelled and delayed ferries that he began staying in Edinburgh at the weekends, claiming it was easier and less stressful for him. The cottage now felt too big and empty. But if Rosie was honest, she did quite like the sense of calm that living on her own had brought to her life. Especially as Dermot, a man of limited words anyway, had become a bloke of even fewer words the past couple of months. When he was there it was as though a dark rain cloud had hung over the cottage, which only lifted when he left.

Rosie frowned as she tried to remember the last time he had shown her any affection. When had he hugged her? Or even *looked* at her properly? He had been completely distracted since Christmas, which he had claimed was due to a work deadline. Dermot worked as an accountant and was seemingly always up against deadlines no matter the time of year.

When he was last home — for the long Easter weekend — he had been particularly on edge, his mind clearly elsewhere. Rosie had asked him if he was okay, but he'd snapped that he was fine and busy with work. She was used to his work taking priority but, if she was honest with herself, she was starting to feel a bit fed up. Tears pricked behind her eyes now, as she thought about how this year would be their twenty-fifth anniversary and they had talked about going away to celebrate it with a special trip, as they did most years. Rosie pondered on this as she realised that it was perhaps *her* that had suggested marking the occasion rather than Dermot. Now, as she flicked through the catalogue with pictures of trips to Sweden — she had always wanted to visit and walk the Osterlen Way — she thought that a holiday was exactly what they needed. A trip away, just the two of them walking and chatting, would give them a chance to reconnect and discover each other again. It would be just the tonic they both needed. The past few years seemed to have been dominated with one drama after another as they negotiated the adjustment of Ben leaving home and then her beloved parents passing away within a year of each other. Then moving over here and starting a new job. Rosie had felt discombobulated for a while now and had been so glad she at least had work to focus on. She taught English at the local secondary school and loved working with young people. Most teachers couldn't wait for the holidays to start but she was always a bit sad that she wouldn't get to see the pupils for weeks at a time.

The summer term started again in two days' time, and she knew that if she got this trip booked, then it would be something to look forward to at the end of June. Especially as the weather would be warm. Suddenly, the thought of walking along the coast of the Baltic Sea, visiting picturesque fishing villages and white, sandy beaches, was very appealing. She would speak to Dermot and then get it all arranged — as she usually did. Travel agent was one of her many other skills in addition to family PA, dog walker (not that she minded that bit), washing and cooking fairy and general dogsbody. Although her duties had lessened lately, with Ben away and Dermot's increasingly erratic visits. If she could get this trip organised for them then everything would all be okay. She took a sip of tea, glad she had it resolved in her mind and now had a plan.

Just then, she heard a car on the gravel driveway. Maybe it was Laura, the postie? Then she heard a car door slam and the front door opening, and she looked at Coisty, still curled up in his bed, his head lifted in surprise. The dog opened his eyes and wagged his tail half-heartedly. The sound of keys being thrown in the dish by the door confirmed that it was Dermot who had arrived. Rosie frowned. How strange. He wasn't due home until the weekend, and he *never* worked from home unlike many of his colleagues who seemed to relish the chance to avoid the office as much as they could. Why hadn't he let her know he was coming? Maybe he'd decided to surprise her. She felt a rare glimmer of hope swirl in her stomach.

CHAPTER TWO

Dermot walked into the kitchen, his face pale and drawn.

'Are you okay?' she asked, sliding from the stool and going over to him. She tried to hug him, but he stood rigid in her arms. Rosie stepped back. 'What are you doing here? You didn't say you were coming home.' She wondered when they had last spoken — was it yesterday or the day before? She couldn't remember. It was so easy to lose track of time.

Dermot set down his satchel on the floor, shrugged off his raincoat and then loosened his tie at the collar. She didn't like the way his eyes avoided hers and she clenched her hands together. *Eggshells.* The feeling of walking on eggshells had come back into the cottage along with Dermot.

'You might want to sit down again,' he said, an edge to his voice.

She felt a chill of horror curl down her spine. 'What's wrong? Is it Ben?'

His gaze softened slightly. 'Er no, Ben is fine.'

Rosie sat down on the stool in relief, though she was still clenching her hands. 'Phew. What is it then?'

He cleared his throat yet still didn't speak.

'Dermot?' she said, pleadingly. She watched, worry mounting, as he stood staring at her. 'Tell me what's wrong, Dermot.'

He shook his head. 'Look, I'm sorry, Rosie. I really am. But there is no easy way to say this.'

'What is it?' said Rosie quickly. Was he going to tell her he was dying?

There was a moment of silence when neither of them spoke. Rosie realised she was holding her breath. A huge wave of panic rose up inside her and her stomach clenched in a knot.

He gestured around the kitchen, then clasped his hands in front of him. 'I am really sorry, Rosie. But I'm leaving you.'

Just like that, Rosie's world tilted on its axis. More than two decades of her life flashed before her eyes. A shared life, packed with family, love, laughter, loss and heartache. And now, it would seem, heartbreak. Almost twenty-five years of marriage. And that was it. Just like that. *How had this happened?* Not knowing what to do, and as though she was having an out of body experience, she picked up her mug of tea, desperate to do something normal and perfunctory. But the cup slipped out of her hand, and she watched as it fell — almost as though in slow motion — and crashed loudly onto the flagstone tile floor. Her mouth formed an 'o' shape but no sound escaped her lips. Coisty yelped in fright and shot out of his bed. He slinked over and sat firmly down on Rosie's feet, staring suspiciously at Dermot.

Dermot bent down to pick up the shards of the mug that had always been her favourite. Ben had painted it for her when he was at primary school and at the time his favourite colour was orange. Back then he had loved everything orange; carrots, lions, satsumas, giraffes, orange Smarties, pumpkins. He'd covered the mug entirely in orange paint and presented it to Rosie one Mother's Day. He had been so proud of it and excited to give it to her. She choked back a sob at the memory. And now the gift from her darling boy was smashed in smithereens all over the kitchen floor. Rosie couldn't help but think how symbolic it was of her life. Dermot may as well have clubbed her world with a sledgehammer.

She looked at him in disbelief as he mopped the tea up with kitchen roll, then went to the cupboard under the sink and got out a dustpan and brush. Rosie couldn't believe he was more focused on tidying up than he was on *her* — the woman he had spent almost half his life with. *His wife*. It was as though he was emotionally disconnected from what he'd just said. Did he actually realise what he had told her? She wanted to scream and yell at him but the words were stuck and she was frozen to the spot.

Meanwhile, he kneeled down and spent what seemed like *forever* carefully sweeping up the debris. Standing up, he tipped the contents of the dustpan into the bin. Finally, he looked at her. There was sorrow, or actually maybe it was pity, in his eyes. 'I'm sorry. I really am. But it's for the best. I will pack some stuff to take until we can chat properly . . . about next steps.'

'Next steps,' she managed to stutter as she felt her cheeks colouring and a pool of incandescent rage start to form at the pit of her stomach. 'What do you mean, *next steps?*'

'I think we need to be grown up about this and admit it's not been working for a while. We've been living separate lives for ages now and I know you're not happy,' he said, as though he had rehearsed his lines and he had suddenly remembered them and better share them before he forgot what to say again. He spoke quickly. 'And I'm not happy either and this seems like the most sensible way forward.' His cheeks were flushed, a tell-tale sign that Dermot wasn't telling her the truth.

She had been married to him long enough to know when he was hiding something and could now feel fury bubbling away inside. 'Just like that? You've completely upended my life after all these years and that's all you're going to say? That you're unhappy and *apparently* I am too?' Rosie didn't think she had been unhappy. She had always been fairly content with her lot. Clearly her husband didn't agree. 'Don't you think you owe me an explanation? And the actual truth?'

He looked shamefaced and couldn't quite meet her eye. But he remained silent.

Rosie tipped her head to one side and eyed him suspiciously. 'You haven't told me why,' she said very slowly.

'What do you mean?'

'You haven't told me why you are you leaving me. Why now? Why have you decided to tell me at *this very minute* that our marriage is over? Especially as we've *apparently* been unhappy for some time.'

Dermot still couldn't meet her eye and his gaze flitted around the room on everything except her. Rosie didn't realise the wall behind her was so fascinating. She cast her eye around for a heavy pot to lamp him with. Typically, the kitchen was clutter free as she had spent the morning cleaning it within an inch of its life. Life in the fast lane, eh?

He took a breath. 'Well, the thing is, Rosie. The thing is I've met someone else.'

Coisty whimpered and Rosie half-wished he had an aggressive streak, and he would sink his teeth into Dermot when she gave him the nod. But, instead, she reached down and picked up one of Coisty's toys — a cerise, squeaky pig — and she promptly lobbed it at Dermot's head.

CHAPTER THREE

Bella stared at the open pages of the notebook in disbelief. She read the sentences over and over again and her heart skipped a beat. Then she slammed the book shut, wishing she hadn't set eyes on it. This was her mother's private journal with her innermost thoughts and feelings. She had no right to know any of this and she had never ever been the type of person who thought it was okay to pry and read someone else's private thoughts — no matter how compelling and shocking it was. Guilt and shame washed over her. Then, a small voice reminded her that she *did* have rights and it was okay to look. She was *entitled* to know. For the last few years in particular, she had tried to get more information from her mum, but Isobel would never be drawn and would very quickly change the topic of conversation. If her mother hadn't wanted her to see her diary then she should have taken more care of it and either got rid of it or hidden it better. Reading the diary was Bella's last resort to find out the truth. Bella's gran, also known as Granny Margaret, had recently downsized from her family home to a small retirement flat and she had insisted that it was time for Isobel to reclaim her stuff. Isobel had muttered about not having any space and had grudgingly taken the box which was part of a larger collection of items from her youth. She had shoved it into the hall cupboard of their tenement flat, under a pile of camping gear, and, seemingly, must have forgotten about it. Bella had only come across her mum's stuff as she hauled out the tent in preparation for a camping trip she was going on at the weekend.

She heard the front door open and her mum calling out. 'Hiya, Bella. Just me.'

Bella panicked. *How could that be the time already?* She looked at her watch. Somehow, she had managed to lose a couple of hours thanks to an unexpected trip down her mum's memory lane. 'Hi, Mum,' she said, hearing the door bang shut, knowing her mum would have used her foot to slam it behind her as she balanced shopping bags. Bella quickly stuffed the book back into its box and shoved it in a corner, throwing a hoodie over it in case her mum spotted it.

'Hi, love,' said her mum, Isobel, popping her head round the door of Bella's bedroom. 'How was your day?'

'Um, it was okay, thanks,' she said vaguely, trying her best to look relaxed as she sprawled herself across the floor. 'Not much was happening, so I got away earlier.' Bella was still trying to get her head round things and, until she did, she would have to act as normally as possible.

Her mum walked into her room and frowned. 'They're not giving you many shifts, are they, love? Maybe you should look for something else?'

Bella sat up and scowled. She wasn't quite sure what else she could do. After leaving college last year — where she studied beauty and complementary therapies — she had managed to get a part-time role at a local beauty salon. But she had also signed up to a temping agency for bar staff to earn some extra cash.

'Everywhere is the same. Everyone else is either working on a short-term contract or on these zero hours contracts, Mum,' she said quickly. She knew she was being snappy but she was very frustrated that her work was so erratic. Since joining the beauty salon, the owner had already let one of the other therapists go as their footfall was down. People just didn't have the money anymore to spend on facials and massages and getting their nails done. Luxuries. The temping agency she had joined had given her jobs in Glasgow's city centre hotels, concerts at the OVO Hydro and football matches at Hampden Park Stadium. But demand was high for the shifts and Bella had hoped that by now she would have more security and a better sense of where she was going and what she would do next. Instead, she felt like she was treading water and nothing had changed. She was saving as much as she could in the hope that she could go travelling later in the year. She and her mum and gran had been planning to visit their friend, Olivia, in California in the autumn but that had been put on hold as her mum was worried about the cost. Everything just felt a bit rubbish lately, especially as Bella was now at the stage of her life where she couldn't wait to get out of Glasgow and explore the world and meet different people. After all, these were *supposed* to be the best years of her life. The world was *meant* to be her oyster. It was a shame it didn't feel like it.

'Okay, love, you know best,' said her mum, rolling her eyes. 'Och, Bella, this room is a total midden.' She glanced around. 'You could really do with picking some of your stuff up off the floor.'

'How was your day?' Bella asked, swiftly changing the conversation and making sure she kept her eyes trained on her mum's face. The last thing she needed was for her mum to bend down and start gathering laundry, which she had a habit of doing when she was stressed.

'It was fine. Just the usual, you know.'

Isobel worked for a children's charity and didn't always like to talk about work. But today wasn't one of those days. Instead, she seemed keen to offload. 'I'll just grab a cuppa and tell you about it. Do you fancy one?'

'Sure,' said Bella, knowing she needed to be kind and listen. She scooped her dark hair into a ponytail and followed her mum into the small yet immaculate kitchen. She perched on a chair at the table as her mum bustled around making the tea.

'There you go,' said Isobel, placing a mug of milky tea in front of Bella.

'Thanks, Mum.'

Isobel reached into her handbag. 'Fancy a bit?' she asked, snapping off a square of dark chocolate. 'It's packed full of antioxidants, don't you know?'

Bella crinkled her nose. 'You're okay, thanks Mum. That stuff is bogging. It's like chomping on charcoal. I'll pass.'

As Isobel chewed the bitter chocolate, she screwed up her face. 'Aye, I'm with you. This won't do. I mean, I know the darker stuff is meant to be better for you especially at *my* stage in life. And you're only meant to eat one square — and no wonder. But you're right. It's actually giving me the boke. It's time to get the emergency stash out.' She spat out the rest of the chocolate into a piece of kitchen roll and put it in the bin. 'Right, don't look, Bella. Cover your eyes.'

Bella knew exactly where all her mum's hiding places were, including her bottle of emergency gin which was behind the baked beans. She pretended not to watch as Isobel reached into the box of bran cereal that neither of them ate but Isobel bought as she felt she should tick that 'eat enough fibre' box. She pulled out a huge bar of milk chocolate covered in purple wrapping. 'Here, this is more like it. This is what we need,' she said triumphantly, holding it up like a trophy. She plonked it on the table next to Bella who reached over, ripped it open and broke off a slab. 'Tough day, Mum?'

'Aye,' she said. 'You could say that. We lost out on another funding bid *and* there's talk of redundancies.'

Bella grimaced. 'But there's always talk of that, Mum. I'm sure it will be okay.'

Isobel shrugged and gave a small sigh. 'I hope so.' She popped a piece of chocolate in her mouth. 'It's all a bit doom and gloom just now.'

Bella knew exactly what she meant. 'But at least you have your trip to see Rosie to look forward to,' she said.

Isobel nodded. 'True. Yes, that will be a nice change of scene. I'm looking forward to seeing her. Just two sleeps to go and we will be living the island life together.'

Isobel and Rosie were friends from a long time ago, having met at a youth festival in Glasgow, and Rosie had always felt like part of the family. 'How is she?' asked Bella.

Isobel sighed. 'She says she is okay, but Rosie has never been one for complaining and she doesn't ever say too much on the phone. She tends to only open up after a while, so I will feel better once I can actually see her for myself and spend a bit of time with her. I can't believe it was almost a year ago we were last on Arran with your gran at the Highland Games. Time flies, eh?'

'I know. Feels like just a few months ago. Not a whole year. By the way, are you remembering I'm away camping at the weekend?'

CHAPTER FOUR

'I was in the hall cupboard before you came in. Sorting some stuff out,' said Bella, watching her mum's face for a reaction or realisation about what was stored beneath the camping equipment. But there was nothing.

'Did you find the gear? It should all be there,' said Isobel.

'Yes,' replied Bella. Her mum had clearly forgotten that her box of stuff was also there. Her forgetfulness seemed to be a constant theme these days. Bella shuddered. She did *not* want to get old. Not that her mum was that old. But she was now fifty-one and that was old enough. To be fair, though, with her chin-length, wavy, dark hair and petite figure she looked way younger. At least a decade younger. Bella just hoped she had inherited her mum's youthful genes. Although she kept telling Bella that once you were past forty everything seemed to go downhill. Though, thinking about her gran, who was now well into her seventies, she seemed to be doing okay even as a *senior* lady. She was even talking about getting a tattoo.

'What do you want for tea tonight?' asked Isobel, looking at the clock.

'I don't need anything, Mum. I'm out meeting the girls. Remember I told you?'

Her mum stood up and dumped her mug in the kitchen sink and looked out the window for a moment. 'Yes, sorry. Brain fog. Again. I guess I'll make something later after I've been to Zumba,' she said.

Bella's phone rang. She could see her gran's number come up on the caller ID. 'Hi, Gran, how are you?'

'Hello, duckie. I'm fine although I can't get hold of your mother. She must have switched off her phone again. Honestly, what's the point of having a mobile if you don't answer it? Sometimes I think she does it on purpose to avoid me.'

Bella chuckled and put her on speaker phone. 'She's right here. And remember Gran that you are on the speaker phone, so Mum can hear *everything* that you say. *Absolutely everything.*'

Isobel smiled at Bella and rolled her eyes. 'Hi, Mum. How are you? What's up?'

'Och, I've been trying to track you down as I need to check something with you. I just wondered if you would mind popping round later. I've just got some papers for you to sign.'

Isobel sighed. 'Yes, of course. I was going to go to my keep fit class though . . .'

'That's fine. Do your class and then come over. You'll be in a better mood after that. You're sounding on edge.'

Bella winced as she watched her mum bristle at that comment.

'But don't worry, I'll even make you some dinner if you want.'

'That's a deal,' said Isobel, seemingly placated by the offer of a meal. 'Bella's out tonight anyway. I'll be over after seven and be as happy as Larry as I'll have more endorphins than I'll know what to do with . . .'

'Righty-ho. See you then. Bye. Bye Bella. Come and see me soon.'

'I will, Gran. Don't you worry. I haven't forgotten I'm your favourite gran'daughter . . .'

Margaret chuckled. 'You're my *only* gran'daughter. See you later alligator.'

'Bye,' chorused Bella and Isobel.

Bella ended the call and then looked at her mum who had turned to stare out the window. Bella wondered what she was looking at and went to stand beside her. All she could see were a few cars driving past on the street below and the woman in the flat opposite standing on her phone frowning. 'Mum, are you okay?'

'Yes, just thinking that I can't be bothered with the exercise class but I should really go as it will make me feel better.' She reached over and hugged Bella.

'Mum... you know how I'm thinking of going travelling?'

Isobel looked at her. 'Uh-huh.'

Bella looked at her mum's face intently as she spoke. 'What do you think I should do? I was wondering about changing my plans to go to South-East Asia and just head straight to Australia and New Zealand. Lily's just back from there and she has been raving about it.' Lily was one of her friends from college and she was already talking about going back.

Did she detect a glimmer of *something* pass over her mum's face?

'Well, they're both big countries. I'm sure you will have a great time.'

'But how did you and Rosie decide where you were going to go when you went off travelling?'

Isobel turned to look out the window again. 'Gosh, it was such a long time ago. Almost a lifetime...' Her voice trailed away. 'We had always wanted to go to Australia and had been saving for years. Then when we started looking at flights the options were to stop off in Bangkok or Singapore. We chose Bangkok which was amazing. Then we flew to Brisbane and down the Gold Coast and onto Sydney.'

'Sounds amazing, Mum. You'll have some top tips then?'

She nodded. 'I guess so. Though it was a long time ago now. It will have changed a lot.'

Bella thought her mum looked a bit wistful. 'Do you wish you had travelled more?'

Isobel frowned. 'Not really.'

'Didn't you plan to go for longer? You don't really say much about it.'

Isobel's face flushed and she fanned her face. 'I suppose it was a long time ago, love. But I think I was quite open to it all and went with the flow. Why, what makes you ask?'

'I just wondered,' said Bella. 'I suppose I just wondered what made you want to come home. Weren't you and Rosie and Ash having the time of your lives?'

'Yes, we were having an absolute ball. But Ash wasn't with us for that long before heading to Brisbane and Rosie was keen to explore more. I missed home and your gran,' she said half-jokingly.

Bella really loved her mum but couldn't imagine missing her so much that she would curtail her travel plans. And leave a hot country where so much fun stuff was happening to come back to Scotland. But then that was her. She had to keep reminding herself everyone had different perspectives in life.

'Seriously, I had seen enough and my life had changed a bit in the time I was away from home. I realised that I didn't need to go abroad to find what I was searching for. I had everything I needed.' Isobel looked at her watch. 'I'll need to keep an eye on the time for my class. Um, Rosie stayed on. Maybe you should chat to her?' Isobel frowned. 'Mind you, maybe now she wishes she had come home with me and then she wouldn't have met that big eejit Dermot after I left her in Australia.'

Bella knew that the window of conversation was starting to close by the way her mum was now frantically fanning her face. 'I better go and get ready and wash my face to cool it down. Feels like you could fry eggs on it.' She kissed Bella on the top of her head as she walked past. 'Enjoy your night with the girls.'

Bella stood for a moment, silent with her thoughts. Why couldn't her mum just open up and tell her the truth about things? She had always told Bella that honesty was the best policy, yet she knew her mum was lying to her. She was starting to think her mum was quite the hypocrite. Even though Bella would be turning twenty-five this summer, her mum seemed to insist on always treating her like a child. Especially as she had written most of what happened down in that travel journal. It hadn't taken Bella long to piece things together. Even though she had been completely blindsided by it. She still couldn't believe it. What she couldn't understand was why her mum insisted on it all being such a huge secret? And it made her wonder what other secrets her mum had.

CHAPTER FIVE

The warm sunshine on Rosie's face was so very welcome and felt like a gentle and loving caress on her cheeks. She sighed as she sat down on the wooden bench in the cottage garden and admired the sea view before her. The garden was bursting with colourful blooms which Rosie had uncovered under the tangle of weeds that had taken over the flower beds.

When they had moved to Creel Cottage permanently two years ago, she had been nervous about what she would find. She hadn't visited the cottage since her parents had passed away the year before that and, although she had someone popping in regularly to check on it, she couldn't help but feel guilty that she had neglected the little house which had belonged to her parents. Dermot always preferred to holiday abroad and if they did spend any time on Arran, he always went reluctantly and moaned that the village, Kildonan, which was on the southern tip of the island, was miles away from anywhere. Which was a slight exaggeration but the fact it was quiet had always been part of its appeal to Rosie. She loved the minute she got on the ferry and stood on the deck waiting to get closer to the island. It didn't matter whether it was sunny, raining or misty; as soon as she could spot the rugged hills beyond the pier at Brodick, she felt like she was coming home. It was comforting to know that her parents had spent their happy retirement years in this house. It had been a sanctuary over the years, and she was so grateful she could now call it home. *Especially* after what had happened with Dermot. Now that she thought about it, he never had been interested in making a life here on the island. He had always been a city boy.

Stretching her feet out in front of her, Rosie shook off any thoughts of Dermot. She *knew* she no longer needed to think about him. She could do what she wanted now she was a free agent. But she had been a wife and a mother for such a long time that it would take her some time to get used to the fact that she wasn't needed — or wanted — anymore. She was on her own. Just at that moment, Coisty nudged his wet nose into her hand to remind her that wasn't entirely true and that, also, if she was having a coffee then he needed his morning treat. She was so glad she had him. He had been such a loyal and faithful friend to her these past few months.

She had to keep reminding herself that it was still early days and only three months since Dermot had announced he was leaving her. Rosie had been longing to stay put and hide out in the cottage since then. But she couldn't let her pupils down, especially those who had their final exams coming up. She had managed to dig very deep indeed and hold her head high and had just about managed to get through the summer term without crumbling. A couple of her close friends had helped her get through, especially her oldest friends, Isobel and Ash. But so many others, particularly those in the city that she had lost touch with, since the move anyway, had seemed to disappear off the radar or side with Dermot. She could feel her blood pressure rising as she thought about their encounter the other day when he had called and told her that an estate agent would be in touch about a valuation for Creel Cottage. It was just as well he'd been on the phone, rather than face-to-face, otherwise she would have gladly throttled him with his tie.

He was now shacked up with his younger lover in her city centre apartment and was keen to *get things moving* as they wanted to buy a house. Bully for them. He reminded her that he had been *patient* and hadn't wanted to rush her but it was now time to think about the future and make a plan to sell and divide their assets, including the cottage and the flat, then split the proceeds so they could both *move on* with their lives. He clearly didn't get the irony in that he already had *moved on*. It wasn't as if Rosie had any ties to the Edinburgh flat. As far as she was concerned, he could keep it. But who did he think he was to announce that he thought they should sell Creel Cottage? What right did he have? Especially when it wasn't somewhere he even liked. He was so flippant and business-like about it all. It was as though their marriage hadn't mattered to him one little jot. She had curtly told him that he could deal with her lawyer directly and then she had ended the call. *How had she ended up being married to such a numpty?*

When she had broken the news to Ben — because Dermot kept avoiding the issue, despite promises to tell their son about the divorce *and* his affair — he had insisted that he would come home. But Rosie had made him promise not to change his plans. 'Your life has to go on,' she said to him on a teary FaceTime call. 'These things happen, love, and you won't be the first of your friends to have parents who split up.' She had managed to keep *her* tears at bay; the last thing she wanted to do was upset him even more and have him worry about her. But her son had always been sensitive and emotional. He had never been afraid to shed tears but it had been even more heartbreaking to bear as she couldn't console him in person. As the weeks had gone on, though, he had bounced back and was full of excitement as he told her about the next part of his travel plan which was to spend a month in Bali. Strangely enough, these plans didn't seem to include Mabel and, when Rosie had questioned him, he was vague saying that it was easier being single. She wholeheartedly agreed.

Now, as she finished the dregs of her coffee, she smiled. She may not be on an exotic island on the other side of the world but this little spot in Kildonan was just as good. There were beautiful beaches, the sky was currently blue, and the sun was shining. Being here would give her the perfect chance to heal her wounds and think about what *she* wanted going forward. Glancing at her watch, she realised it would soon be time to get ready to collect Isobel from the terminal. For the first time in weeks, Rosie felt something that resembled excitement. Her friends were exactly what she needed to help her move on.

CHAPTER SIX

A few hours later, Rosie hopped around anxiously as she tried to spot Isobel with all the other foot passengers coming down the stairs and out of the terminal building.

'Rosie!' hollered Isobel, grinning and waving madly at her as she spotted her friend. She hauled her bag on wheels behind her.

'It is *so* good to see you,' said Rosie, throwing her arms around Isobel and hugging her tightly. She held her back at arm's length and studied her. 'I can't believe you are actually here.'

'Well, you'd better believe it,' Isobel replied, laughing. 'I am here, and I can't wait for the holiday to begin. Here, my bag weighs an absolute ton. It's all the plonk I've brought. Give me a hand, will you, and take my handbag? Jeezo, I feel as though I've spent the whole day doing a million Body Pump classes, lugging these bags around.'

'Of course,' said Rosie, reaching over to take the huge handbag from Isobel, wincing at the weight of it. 'Are you sure there's not bricks in here?'

'Nope. Just an extra bottle of Prosecco,' she said with a wicked grin. 'There was only so much I could fit in my wee case.'

'Come on. The car's over here,' said Rosie, pointing to the car park.

'Oh, it's good to be back,' said Isobel, looking around. 'What is it about this place? Whenever I get here, I just feel immediately at home.'

Rosie knew exactly what she meant. Even though the island was now her home, it had always had something magical about it. No wonder it was so popular with tourists.

'It was a shame we didn't get to see you last year when we were over at the Highland Games. That was a great weekend,' said Isobel.

Rosie nodded. 'Yes, it usually is. And to think I was away celebrating my wedding anniversary and now look at me . . .'

Isobel reached over and gripped her hand. 'Yes, Rosie. Look at you. Independent and beautiful and kind and well shot of that useless dick.'

Rosie couldn't help but laugh. Isobel was always so feisty and outspoken. She was a breath of fresh air. 'Come on, in you get,' she said to Isobel as she pressed her key and unlocked the car. Opening the boot, she took her friend's small case and lifted it in with a wince. 'Jings, I see what you mean! Is it full of cement?' She pointed to the passenger door. 'Come on, let's get going. I thought I would start the tour now and take you for a coffee and cake in Lamlash.'

'Ooh, now you're talking,' said Isobel. 'Is it the place that sounds like cake and I can never remember what it's *actually* called?'

'Aye. It's called Cèic.'

'That's it. That's the place my mum has been raving about,' said Isobel. 'She went there when she visited Beth last year and has been talking about the cakes ever since.'

Beth was a reporter on the local newspaper and Rosie knew her from the work she had been doing at the school. She had been helping the kids set up their own newspaper and had been a bit of a hit with them all. Isobel had previously filled Rosie in on the fledgling romance between her mum and Beth's dad.

'How is your mum doing?' asked Rosie as she started the ignition and pulled out the parking bay. 'I can't believe that every time she's been here lately, I haven't.' Rosie had been away doing some Christmas shopping in Edinburgh that weekend.

Isobel raised an eyebrow. 'Very well indeed. Loving her new flat. In fact, it is near impossible to get her in. She's always out and about and living the highlife.'

'And the romance?' asked Rosie with a laugh. There was always a bit of a queue to get out the car park, but the traffic moved quickly and she indicated left to take the road to Lamlash.

'Seems to be going well too. Bill is a lovely man. Though she is a bit coy when I push for details.'

'Erm, what kind of details do you need, Isobel?'

Isobel chuckled. 'True. Less is more. As long as she's happy, which she is, that is the main thing. And she's certainly having better luck with the opposite sex than I am.'

Rosie giggled as she focused on the road and let Isobel admire the scenery. Isobel had broken up with her partner last year and there hadn't been anyone significant since. Not that it seemed to bother her in the slightest. As she reached the brow of the hill which led them into Lamlash she smiled. The Holy Isle sat across the bay and the water was as still as a pond. It was a view that she would never tire of.

Isobel sighed. 'Will you look at that? What a view.'

'I know. I love this bit when you drive down towards the bay. It's one of my favourite views, I think.'

The friends enjoyed the view in silence for a few minutes while Rosie drove into the village. It didn't take her long to find a parking spot near the café. 'We can sit outside if you want?' The seating area was bathed in warm sunshine and there were plenty of free tables and chairs.

'Ideal. Wow, I already feel like I'm on holiday,' said Isobel, staring at the bay ahead. The women got out the car and Isobel gestured over at a free table. 'You have a seat and

I'll go in and get us some drinks. I want to have a nosy at the cakes. What do you fancy?'

'A latte would be lovely, thanks. And whatever cake looks nice. You choose.'

Rosie sat and enjoyed people watching while she waited for Isobel. Freya, a teacher from one of the primary schools, waved and smiled as she walked past. Then she saw Edie, who knew *everyone*, stroll past with her dog, Molly. Edie was always dressed in bright colours and today was no exception. She wore a long, turquoise, linen dress and a set of long, bright-pink beads, which she had slung around her neck a couple of times.

'Hello there. Beautiful day, isn't it?' she said as she beamed at Rosie. 'How are you, dear?'

Rosie was very fond of Edie and, last month, she had taken part in one of her pottery workshops. It turned out that a bit of creativity was just the therapy that Rosie had needed. It had been lovely to immerse herself in the process of playing with the clay and it had been a good distraction from her marriage woes. Even though she had ended up with a vase which looked as though it had seen better days. Edie had seemed to have a knack of knowing what to say at the right time without ever prying too much. It was as though she had been able to read Rosie's mind and knew she needed a bit of kindness at that time.

'I'm really good thanks, Edie,' said Rosie with a warm smile. 'I've just collected one of my best friends from the ferry, she's here for a visit.'

'Oh, how lovely,' she answered enthusiastically. 'You look well, dear, and a lot more relaxed. The summer holidays are obviously agreeing with you.'

Rosie gave her a grateful smile and a nod. It was good to be on holiday at the moment especially as they had been a bit short-staffed. She had been rushed off her feet which had turned out to be a positive thing as it had kept her very distracted.

'What a place,' said Isobel, appearing from inside the café and sitting down next to Rosie.

'Edie, you must meet my friend, Isobel,' said Rosie to Edie. 'And Isobel, this is Edie . . . she's a very talented lady and also makes beautiful mugs.'

'Edie!' exclaimed Isobel. 'I know exactly who you are. My mum has been raving about you.'

Edie blushed and looked a bit bemused. 'Oh goodness . . .'

'Sorry, it is all in a good way, so don't worry. I should explain . . . my mum, Margaret, was here visiting her friend Beth, from the paper, last Christmas. She came round to buy some of your mugs in the gift shop.'

Rosie watched as Edie pieced together the dots and her face was a picture of delight. She clapped her hands together. 'Oh yes, I remember Margaret. And you're her daughter?'

Isobel nodded. 'That's right.'

'Oh, it is so good to meet you properly. Tell me, how is your mum, and how is Bill doing now? I haven't seen Beth for a while to ask her.'

'He is very well, thanks. Looking after himself after that wee scare over Christmas, and he and Mum seem to be very happy together.'

Edie looked thoughtfully between Rosie and Isobel. 'I am so glad to hear that. Isn't life a funny thing? We are all connected, aren't we? And it's such a small world.'

Rosie nodded in agreement. 'It certainly is.' She hesitated for a moment. 'Would you like to join us, Edie?'

Edie groaned. 'I would love to, however I have guests arriving at Coorie Cabin any minute. And I just nipped out to get some milk for them.'

Coorie Cabin was a beautiful shepherd's hut at the bottom of Edie's garden which she rented out to tourists. Sometimes Rosie wished she didn't live on the island as it was the sort of place she would love to stay. Although from what

Edie said, it was really popular and people tended to book it up months in advance.

'Lovely to meet you, Isobel, and you two ladies enjoy your time together. And tell your mum I say hello.' She winked and gently tugged at her dog, Molly, who had been lying down beside her waiting patiently. 'Toodle-oo,' she said, and gave a little wave.

Isobel smiled. 'What a lovely woman.'

Rosie nodded. 'She is. She's the type of woman who knows everyone and everything but is very discreet.'

'Ooh,' said Isobel. 'Does she know everyone's secrets?'

'I'm sure she does,' said Rosie. 'But she's far too kind to gossip.'

'Well, I had no idea what to choose in there,' said Isobel, changing the conversation. 'Oh, my gawd! I could have eaten everything. I had to ask for some help as I couldn't decide.'

'What did you get in the end then?'

She smacked her lips. 'A slice of chocolate cake and a piece of salted caramel traybake. I thought we could share. Though I also had my eye on the carrot cake and the coffee cake. Oh, and the banana bread. I really think we'll need to come back.'

Rosie laughed. 'We can do that. That's what holidays are for.' Just then the owner, Cano, arrived at the table.

'Here you go,' he said, placing down the tray and taking the cakes and drinks off and putting them next to the women.

'Thank you so much, Cano,' said Rosie, smiling at him.

'You are welcome. It is nice to see you. It's been a while.'

Rosie shrugged. 'I know. But now it's the holidays I am sure you will see a lot more of me.'

'I hope so. Enjoy,' he said with another smile and then moved to the next table to clear it.

'This is bliss,' said Isobel, stirring her coffee with a teaspoon and gazing at the still water ahead. 'It's so nice to sit down and not have to rush about anywhere. And eat cake.'

Rosie then watched Isobel as she took her knife and cut up the cakes before handing Rosie a napkin.

'Dig in,' said Isobel.

Rosie smiled fondly at her friend who still had her youthful looks and figure even though she was now in her fifties. Rosie was convinced Isobel had hollow legs as she had the appetite of a teenage boy yet never seemed to gain an ounce.

'I should have brought my suntan lotion with me,' said Isobel, shielding her eyes from the sun. 'Though, do you think putting on the suntan lotion is wishful thinking? You know as soon as I do, it will probably cloud over and start pishing down.'

Rosie laughed and dug her fork into the cake.

'So,' said Isobel, eyeing her friend critically. 'Penny for them?'

'What do you mean?' asked Rosie, trying to be flippant.

'How are you doing? I mean, how are you doing *really*?'

Rosie thought she had done an okay job of putting on a brave face these past months, but now she was with her old friend, she could feel her face crumple. 'Erm, just, you know, trying to get on with things . . .' She felt her bottom lip wobble slightly and shook her head. 'Don't be nice to me as you'll just make me cry. I am okay, it's just because you're here and you're asking that I'm starting to get upset.'

Isobel regarded her carefully. 'Okay. Well, if you want my opinion, you're well shot of him. I always thought he was punching well above his weight . . . Rosie, you are a goddess.'

Rosie felt her cheeks redden. 'Away you go,' she said, embarrassed.

'You are beautiful inside and out, Rosie. Don't you forget it. And you've always been really rubbish at accepting compliments.'

'The cake's nice, isn't it?' said Rosie, desperate to change the subject.

'Delish. But the traybake is even nicer. And stop trying to change the subject. I know you, Rosie. What you need is a steamy fling with some island hunk.' Isobel glanced around the café. 'I don't see any here right now but worry not, my friend, I will be on the lookout for you while I'm here.'

Rosie groaned. 'Tell me about you. What's going on in your world, Isobel? For all I know you've got a man back in Glasgow?'

Isobel stared at her open-mouthed. 'As if. I may be single, Rosie, but I am definitely not keen to mingle.'

Rosie laughed. 'And how is Bella?' She watched as Isobel frowned. 'She'll be enjoying having an empty house while you're away. And having the car to herself too?'

Isobel pursed her lips and nodded. 'Yes, she's okay, though a bit worried about work. Things at the salon seem a bit up and down at the moment. Anyway, I'm sure she will be enjoying a bit of space from me but she's actually away too — camping this weekend at Loch Lomond. I'm sure that give her a wee boost.'

Rosie shuddered. 'Don't. Even the thought of it makes my back sore. Remember that trip in Queensland?'

Isobel nodded, remembering when they slept outside under the stars.

'That was the first and last time I went camping,' said Rosie. 'Never again. I like my home comforts far too much.'

They sat in companionable silence for a while.

'But the thing is, Bella's starting to ask questions . . .'

'Questions are good,' said Rosie, who had always been naturally inquisitive and interested in people. Isobel always told her she should have been a journalist. Or a politician as she was good at asking questions and very skilled at *not* answering them.

'Mm,' said Isobel.

'What kind of questions?'

'Um,' said Isobel. 'Travelling and if we enjoyed it and . . .'

Rosie raised an eyebrow. 'And?'

'Well, I just get the feeling that she is about to start asking about her dad again.'

Rosie scuffed her foot against the ground and reached into her handbag for her bottle of water. She opened the lid and took a drink. 'Okay, I see. But she has asked before and you told her that he was a one-night stand who you met on a night out in Glasgow when you came back from Australia, right? So, what's the problem now? Why do you think she would start to ask again?'

'I don't know. It's just on my mind, there is just something about the way she's been looking at me lately. Call it my maternal instinct. *Or* maybe it's just me overthinking it,' she said, attempting to make light of it. 'I must be hitting that age, Rosie. I'm all over the place overthinking stuff and overly worrying at the moment.'

Rosie nodded in concern. 'I know there is a very valid reason why you don't want to get into the details with Bella and I totally understand that. But . . .'

Isobel drained the last of her coffee and put the mug down on the table. 'I was on Instagram the other day and I seem to get bombarded with motivational quotes and sayings . . . there was something from a French writer who had said that when truth was buried, it grew and gathered such an explosive force that on the day it bursts out, it blows up everything with it. Which I guess is very dramatic. But you know me.'

'O-k-a-y,' said Rosie slowly. 'To be honest, that kind of rings a bell. Sounds like my life of late.'

Isobel clapped her hand over her mouth. 'I'm so sorry, Rosie. You must think I'm a complete idiot. That was so insensitive for me to say. Ignore me.'

Rosie reached over and patted her hand. 'Don't be silly. It's okay. But I suppose a lot of the time we could all find meaning in lots of these Instagram posts, depending on how we are feeling day-to-day. It's like horoscopes, isn't it?'

Isobel nodded. 'You're right. Thank you. And I'm sorry. I still haven't lost that knack of managing to put my foot right in it.'

'That's why I love you so much,' said Rosie, chuckling. 'But for the record you haven't put your foot in anything.'

'Enough of me, tell me about Ben,' said Isobel. 'How is he getting on?'

Just then Rosie looked up and spotted Fergus, from the outdoor centre, coming out of the café with a takeaway coffee. Ben had worked there the previous summer and she'd got to know Fergus quite well. She waved at him and was about to call him over but, although he had smiled back at her, he had quickened his pace and kept going. How strange. Fergus always stopped to talk to her, and she hoped that everything with him was okay.

'He's a handsome chap,' said Isobel, who was watching.

Rosie laughed. 'Ben used to work for him.' She pulled out her phone and showed her the latest beach shots from Ben's trip.

'Oh, my goodness, I can't believe how grown up he is now. And so handsome. Obviously takes after you with his good looks. Where has the time gone?' said Isobel, shaking her head. 'It seems like no time ago they were wee tots. And now they are proper adults.'

There was less than a year between Bella and Ben and they had always been great friends when they were small. But then they'd got absorbed in their own lives and own friends, especially during the awkward teenager phase, and their friendship had drifted.

'I know,' said Rosie wistfully. 'They're both all grown up.'

Isobel bit her lip. 'I just don't know if I did the right thing by her,' she said pensively.

Privately, Rosie had always been a bit worried that this might happen, and that Isobel would wonder if she had made the right choice all those years ago. Especially now that Bella had started to probe. It was a secret that they had carried all these years and Rosie wondered if things were now starting to catch up with them. Rosie had a feeling that there was every chance that things could get complicated, despite her earlier attempts to reassure Isobel. Then she reminded herself that she had already dealt with one life explosion. You couldn't plan for when curveballs might be chucked in your path. Rosie had learned that you just had to be ready to catch them. She smiled brightly at Isobel. 'Try not to worry too much about it. You're here for a holiday so put it to the back of your mind. You can think about it again when you get home. And I'm sure when Bella gets back from camping with her friends, she will have forgotten all about it.'

CHAPTER SEVEN

Over on the mainland, Bella yawned and pulled down the visor to shade her eyes. The sun was bright and she didn't want to risk crashing her car by rummaging around in her bag for her sunglasses while she drove. Bella was currently driving in the opposite direction of where she should have been heading. She had called off the camping trip to Loch Lomond at the last minute, hastily telling the girls that someone had called in sick at work and she had been asked to cover. She did feel a bit guilty about lying to them, but she thought it was better this way. The fewer people who knew about what she was planning to do, the better.

She had left Glasgow fairly early this morning to make the journey to Troon in Ayrshire. According to her Sat Nav it would take her less than one hour to get there. She was extremely relieved that her mum was already away on her trip to Arran. Bella couldn't face the barrage of questions she knew that Isobel would ask if Bella had told her about her change of plan. She wasn't sure she could have pulled it off with Isobel around. *Good old Google*, she thought. When she had done some research online and realised what was happening — a celebrity golf match, very close to home — knowing who would be there, she had made a swift change of plans and abandoned the camping trip. It was now or never, and if she didn't follow it through, she didn't think she ever would. There might not be a chance like this again. She told herself that the timing of all of this was a *sign*. It was meant to be. She needed to strike while the iron was hot and before she lost her nerve.

Bella bit her lip as she thought about the bizarreness of this whole situation. She did kind of wish she had asked one of her friends to come along as a wing woman to offer moral support. But there was no way she could have explained what she was going to do today without one of them spilling the beans or getting overly dramatic about it all. She was also very glad to be single right now. The last boyfriend she had had was Dudley, a guy from Carlisle who she had met on holiday in Corfu last summer. But it had petered out. She thought about the times her mum had met him and winced. He'd been so over the top, which she had put down to nerves. Her mum hadn't said very much at all which, in itself, spoke volumes. It was only afterwards that her mum admitted she thought he was a bit of a plonker. He was always checking his reflection out in windows, mirrors, shopfronts — basically anything he could see himself in. Bella had wondered if he was perhaps insecure then realised he was just vain. He was a bit of a peacock. And when she had visited him and heard his mum call him Diddly Duddles, she knew they were not destined to be together.

Bella took a deep breath in and exhaled slowly. This was something she had to do alone. Her hands were white as they gripped the steering wheel. Bella, who was usually calm, confident and collected, was a bag of nerves. She had no idea where to even begin other than to get herself in the place where she knew he would be.

As she drove down the M77, she told herself that it would all be fine. It just *had* to be. But even the jaunty voice of the radio presenter and the upbeat songs did anything to quieten her nerves as she drove. In fact, they started to irritate her.

Her mouth was dry, her heart was racing and she was the most nervous she could ever remember being. Even her exams at college last year had been a breeze compared to this. She changed the music and her favourite singer, Loyle Carner, started blasting from the speakers. The lyrics struck a chord with her, and she truly hoped she had a guardian angel looking out for her like he described in the song. Eventually, she felt her pounding heart start to calm down slightly and, as she started to see the signs for Troon, she felt herself driving more and more slowly willing time to slow down. Following the signs for the town centre she hoped that she would find a space to park, especially as there was so much traffic, given the event. Bella followed the road round to the South Beach Esplanade Car Park, already busy with cars. She sighed in relief when she saw a dog walker returning to their car and give her a wave. Bella waited for them to move and then pulled into the space. She switched off her engine and took a few steadying breaths. She was just over a mile away from the Royal Troon Golf Club where the competition was happening. All she needed now was a strategy.

For a moment or two she felt light-headed as the enormity of today dawned on her. *What was she doing?* She gave herself a shake. Coffee and fresh air. That was what she needed. An injection of caffeine and a dose of sea air would help her think. She made her way to a small café that she had driven past moments ago. Ordering a coffee and a flaky almond croissant, which she didn't particularly want but she knew she should eat as her stomach had been growling at her for the past couple of hours, she found a picnic table outside and sat down to think. She tore off a piece of pastry and chewed while she stared up at the blue sky streaked with white clouds.

The outside sitting area was getting busy and four women, who Bella thought might be Canadian, asked if they could join her. Bella smiled and nodded, moving up the bench to make room for two of them and the other women sat on the bench opposite. She listened to snippets of conversation about their trip to the town. They had also visited Glasgow and were due to go to St Andrews and then London before flying back to Toronto. It always amazed Bella how much information you could learn about people from simply listening. But she pulled out her phone and started to scroll so it didn't look like she was completely eavesdropping. Even though she was.

'Excuse me, *ladies*,' said a voice.

Bella glanced up to see a tall man, dressed in bright pastel coloured golfing gear, lingering by their table. Bella frowned, wishing he would move on, especially as he was managing to block out the sun.

'Do you mind if I join you?' he said in his affected accent.

'Sure, budge up, Jess,' one of the women said to her friend.

By now, Bella was practically hanging off the edge of the bench as they were all packed on so tightly. She was glad she'd kept up with the squats in the gym. At least her thighs could handle almost having to hover. The woman, Jess, gave Bella an apologetic look. Bella shrugged. She was almost finished her coffee anyway. Perhaps this was a sign she should move on. Even though she had no idea what to do next. She reckoned it would take her at least half an hour to walk along to the golf course.

'Well, well, well is that American accents I can detect?' said the man.

'No, Canadian actually,' said one.

'Ooft,' he said with a loud gurning laugh. 'I am sorry. My mistake. I'm sure you get that all the time,' he said smoothly, raising his sunglasses onto the top of his head and winking. 'I've spent a lot of time there myself, of course. I should have known better than to assume you are American. Canada is a great place. I've travelled to Ontario, the Rockies and British Columbia. And, of course, skied at Whistler.'

Bella frowned. She didn't recall the women asking for details of where he had been in Canada or the type of leisure pursuits he had engaged in.

'Is this your first visit to Scotland?' he asked.

'No, we come here quite often. And we have been so lucky with the weather. It has been stunning.'

'Are you here with your husbands?' he asked. 'Are they golfers?'

Bella inwardly groaned. What a dick.

'No, it's just us,' said one of the women tensely. 'And believe it or not we can all actually play golf. Imagine that, eh?'

'That's nice,' he said, clearly not realising she was being sarcastic. 'Good you're getting out there and enjoying the fresh air.'

Bella couldn't help thinking he sounded rather patronising.

He scratched his head. 'Which course did you play? The wee nine-old course?'

Jess laughed. 'No. Can you believe we *actually* managed to play a full round.'

The man looked completely taken aback.

'I know, right? All eighteen holes,' she continued. 'We all play off scratch and it's been a really great course to play.'

'Ah, right, I see,' he said, clearly flummoxed. 'You did well to get tee off times, especially with the celebrity competition that's been on.'

'We've got friends in the right places,' said one of the women who rolled her eyes at her friends.

'I'm glad it's finishing up soon. This is the last day. I'm looking forward to things getting back to normal. Much as I have enjoyed watching the competition, I do get a bit fed up with these celebs hogging the greens.' He chuckled.

'Do you like the nine-hole course?' said Jess. 'I believe it is a favourite for juniors *and* seniors.'

He looked at her blankly, clearly unaware that she was making a dig. 'And where are you *ladies* off to after Troon?'

'To St Andrews and then to London for a few days.'

The golfer took a sip of his coffee, which left a ridge of foam on the top of his lip, and then proceeded to tell them where they should visit in St Andrews and London.

Jess caught Bella's eye and shook her head as the man continued on his monologue of the best restaurants he thought they should go to in London and how they should really take care when using the underground. It was a fine example of mansplaining at its best.

'Anyways,' he said, standing and crumpling up his coffee cup in one hand.

Bella half-wished that the coffee would dribble down his lemon polo-shirt.

'Nice chatting. Enjoy the rest of your trip, ladies.' He glanced at his watch. 'I'd better be off.' And with that, he strode away.

'What a tool,' said Jess.

'Completely,' agreed her friend and the other one sniggered.

Bella couldn't help but laugh, which then made the other women giggle again and soon they were all holding their sides. 'What a total eejit,' she said.

'I love that word. *Eejit*,' said Jess repeating it back to her. 'No need to hang off the bench any longer,' she said and moved up to make more space.

'Aw, thank you. But I should really head off myself now. But thanks for that. It was most entertaining.'

'I know, right? He was so condescending. No wonder golf gets a bad name with sexist bores like him. Did you see his face when I said we all played off scratch? Which we don't by the way,' she said conspiratorially to Bella. 'Well, Rhona does,' she said, pointing across to her friend. 'But I couldn't help winding him up.'

'It was great to watch. Thanks for brightening up my day,' said Bella, who knew very little about golf. It was a sport that held zero appeal. 'I hope you enjoy the rest of your stay.' Bella hesitated for a minute. 'I hope you don't mind me asking but where is the best place to see some of the golfers in the competition?'

'Do you have a ticket?' asked Jess.

Bella wished the ground would open up and swallow her. Of course, she needed a ticket. *Why didn't she think of that?* Her cheeks flushed as she shook her head and she shuffled her feet awkwardly.

'It depends on who you want to see,' said Jess kindly. 'The younger ones will get mobbed by the hordes when they come off the course. But there is a bar in our hotel where we have seen a few the last couple of evenings, say from around four o'clock. The guy from the eighties American rock band.'

'That hideous English TV presenter,' said her friend, pulling a face. 'Piers something or other. He was arguing with a footballer last night. Though I almost don't blame him. They were both as obnoxious as each other.'

'And the guy who was in that boyband, GFC or something . . . he turned to acting.'

'Do you mean the Get Fresh Crew?' said Bella.

'That's the one. Luke . . . Giles. He's quite easy on the eye, if you get my drift. Though will be positively ancient to a young thing like you.' Jess gave a dirty laugh.

Bella's eyes widened. Luke Giles. *Bingo.*

'It's a bit quieter and less showy than the hotel they're all staying at,' said Rhona, telling her the name of the place they were staying in.

'Thanks so much,' said Bella, and she smiled gratefully as her mind started to race. Glancing at her watch she realised she had quite a long time to hang about. In fact, she had a number of hours to kill. But hopefully she would get a chance to talk to Luke and the wait would all be worth it.

CHAPTER EIGHT

Luke was extremely glad he had Andrew with him, a very patient caddy, who didn't mind the numerous flunked shots and lost balls. When they were both searching for yet another lost ball in the rough, they were distracted when they heard a kerfuffle on the fairway. Looking over they could see that one of the team — the former Premier League footballer, Warren — was having a full-blown tantrum after slicing his shot. He slammed his club to the ground and actually *stamped* on it. Then he screamed. Luke and the caddy made eye contact and both grimaced. If it wasn't so ridiculous, it would be very funny. In fact, Luke couldn't help but chuckle. He just hoped for Warren's sake that nobody had caught any of it on film. It wouldn't enhance his tattered reputation one bit. Especially after the torrid year he'd had. Earlier that year, Warren had been caught in a compromising position with a popstar who was very much not his wife, and her popstar rival to boot. It was all very complicated and a bit clichéd. But the tabloids absolutely loved it and Warren's ongoing games off the pitch provided them with plenty of material to write about.

Luke certainly wasn't perfect, but he had hoped he had learned from the mistakes he had made over the years — and there had been several that he wasn't proud of when he was younger. But Warren still seemed as arrogant as ever despite his private life having been splashed across the press. Or maybe because of it.

'There you go, mate,' said Andrew, the caddy, who bent down to pick up the ball. 'Told you we'd find it. It's your lucky day.'

'Brilliant. Thank you.' He glanced over at Warren whose face was now puce. 'I don't think it's his lucky day though. Someone should tell him it's only a game,' he said drily.

Andrew nodded and rolled his eyes. He was too discreet to say anything else, however Luke was sure the caddy had seen it all before — and probably much more.

Now, as he put his putter into his bag, he gave a huge sigh of relief. Much as he loved his golfing trips to Scotland, which were fairly frequent, he was very glad he had swung his last shot on this trip. 'Thanks, Andrew. You've been great,' he said, shaking his hand and making loose plans to buy him a drink later. Luke much preferred going to a different bar he knew that was quieter than the one in the hotel that the celebrity players, including Warren, enjoyed hanging out in as they loved the attention from adoring fans. Luke, on the other hand, did not. His days of adulation were well and truly over.

'See you in the bar, mate,' said Warren, sauntering past him, clearly recovered from his hissy-fit on the fairway.

'Sure thing,' said Luke casually, not wanting to commit to spending a minute more with the odious man than he needed to. He'd learned over time that it was easier to go with the flow and keep his plans vague. If he told Warren that he had no intention of meeting him in the bar, the sport star would throw another tantrum which Luke could not face. It was far easier just to nod and let the poor sod assume Luke would be there.

Stepping aside, he switched on his mobile and saw the raft of messages and missed calls flash up on the screen. His agent, Linda, had left another voicemail about the upcoming deadline for his book. Luke had been contracted to write a book about his life — he was a founding member of The Get Fresh Crew, one of the world's biggest boybands in the nineties — and had, foolishly, he now realised turned down the option of working with a ghostwriter. With a slight pang of worry, he wished he had taken Linda up on her suggestion to collaborate with someone else, as procrastination was becoming his full-time occupation rather than just sitting down and writing. He couldn't remember having done so much housework in all his life. His flat was the tidiest it had ever been and he had also bought himself a soup maker and was now becoming quite the pro at producing every type of soup that you could imagine. It was yet another distraction from writing. Meanwhile, he had constantly reassured Linda that it was all fine and coming along nicely.

'Then send me some over,' she said, when they last spoke. 'Just so I know how it's *flowing*.'

'Of course,' he told her smoothly. 'You don't need to worry about a thing. It's all in hand.' Except it wasn't. He needed to go and lock himself in a cupboard for the summer and just write the damn thing. As soon as he was out of here, he would head back to London and do it. Though the thought of being stuck in his rented flat in Notting Hill didn't appeal one jot. Maybe if he had made more of an effort with Elton John, back in the day when they were close and the GFC had worked with him and George Michael, he would have the option of using Elton's home in the south of France as a bolthole to write his book. Right at this moment, he didn't have the energy to have a conversation or argument with Linda. Instead, he sent her a message saying he would be in touch soon, all was great and the writing was going well and then switched off his phone.

* * *

An hour later, Luke had packed up most of his things ready for an early departure in the morning. He showered and changed into a pair of beige chinos and a navy polo shirt. Then pulled on his trainers and quickly raked his hand through his dark blonde hair, grateful that he still had it all. Especially when so many of his friends were now thinning, completely bald or had gone for the hair transplant option which he hoped he would never have to resort to. He left his hotel room and quickly scanned the corridor for other guests then headed straight for the exit and jogged lightly down the stairs. He didn't want to take the lift which opened out into the lobby. That would mean walking right past the bar and potentially being spotted — and then collared — by Warren, which was not an option. Instead, he left by the hotel's back entrance and made his way towards the smaller, boutique hotel a few streets away to wait for Andrew where he knew they could have a drink and a chat without being disturbed.

As he walked, he sensed he was being followed and he turned round to see a young and very pretty woman, with brown, wavy hair, looking at him. He frowned. He had clocked her somewhere earlier. Was it outside the clubhouse or somewhere else? He remembered her because of the eye-catching bright blue sun dress she wore. He kept walking, and as he reached the hotel entrance he turned round again, she was still there, not that far behind him, and still staring at him. She wasn't his usual type of fan — they tended to be much older — although the last tour with the band had surprised him as all ages of fans were there. Mothers *and* daughters. He paused and smiled giving her a wave in case she was a fan. A wave and a grin was usually enough to placate people who thought they recognised him from somewhere. She didn't reciprocate but instead walked towards him with a grim look on her face. Oh dear, this didn't bode well, he thought to himself. Her face was white and she looked very worried. Luke quickly racked his brain. *Did he know her?*

'Hey, how are you?' he said, flashing his best smile as she stood yards away.

She bit her lip anxiously.

Okay, he said to himself. His usual charm clearly wasn't working today. He needed to ramp things up a notch or two. 'Would you like an autograph?'

She wrinkled up her perfect nose and shook her head in confusion. 'Erm, no, I don't want an autograph.' She had a Glaswegian accent and looked utterly baffled at the thought. He may as well have offered her a pair of his dirty underpants.

Luke brushed his hand over his chin. What had he done or not done that had caused this woman to be so annoyed with him? He couldn't help wishing he hadn't bothered to stop. In fact, maybe chatting with Warren might have been easier than this. Then he saw a brief look of vulnerability pass over her face. He smiled encouragingly. 'Hey, are you okay?' he said, his voice full of concern.

She was now looking down, fiddling with her hands. 'Um, look I need to have a word with you. It's a . . . it's a personal matter.'

Out of the corner of his eye Luke saw a photographer he recognised walking down the street, headed in their direction. *Brilliant*. Being snapped with a young woman was the last thing he needed right now. He could just see the headlines. *Luke Finds Love Again* or *Lovestruck Luke*. His estranged wife would go nuts and he could already hear her instructing the lawyer to screw him for even more money in the divorce. Even though *she* was the one who had strayed — and with his very own brother, at that. Even though they had now been together for a few years, the thought still sickened him to the core.

'Mr Giles,' she said firmly.

His eyes widened in shock. Nobody ever called him that. Well, apart from his GP and bank manager and when they did, it made him feel about ninety.

'I need to tell you something,' she said, chewing her bottom lip.

He sighed. He was used to people approaching him all the time with different and random requests. Which usually involved money. But this was different. There was something clearly troubling the woman. He knew he should be careful but she didn't look like a crazed stalker who was dangerous. Though a voice in his head reminded him that you never could tell.

'Shall we step inside?' he said, gesturing to the pub and trying to move things away from the gaze of the photographer who was almost upon them. He opened the door for her and allowed her to pass through. He didn't have a good feeling about this *at all*.

CHAPTER NINE

Bella followed Luke into the bar which thankfully was quiet with only a few others there. It had an air of sophistication about it with its polished wooden floors, intimate seating areas and jazz playing in the background. It made her think of how different her local pub at home was which had sawdust sprinkled on the floor and smelt of warm apples. She had a pang of longing for home and for her mum. Then she felt a wave of guilt wash over her. But she knew if she'd told her mum her plans, then she would have flipped her lid. Bella had no choice and she needed to get this over and done with now. She had been waiting to catch Luke for hours, growing more and more agitated by the minute. She stood awkwardly while he had a brief word with a man standing at the bar.

'Take a seat,' he said, gesturing to a small booth tucked away discreetly in the corner. 'Can I get you a drink?'

'Um, just some water, please?'

He nodded curtly. 'I'll bring it right over.'

As she waited for him to get the drinks, she felt herself panicking. This had been a really stupid idea. What if he got angry with her? There were only a few people in the bar but at least they were in a public place which had to be better than nothing. He wouldn't erupt in front of an audience, surely? He was famous, he couldn't afford to make a scene. Oh, why had she been so hellbent on doing this? Her mum had always said she was stubborn and acted on impulse. And as she was getting older, she was starting to realise that her mum was usually, though not always, right. Bella should have thought more about this instead of racing here and confronting Luke. Now, her mouth was completely dry, and she was glad he was getting her some water otherwise she wasn't sure she could actually speak. *You're here because you have to be*, she reminded herself firmly. *It might be the only chance that you get. You need to get some answers. For your own sanity if nothing else.*

'There you go,' he said, placing the glass down and sliding into a seat opposite her.

'Thanks,' she said and then took a gulp of water. She couldn't believe she was now sitting across from Luke Giles. *The* Luke Giles. And he actually looked quite normal for someone who was famous. She had been researching him extensively these last few days and had pored over all the details she could find and stared at all the pictures that were online. His face was actually fairly unlined for someone of his age, no doubt thanks to some Botox. *And* his hair was still thick and sandy, like it belonged to someone who regularly went yachting. She had no idea, though, if he liked sailing or not. Her mum was always telling her off for making assumptions about people. As she studied his face closely, she looked for something that might be familiar. But the only passing resemblance she could detect was that he might be described as looking like the older brother of Sam Heughan from *Outlander*.

'Is that a Glasgow accent?' he said.

She nodded, clearly surprised. She never thought her accent was particularly strong. Unless she was angry. She had inherited that trait from her mum who claimed she had inherited it from her gran. Granny Margaret got very hot under the collar at social injustices and rudeness. Of which there seemed to be a lot in the world these days. Suddenly, Bella wondered what her gran would think of her being here and quickly pushed that thought well away. Knowing Granny Margaret, she would have a few choice words to say.

'I've got some good friends from Glasgow,' he said as a way of explanation. 'And I've visited a lot. It's a great city. Everyone's very welcoming and very friendly.'

Aye, maybe too friendly, she thought to herself. *That's perhaps been the problem.*

He focused his dark blue eyes on her. 'You said you had something you wanted to talk to me about?'

Bella gave herself a shake. She knew he didn't have all night to hang about and he was doing her a favour by even giving her the time of day. She could be a serial killer for all he knew. His hands were clasped in front of him on the table and his fingers were long and slender. She looked down at her own hands. She had always been proud of them and her nails were always manicured. Looking up at him, she grimaced. 'You've travelled the world, haven't you?'

He nodded, looking unsure as to where she was going with her line of questioning.

'I'm hoping to go travelling too,' she said quickly. 'Australia and maybe New Zealand. I'd like to go to Bali too. And Thailand.'

'Great places,' he said. 'It's good to travel while you're young.'

'Yes,' she answered.

'You were in Australia in 1999?'

He gave her a rueful smile and nodded. 'Erm, yes, that's right. Though I have been back since then. That was when we were on a world tour. I always wished we had stayed on to celebrate New Year there — how amazing would that have been? But by then we had to move on to do the next leg in the States. That was a very long time ago and a very crazy period in my life. In fact, it feels like a completely different lifetime, if I'm honest. A lot has happened since then.'

'I'm sure.' She took another sip of water, aware that he was now staring at her and waiting. 'The thing is, that I believe you met my mother over there when you were touring.'

'I see. Well, if I'm honest, then I met *a lot* of women when I was touring,' he said, raising an eyebrow. 'As I said, it was quite a crazy time in my life.'

'I can only imagine,' she said.

He had started to drum his fingers gently on the table. 'Look, is there something specific you wanted to talk about? Do you need help with getting into the industry or something?' He paused. 'Or did you want an interview?'

She didn't reply.

'Normally I wouldn't do this,' he said, indicating the drink at the table, 'just agree to have a drink with a random woman. But there is something about you that looks familiar,' he said. 'Do I know you from somewhere?'

Bingo, thought Bella. That was *exactly* what she was hoping he would say. It just confirmed that she had been right to come here and confront him. She knew that there was a reason he had been in Scotland. Finding out about it had indeed been a sign. 'Erm, yes, well the thing is . . . I have reason to believe that you are actually my dad.'

CHAPTER TEN

The words had tumbled from Bella's mouth before she could stop them. And now she wished she could claw them all back. Especially as Luke's eyes widened in utter shock. Meanwhile, the walls of the bar seemed to close in on them, making Bella feel as if they were the only two people in the room. She traced a bead of water which was running down her glass, willing him to say something. *Anything*.

'Sorry . . . but can you, can you say that again?' he whispered, looking at her in disbelief. 'I'm not sure, I'm not quite sure I heard you properly.' He leaned in towards her digging his nails into the table.

Bella's heart was now thudding and her mouth felt as though it was full of marbles. She took a long drink of water and it caught the back of her throat causing her to choke and splutter.

'Here,' he said, reaching over and gently patting her on the back.

When she had caught her breath, her voice was soft as she repeated the words. 'I have reason to believe you are my father . . . I think you might be my dad.' She watched as he swallowed hard and cleared his throat several times.

'O-k-a-a-y,' he said, drawing the word out. 'And what makes you think that?' He sat back and narrowed his eyes, frowning.

'Because you and my mum had a *thing* many years ago. In Australia. In Sydney, to be precise.'

Luke was looking irritated now. 'You're going to have to be a bit more specific than that and unless you have something particular to prove this then I think our conversation is over,' he said curtly. 'Tell me why I should believe what you're saying?'

'I don't make a habit of doing this type of thing,' said Bella, now feeling a bit tearful. She wasn't quite sure how she had expected him to respond. Had she been naive enough to think he would welcome her with open arms? Especially when it seemed obvious that he had no idea her mum was pregnant. He had every right to be short with her. She had just launched a huge grenade at him. She took a steadying breath and then started to explain. 'My mum — she's called Isobel — was travelling in Australia and in Sydney when she fell pregnant with me. I happen to know for a fact that she was having a bit of a thing with you when you were there on tour.'

Luke groaned out loud. 'Look I'm not proud of any of my behaviour back then. I was young and single and there were a lot of women. *Many.*'

'So, you're saying that you don't remember my mum then? You used to go to the Q bar together.' Bella sat back too and crossed her arms.

'Well, um, not off the top of my head. You're talking about over twenty years ago. It's a very long time ago and my memory isn't always as sharp as it used to be.'

'I know it happened a long time ago . . . but please think. Her name is Isobel and she is from Glasgow. She looks like me, she can't sing to save herself and *apparently* was head over heels in love with you and you had several nights of *passion* together when you were in Sydney. And you told her she was *special.*' Bella pulled a face.' You got chatting in a bar after one of your gigs and that was that. Until you then did a midnight flit and buggered off to the other side of the world without telling her.'

Luke was quiet as he sat thinking. Bella watched him, waiting for a glimmer, even a *tiny* one, of some kind of long-lost memory to unearth itself. Maybe he was one of those popstars who had taken far too many drugs in their youth and their brain had been fried as a result and wiped their memories. That would just be *typical*.

'I do remember a girl from back then,' he said softly. 'I've always had a soft spot for Scottish accents.' He gazed beyond her as he seemingly tried to remember more details. 'There were a few women in Australia,' he said with a shrug. 'But I do remember one who was from Glasgow, I think. Though I'm sorry but I don't remember her name being Isobel. But, yes, I do vaguely recall that we had a few nights together. She was really pretty . . . and funny . . . and, damn, that's all I remember . . .' his voice trailed off. 'I'm really sorry that I don't remember your mum exactly. As I said, my memory isn't as sharp as it used to be. I'm not proud of it now but there were many women back in the day.' He shrugged helplessly. 'That was just the way it was then.'

Bella sighed. She could feel tears starting to trickle down her face. Maybe her mum hadn't even told him her real name. *What a mess.*

'Hey,' he said, passing her a napkin. 'Please don't cry.' He paused. 'If you are my daughter then I had no idea. And I am sorry. Especially as I don't even know your name.'

'It's Bella,' she said, through her tears.

'Okay, Bella. Well, I think we need to find out a bit more from your mum. And find out the facts. Are you sure she is telling you the truth?'

Bella glared at him. Then she reminded herself that her mother hadn't told her any of this. And she would go absolutely mad once she found out what Bella had done. 'Um, she doesn't actually know that I'm here.'

He tilted his head at her. 'Right.'

'She will go absolutely *tonto* when she finds out what I've done.' Bella's stomach tightened at the thought. 'Tonto means crazy by the way.'

'Yes,' he said with a nod. 'I gathered that.' He shrugged. 'But I do think if this is the case and you do think that I might be your dad then we need to find out either way. Where is your mum now? Could you call her and ask her?'

Bella hesitated, wondering whether she should phone her mum. But for a start it wasn't the type of question she could just slide into a phone call. It really was the sort of conversation she needed to do face-to-face. But she wasn't sure it could wait until her mum returned home from Arran. Just then the man at the bar, who Luke had spoken to when they had first arrived, came over to the table. She wondered if he was his security guard.

'Hey, sorry to interrupt. Luke, can I have a quick word?'

Luke nodded and excused himself, walking out of earshot to talk with the man. Bella watched him and he looked grim-faced as he listened to what the man said. A few minutes later, they shook hands and the man left the bar. Luke sat back at the table with his hands steepled together. He worriedly glanced over at the door.

'What now?' she said, looking at him questioningly.

'That's my caddy, Andrew. He was just filling me in on what's been happening up at the main hotel where all the players are staying. It looks like my golfing partner has disgraced himself. *Again.* I saw a photographer earlier who I know will now be all over it, desperate to get some shots to sell to the press. He'll be looking for me, too, and wanting a reaction. If I'm honest, I'd rather not be here. I'd rather be as far away as possible.'

'Who is he?'

'My golfing partner? Warren Bruce. The footballer,' he said grimly.

'Oh dear,' said Bella, rolling her eyes. *Everyone* knew who he was and all about his off the pitch antics. Even her gran knew who he was. Whenever he was on TV, she called him a big dunderheid, which wasn't a compliment.

'Exactly. I could do with getting out of here ASAP before the place is swarming with journalists. I'm sure his wife is playing in Glasgow tonight, which will give the press even more ammunition.' He gave her a wry smile and tipped his head to one side as though he was formulating a plan.

'Yup, she is in Glasgow tonight. She's playing at the Hydro. I got a message this afternoon to ask if I could work at one of the bars. I turned it down,' she said, by way of explanation as to why she was still here.

'Hmmm, is your mum in Glasgow just now?'

Rosie shook her head. 'No, she's on holiday at the moment on Arran. The island. Not too far from here.'

'Okay,' he said suddenly, his eyes flitting across to the door. 'Let's go and see her then and try to get some answers.'

'Seriously?'

'Yes,' he said. 'Apart from anything else I need to get out of here fast and Arran is a place I have always wanted to go.'

Bella nodded, so swept up in the moment and relieved that he was taking her seriously. She didn't even stop to think about what he had actually agreed to. She just nodded and took a deep breath. 'If you are sure?'

'I am,' he said. 'I'm happy to come and talk to your mum ... and I believe there are some great golf courses there ...' He shook his head. 'Although I am seriously considering quitting,' he said as a bit of an afterthought. But Luke knew this was the opportunity he had been secretly wishing for. If he was being entirely selfish then this would give him the chance to escape the press, and his manager, and hide out and get the book written. He smiled at Bella. 'I'm up for it if you are?'

'Sure,' said Bella in disbelief, not quite wanting to believe that he wasn't winding her up.

'I'm game for an adventure and it sure beats going back to London.' He glanced at his watch. 'How long do you reckon it will take us to get there?'

Bella quickly did some mental calculations. 'It will take us half an hour to get to Ardrossan. But the last ferry is at six.' Bella looked at her watch. 'So, we'd better get a bend on. We might not even get on it. Especially as we haven't booked.'

He glanced over at the door. 'If you're game, then let's just get on the road and hope for the best. Do you have a car?'

Bella nodded, glad that they could be inconspicuous in her mum's small Peugeot.

'I just need to work out how to get into the hotel to get my stuff without anyone seeing me. It's all packed and ready to go.' He frowned. 'Apart from my toothbrush.'

'You can leave that to me,' said Bella firmly. 'Give me your room key and I'll go and collect it. Nobody will recognise me.'

He grinned. 'You're on. Let's go, Bella. Let's do this.'

Hope bubbled up in Bella. Maybe things would work out okay. Her mum might be angry to begin with but she would understand. Bella tried to ignore the niggling voice in her head that said, *will she though?* Bella had always wanted to know who her father was and now she had *hopefully* found him, she felt a sense of relief. At least the journey to Arran meant they would have time to get to know each other a bit more. It would be quality father and daughter time.

CHAPTER ELEVEN

When they arrived at Creel Cottage, Rosie wasn't quite expecting Isobel to wax lyrical as much as she was currently doing.

'This place is magical,' said Isobel, her eyes wide in wonder, as Rosie showed her around. 'I feel at home already. I mean, I know I've seen photos of it and everything. But wow, Rosie, this is such a special place! No wonder you love being here. It's worth the drive to get away from the busier spots. I'm just sorry it's taken me so long to actually get over and see you.'

'Life is so busy though. It's not always the easiest place to get to. Anyway, the main thing is that you're here now.'

Rosie was just grateful she could show off Creel Cottage to her friend. There was something about these four walls that had always felt like home to Rosie. Even though her parents were no longer here, she still felt connected to them in this house. It felt weird to say but it still smelt of them. A familiar and welcoming scent, a bit like the smell of sweet and buttery shortbread baking in the oven, mixed with laundry powder, which made her feel so at home. Although she had cleared lots of things out since her parents had passed, there were plenty of reminders that it was once their home. There were a variety of hand-painted flowers on plates, by her late grandmother, hanging on the wall:

paintings of Kildonan beach which her dad had done during his retirement when he had started going to art classes; her mum's faded old recipe book, held together by two elastic bands which secured the additional pages; magazine cuttings that had been added to the collection. Seeing her mum's spidery handwriting on the book, additions of her own cooks' notes, made her sad with a pang of longing for her mum. But then she realised she was grateful that her mum had left that legacy for her to enjoy. She had every intention to work her way through the recipe book over the summer. Even more so now that she had another body in the house who loved to eat. Since Dermot had left, she had lost all desire in cooking and eating and had just picked at things that were easy. Like crackers and cheese and eggs on toast.

Coisty had sprung to life and was happily trotting around after Isobel, delighted that he had someone else to dote on him and rub his tummy on demand.

'You are just so cute,' said Isobel, when he bounded into the bedroom that Rosie had just shown her to and jumped up on the bed.

'Oi!' said Rosie firmly. 'Off the bed.'

Coisty looked at her defiantly, before turning to lie on his back with his legs in the air. Isobel burst out laughing. 'You're a disobedient wee sausage,' she said, sitting next to him and rubbing his belly before looking at her friend thoughtfully. 'Was it hard moving here after your parents died?'

'To be honest, not as hard as I thought it might be,' said Rosie, sitting on the other side of the bed across from Isobel. 'I think it has actually helped. I feel they're here with me. I don't mean that in a weird and creepy way,' she added hastily. 'I just feel their presence in the house, if that makes sense?'

'I get that,' said Isobel. 'And that must be a wee bit of comfort to you.'

'Yes, it is,' said Rosie.

'I'm sure my mum will *definitely* make her presence known in more ways than one when she's on the other side,' she said drily. 'You know what she's like.'

Rosie chuckled. 'I'm sure she will.'

'Tell me what you've done so far then,' said Isobel. 'The photos that you sent me don't do the place justice.'

'Well, I've made good progress with the garden and gone through most of the cupboards and drawers, sorting out stuff.' She had promised herself that she would use her time wisely and not mope around thinking about Dermot. A couple of times, the feelings of sadness about her broken marriage did catch her unaware and she felt a wave of grief wash over her. But she was trying her best to let it go. Fortunately, he hadn't tried to call her again to talk about the sale of the house. That was one conversation she wasn't ready to have again right now. She was glad it was in the hands of the lawyers. She would tell Isobel about that later. She didn't want to do a total information dump on her when she had just arrived. 'I've painted all the bedrooms and the bathroom. Next up is the kitchen and the lounge. Though I might get someone in to do that. I'll see how it goes.'

'Look at that view,' said Isobel, standing up and walking to the window with its splendid views of the sea.

'I know. It's not something I will ever tire of. And it's always changing.' Rosie thought of the windows like ever-changing photo frames which captured the sky and the sea in different phases and stages. Sometimes the sky could be milky grey, black and several shades of blue and the ocean could be black, turquoise and sparkling blue as though it had been scattered with diamonds. She loved lying in bed and watching the scene frequently change. It was magical. 'Right, how about a cuppa outside? I'll go and put the kettle on. We need to enjoy the sun while we can.'

'Or,' said Isobel wickedly, glancing at her watch, how about a wee glass of fizz. 'It is surely wine o'clock time somewhere in the world?'

'That sounds like a plan,' said Rosie. 'I'll go and get the glasses.'

Just then Isobel's phone started to ring. She frowned. 'It's Mum. I better take it just in case there's anything wrong. I'll be there in a minute.'

Rosie went downstairs and sat on the bench outside while she waited for Isobel to finish her call. It was so peaceful with the only sound that of chirping birds and a few lazy bees buzzing by. Rosie was glad that the cottage next door appeared to be empty. There had been no sign of anyone since she had arrived and she hoped it would continue to stay vacant. For as long as she could remember it had been a holiday let, but a *very* expensive one. But not everyone wanted to pay through the odds to holiday in Scotland when the weather could be a bit of a lottery.

Like Creel Cottage, Beach Cottage was a traditionally built three-bedroom cottage which had been restored over the years and now had a wood-burning stove in the lounge and an outside hot tub surrounded by decking in the enclosed garden with sea views. Fairy lights were strung around the garden and they did look lovely in the website pictures when they were turned on and twinkling at night. The bedrooms were decorated to the highest specification with Egyptian cotton sheets and thick white duvets. The kitchen had a top of the range stove and coffee machine and was very sleekly designed. When she had a nosy at the cottage online, it made her cottage look positively shabby. Before they had moved over to the island, Dermot had tried to persuade her to makeover Creel Cottage and let it out but she had dug her heels in and refused. Even though she knew some of the downstairs rooms were still in need of attention and a lick of paint she wouldn't swap it for the world. It felt homely and had character which she felt next door didn't as it had been renovated to capacity.

Her stomach rumbled and she realised how famished she was, despite the cake earlier. Rosie had always been a good eater and had always been curvy rather than overweight but Dermot's news had destroyed her self-confidence and her appetite. Especially as his new woman was as svelte as a pin. When Rosie had found out her name, she had googled and seen photos on her employer's website. In her darker moments she had wondered if she had brought this on herself. Maybe if she had been a better wife, a prettier or thinner wife, then this wouldn't have happened. Dermot wouldn't have wanted to leave her. But then she had given herself a shake. She knew this was nothing to do with her, really. And Isobel would kill her if she knew her friend was thinking like that. There was no point in going back to that dark place again. What was done was done. Dermot had made his choices and moved on and perhaps had done her a favour. She had to remember that *and* she had to move on too.

She sat for a moment watching a blackbird hopping around the patio and admired the pale pink petals of the rose bush that had always been her father's pride and joy. She told herself that both were signs from nature that, despite the past few horrid months, life goes on.

'Mum sends her love,' said Isobel, appearing in the garden.

'Is everything okay with her?'

Isobel shook her head in despair. 'Yes, she's just having a problem logging into Netflix and needed my help. I feel like her on-call IT person and I don't even understand how to sort it most of the time. Anyway, she's all sorted. There's some new boxset on that she and Bill are keen to watch.'

'Two ticks and I'll sort the drinks.' Rosie went inside and quickly poured two glasses of Prosecco and brought them out to Isobel who was now sitting at the small patio table.

'Cheers,' Isobel said, clinking her glass against Rosie's.

'Slainte,' said Rosie. 'Thanks for coming over to stay. Here's to a great summer on Arran.' Rosie took a sip of the fizz and smiled. Things could only get better now that Isobel was here.

Isobel laughed heartily. 'Cheers. And thanks for having me over. We will have a ball. Us two together, what could possibly go wrong?'

CHAPTER TWELVE

Luke had tightly gripped the grab handle of the passenger seat as though his life depended on it. He could hardly look at the road ahead as Bella put her foot down, desperate to get them to the ferry terminal at Ardrossan as soon as possible. Her car was packed to the gunnels with his stuff and he was impressed by her organisational skills, even managing to wedge in his set of golf clubs. Then she had ordered him to get in the car. *Pronto.* He had barely secured his seatbelt when she had put her foot down and accelerated away from the hotel. He was surprised she hadn't left skid marks on the road behind.

'I need you to check the ferry online and see if there is space for us to get on the next sailing,' she had said as she navigated her way out of the town. 'I reckon we can be there in around twenty-five minutes if I put my foot down.'

'You don't want us getting stopped for speeding though,' he said and then realised he sounded about ninety-five. He frowned as he called up the ferry website on his phone. 'Mm. Looks like it's full.'

'Try phoning them. Sometimes it's easier when you can just speak to an *actual* human being.'

Luke didn't like to disobey though he couldn't help laughing as it was rare to hear someone of the younger generation talk like that. He just assumed they all preferred communicating digitally like his sons did. He hit the call button and managed to get through to a helpful woman in the ticket centre who told him that his best chance was to join the standby queue. He relayed this to Bella who was chewing a piece of gum impatiently.

'Okay,' she said grimly. 'I didn't think it was likely. The ferries can be a nightmare to get on in the summer and that's even if you have a booking. But I say we just get there and join the standby queue and keep everything crossed. Let's be positive. You just never know. If we think positively, we can manifest it.'

Luke admired her approach but also knew that no matter how much manifesting she did, there was no guarantee that they would get on that boat. He didn't like to ask what they would do if they missed the last ferry for the evening. He didn't fancy sleeping in the car for the night. Anyway, they could worry about that later. He was sure they could book into a hotel for the night. He reminded himself that taking off like this, was probably the most exciting and spontaneous thing he had done for years. It made him realise what a boring old codger he had become. Now, as Bella sped down the dual carriageway, he felt a wave of excitement ripple through him. He'd cancelled the taxi that was supposed to be taking him to the airport for his flight home tomorrow. London could wait.

As they followed signs for Ardrossan and then the harbour, he looked at the clock. He really hoped they would make it. So far, so good. Then they hit a set of red traffic lights. He watched as Bella drummed her fingers off the steering wheels. 'Come on,' she muttered, waiting for the lights to change. When they did, she had sworn under her breath then shouted at the driver in front, who was in no rush to move. 'The lights are green. Get a bend on!'

He raised an eyebrow. Good God, he wouldn't like to get on the wrong side of her. His initial impressions of Bella were that she was a bit shy. However, she had quickly overturned this in the past half hour with her decisive delegating, speedy driving and demonstrative gestures to several male drivers. He had watched the scenery flash past as he desperately tried to rack his brains for a glimmer of a memory that would help him remember Bella's mum. But try as he might he really couldn't recall very much about that time in Sydney. He definitely couldn't remember being with a woman called Isobel. He snatched the occasional glance at Bella wondering if he really could be her father. He was desperately trying to compare any similarities. They definitely didn't have the same nose: hers was petite and perfect whereas his was much bigger and also slightly crooked thanks to someone punching him and breaking it when he was younger. Could he really allow himself to think he might have a daughter? He had two sons from his marriage. Scottie was twenty-three, and studying sound engineering in Bristol. Ralph had just turned twenty-two and had taken a year out to travel in South America. Scottie had flown out to join his brother for the summer and if their last WhatsApp messages were anything to go by, then it didn't sound like either of them were in a hurry to get back to the UK. Mind you, he didn't blame them. It was all doom and gloom. The country was in a mess.

Just then, Bella skidded into the terminal and interrupted his thoughts. She rolled down her window to speak to a man in a high-vis vest.

'Are you booked on, love?' he asked.

Luke didn't speak and watched as Bella took charge.

'No,' she said, smiling sweetly and batting her eyelashes. 'I thought I would take my chances. It's a bit of an emergency, you know?'

'Mm,' said the man in the vest, sucking air in between his teeth and shaking his head. Then he flashed a grin at Bella. 'I think you might be lucky. There's roadworks on the M8 at Glasgow which has caused a tailback so there have been quite a few cancellations. People are raging, as you can imagine. Can you believe some geezer actually asked if we could hold the ferry for him?' He shook his head in disgust. 'Honestly. The cheek of some folk.' He looked towards the ferry. 'There are two cars ahead of you at the moment.' He made a clicking sound with his tongue.

'Och, I do hope we get on. I've got my friend with me who's here from Australia. And getting to Arran is on his bucket list before he . . .' she sniffed dramatically. The man in the vest widened his eyes, clearly hoping she didn't start to cry.

Bella reached into her pocket for a tissue and dabbed her eyes. 'It was a last-minute thing to come over to Scotland. He wasn't sure he would make it and, well, we want to surprise my mum . . . ' Her voice trailed off and she sighed dramatically.

Luke watched in bemusement, trying his hardest not to look shocked. Australia? Bucket list? Was she trying to finish him off? Maybe she *was* his daughter. She certainly had the performance gene.

The two cars ahead were waved on and Luke held his breath as Vest Man flushed and apologised.

'Right, love. On you go.' He held out the card machine to her.

Bella quickly made the payment with her card, bid him a grateful thanks and flashed him another smile, then pressed the button to close the window. 'Bingo,' she said. 'We're on. Let's get to Arran.'

CHAPTER THIRTEEN

Rosie was now wishing she had prepared dinner earlier as the thought of chopping and slicing did *not* appeal. As she sat in the garden, she realised how tired she was and stifled a yawn.

'I think I could do with another cup of tea,' said Isobel. 'Otherwise, I will faceplant onto the table.'

Rosie sighed. 'I know what you mean. Check us out, living life on the edge. A change from our younger days, eh?'

'I know, I forgot too. What are we like? But I'll go and make the tea. That's as long as you don't mind me rummaging around,' said Isobel, standing up.

'Make yourself at home,' said Rosie, thinking how nice it would be for someone else to make her a cuppa for a change. 'I'll come in and sort the wine and glasses too.'

'That sounds like a good plan,' said Isobel.

'Are you hungry?'

'Not hugely,' said Isobel.

'How about I just bring out some picky bits we can snack on?' suggested Rosie, who had now lost her appetite too.

'That sounds wonderful to me,' said Isobel. 'I'm still quite full of all that cake. Honestly, we're like a pair of grannies.' She clocked Rosie yawning again.

Rosie groaned as she rolled her shoulders. 'I feel about eighty-five at the moment. Definitely not youthful in the slightest.'

'Well, I am the opposite. I feel like a teenager again but for all the bad reasons. Like the hormones and the mood swings,' said Isobel. 'Sometimes I feel like I'm fifteen again — and not in a good way. I just want to eat chocolate and go to sleep and wake up when this is all over.'

Rosie realised that she must have been lucky so far with hot flushes and the *change*, although she reminded herself that her mind had been otherwise distracted with the breakdown of her marriage. She now wasn't sure if the murderous rages she felt towards Dermot were due to the perimenopause or the fact she actually couldn't stand him. Or both.

Isobel stood with her hands on her hips. 'And I am so easily distracted. I went online the other day to order something and then all of a sudden, I found myself looking at competitive swimming costumes on Amazon. How that happened I have no clue. I can't remember the last time I went swimming and I certainly don't plan to.' She shook her head. 'I wish I could bottle your serenity, Rosie. You've always done a good job of looking calm, regardless of what is happening.'

Rosie laughed in disbelief as she followed her into the kitchen. 'I must be a good actress as I don't feel serene.' Then she suddenly grinned. 'Do you really want to know my secret to happiness and wellbeing?'

Isobel had just filled the kettle and she turned to her, eyes wide. 'Wild sex parties? Don't tell me you've got a secret man stashed away somewhere? Or is it magic mushrooms? Rosehip tea?'

Rosie reached down and ruffled Coisty's head. 'This wee furry chap. He has got me through it. Coisty is the love of my life. Obviously apart from Ben,' she added hastily. 'Coisty loves me unconditionally, gets me up in the morning and forces me to go out and walk, even when it's pishing with rain or snowing. He seems to know if I'm a bit down and plonks his head on my lap and makes me sit down. And he cuddles up to me at night. Who needs a bloke when I've got this wee fella? I can highly recommend dogs. Coisty has changed my life.'

Isobel grinned. 'I still can't quite believe that he is called Coisty though.'

Rosie laughed. She had named him after her favourite Glaswegian footballer, Ally McCoist, who was now a leading TV sports commentator. It was now even more pleasing to think how much it had annoyed Dermot at the time. He was a lifelong fan of the Edinburgh team, Hibernian, and had no time for Ally McCoist and his cheeky chappy commentary. He disliked him so much that he changed the channel whenever he was commentating.

'You're actually going to shout "Coisty" at the park?' he had said in abject horror.

'Indeed I am,' she had said stubbornly. 'What better name than Coisty?'

Rosie now gazed at Coisty with complete adoration, glad she had stood her ground.

'I think a pet would tip me over the edge,' said Isobel good-naturedly. 'Much as I love Coisty, I don't know that he would fit in with my lifestyle.'

'Maybe you should go and see the GP then and get yourself checked out. Especially if you're feeling so rubbish,' suggested Rosie gently, taking the wine bucket outside and plonking the glasses next to it.

'Maybe,' said Isobel. Just then a Calvin Harris track started blaring from Isobel's phone. She snatched it up from the table. 'Hi Bella, love, how are you?' There was a pause.

'How's the camping going? I'm just with Rosie, relaxing in the cottage. In fact, I'll just put you on speakerphone so you can say hello to her.'

There was a pause before Bella spoke. 'Hi, Rosie, . . .'

'Hi, Bella, so what is life in a tent like?'

'Um, so I didn't end up going camping,' said Bella.

'Oh. How come? Though we were just saying camping is our idea of hell. I don't blame you for—'

Bella cut her off. 'Um, Mum, I'm actually here. I'm on Arran.'

Rosie watched as Isobel suddenly sat bolt upright. 'What do you mean, you're here on Arran? Did you change the camping location?'

'No,' said Bella.

'Is everything okay?'

Coisty jumped up to attention and barked.

'Kind of. But I need to talk to you. Now. Can I come round?'

Isobel looked at Rosie who nodded.

'Of course. Come now.' Isobel gave Bella directions. 'I'll see you soon.'

'Okay thanks, Mum,' said Bella in a wobbly voice.

Isobel ended the call and looked at Rosie in shock. 'I've no idea what's going on, but it must be serious if she's here on the island.'

Rosie nodded in concern watching her friend and knowing her mind would be racing wildly.

Isobel's hand flew to her mouth. 'What if she's pregnant?' She grimaced. 'Surely not? She doesn't even have a boyfriend. Not since that fella she was seeing that she met in Corfu. But that fizzled out. Mind you who am I to talk. I didn't have a boyfriend and look what happened to me.'

Rosie tried to stay calm. But she knew how level-headed Bella was and she wouldn't normally just get the ferry over to Arran on a whim. Bella's sensible approach to things was a quality she must have inherited from her father as Isobel tended to do *drama*. She had a sense that whatever it was that Bella needed to talk to her mum about was going to be serious. *Huge*. And Rosie had a feeling that their summer plans were about to change. A lot.

CHAPTER FOURTEEN

A few moments after they had driven off the ferry, Bella had pulled into the car park and taken a big breath explaining that she was going to give her mum a heads-up rather than just arriving unexpectedly. Luke watched Bella as she anxiously paced up and down on the pavement next to the car, telling her mum that she was on the island and had *news*.

He was in no rush to go anywhere else right now. It was strange, but from the moment Bella drove onto the ferry, a sense of calm and peace descended over him. It was as though his life had actually slowed down. Just like that. He had followed Bella onto the deck outside, pulled on his beanie hat and been completely transfixed as he had watched the sea. Maybe it was the fresh, salty air and the trails of frothy waves the ferry left behind as it ploughed through the water. But Luke was incredibly excited about this journey. Most of all he was excited that he was going off grid. He felt as though he had come home. Which was strange as he had never set foot on this island before.

A few moments later Bella stopped pacing, ended the call and looked over at him. He gave her a questioning look and a thumbs up and then down. If truth be told, he had grown very fond of her in the past few hours that they had spent together. She was a lovely young woman and her mother had done a great job of raising her, especially as she had done it solo. Although he and Cindy, his ex-wife, were now apart he was grateful they had been together long enough to raise the kids. Though he did have to acknowledge that she had been left holding the babies plenty of times when he was touring with the band or away with work. But he had always been faithful to her and couldn't wait to return home to his family after being away on the road.

He could only imagine how Bella must have felt all these years not even knowing who her father was. He could only trust that her mother had her very good reasons for not telling Bella. And he had to ask himself that if he had known about her when she was a baby would things have been different? Or if he had known her mother was pregnant at the time it could have changed the course of his life completely. Maybe he would never have met Cindy and married her. But then that would have meant that his sons wouldn't exist. He realised that his whole life might have been completely different. He momentarily wondered how his sons would react if they learned they had an older sister. Then, realising that he was getting way ahead of things, he gave himself a shake. There was no guarantee or proof that he was indeed Bella's dad. Only her mother could shed light on that fact. And then they would have to do a paternity test. He watched as Bella slipped her phone into her pocket. It looked like they would soon find out.

'Okay,' said Bella, getting back into the driver's seat and puffing. 'She knows I'm here and that I need to talk to her. And I know she will now be flipping her lid and be worrying that I'm pregnant or have killed someone.' She was talking very quickly and he knew she was worried. His son, Scottie, was exactly the same when he had something on his mind.

'Extreme, huh?' said Luke.

'You don't know my mother . . .'

He only had to look at the expression on her face to tell she was very nervous about this. 'Where is she staying?'

'It's in Kildonan, about half an hour away. Mum is here with her best friend. She lives here permanently.'

Luke tried to give her a reassuring smile even though he now felt very skittish. 'Come on then,' he said, 'let's go and get this over with.'

She gave an excitable laugh. 'Yes, I suppose so. We will soon find out the truth and whether or not you are my dad.' She glanced over at the departing ferry which was returning to Ardrossan and then clasped her hand over her mouth. 'That's the last ferry for the night. You do realise that you're stuck here regardless of what mum says?'

Luke shrugged. 'I have everything that I need here.' He gestured to the back of the car. 'Don't worry about that. I am in no rush to go anywhere. In fact, I have a confession to make.' He watched as she looked at him quizzically. 'When we were on the ferry and I was outside on the deck, I made a couple of calls, booked a place to stay. I'm going to stay on here for a bit. *Regardless* of what your mum says . . . I've got some work to do and could do with hiding out somewhere quiet for a while where I won't be disturbed. I'm not in any rush to go back to London and I've managed to get a cottage to rent here.'

'Oh, okay. I wasn't expecting that but well, why not, I suppose,' said Bella, starting the ignition. 'Especially if you don't have to be anywhere. That's a nice position to be in.' She indicated left out of the car park and followed the road that would take them over to Lamlash and to the south of the island towards Kildonan. 'I was supposed to be camping with friends this weekend. That's why Mum is even more freaked out.'

Luke pursed his lips. 'Parents *always* jump to these conclusions. It's just what happens. It's the way we're wired. I think it's a design flaw. We always worry. It doesn't matter how old you are.'

She glanced sideways at him. 'Do you worry about your boys?'

He had told her earlier about his sons and explained that they were away travelling. 'Of course I do, though my ex probably worries about them more. She had an awful time with empty nest syndrome when they both left home. She just didn't know what to do with herself . . . she became quite lost . . . ' his voice trailed off. Cindy soon found herself again though *and* someone else to focus her attentions on and it wasn't him. He blinked. He really needed to try and get over this.

'Earth to Luke,' said Bella.

'Oops, sorry,' said Luke, realising he had got lost in his own thoughts. 'Do I worry? Yes, I do, though I think it's probably a bit different with sons. It shouldn't be, but it is,' he added hastily. 'If I had a daughter then I think I would worry a whole lot more.' His words hung there, layered with uncertainties. *If* he had a daughter. Maybe he did.

As Bella drove down the hill towards Lamlash, Luke admired the view of the Holy Isle and kept his eyes glued to the window as he took in the still blue waters of Lamlash Bay. 'Wow, what a beautiful spot,' he said quietly. It looked so tranquil and, despite the cause of the trip over here, he also felt a sense of peace descend over him which he never felt in London, despite his many attempts at meditation. Staring at the water made him realise how parched he was. 'Do you mind stopping so I can just nip in there to grab some water?' He pointed at the Co-op ahead.

'Sure,' said Bella, her voice shaking. 'That will give me a chance to mentally prepare.'

'Can I get you anything?' he asked kindly.

She shook her head. 'No thanks.'

'I'll just be a few minutes.' He unclipped his seatbelt and got out the car, walking briskly across the road. As Luke entered the store, he headed straight to the chiller section and reached for a small bottle of water. Turning, he collided with a customer who had her head down as she studied her list. 'I'm so sorry,' he said immediately, checking that she was okay.

Usually people would give him a second glance when they realised they recognised him from somewhere and would stare at him while they tried to place his face. However, the woman walked on, oblivious. Luke was thrilled that he was seemingly invisible. As he got older, he much preferred keeping a low profile and staying under the radar. It was a change from his younger days when he had loved all the attention. And he wasn't too proud to admit that he had developed quite the ego when he was younger.

Staring at the bottle of water in his hand, he realised it might be a good idea to grab a few other provisions to keep him going. He quickly found a loaf of bread, some cheese, a box of eggs and some bananas. It was a random assortment of things but he was aware that Bella was waiting in the car and at this rate would think he had done a runner. The sooner they saw her mum and cleared all of this up, the better. He momentarily wondered how long it would take to get from where Bella's mum was, to the holiday cottage he'd booked. Hopefully he could call an Uber to take him. He paid for the groceries, carefully bagged them in a bright blue bag for life, and walked out of the shop towards Bella, who was waiting in the car.

CHAPTER FIFTEEN

There was a loud rap at the door of Creel Cottage. Isobel had been pacing around, frantic with worry ever since Bella had phoned, and Rosie had been doing her best to calm her down. 'Let's just wait until she gets here and she can tell us what's going on,' she had said soothingly, in a bid to placate Isobel. 'There's no point in jumping to conclusions.' But her words had been in vain, which she knew would be the case. Isobel had always been the type of person to catastrophise and had become increasingly frantic as the minutes passed. She ran to the door and flung it wide open.

Rosie held herself back, wanting to give them some space. From where she was standing in the hallway, she could see a white-faced Bella. Isobel threw her arms around her daughter. 'Bella!' she shrieked. 'What's wrong? You're worrying me. Come in and tell me what on earth is going on.'

'Mum . . .' Bella's voice trailed away and she pointed at a man who came to stand beside her on the doorstep.

'Who's this?' asked Isobel suspiciously.

Rosie hadn't even realised Bella had company. Oh dear. This did not bode well.

'Mum, this is Luke.'

Rosie wished she had her glasses on so she could see properly. From where she was standing, she could see a man who was around the same age as her and Isobel and was wearing chinos and a navy polo-shirt. He definitely fell into the good-looking category. He stepped forward to shake Isobel's hand. If only she could get a better look.

'Hello there, Isobel,' he said. 'I'm Luke. Nice to meet you. Bella has told me so much about you.'

Rosie clocked his London accent. He sounded very confident. But she was so frustrated that she couldn't make out his features. It was no use; she needed to go and get her glasses. With as much stealth as she could manage, she crept into the kitchen. She could still hear them talking and she paused when she heard Isobel's voice rise an octave.

'What's going on, Bella?' Isobel said slowly, clearly trying her best to keep her voice as even as possible. 'Who is this?'

'It's probably better that we talk inside,' said Bella.

'Come in,' said Isobel loudly.

Rosie heard the door close and footsteps go down the hall and into the living room. She heard Bella ask very loudly and clearly, 'Where is Rosie?' She knew Bella would be hoping that she would take her side and smooth things over like she always did when she and Ben were younger. Just then Coisty ran out the kitchen, barking and wagging his tail. Rosie knew within seconds he would probably be sitting on the man's feet and gazing up at him. He was a shameless flirt with both sexes. Rosie put her ear to the kitchen door that opened through to the living room.

'Look, why don't you take a seat,' said Isobel.

'Is Rosie here?' said Bella again, sounding nervous.

'Yes. She just must have nipped to the loo.'

'Take a seat,' Isobel said again and waited for them both to sit down. 'Now is anyone going to tell me what this is all about? Am I missing something?'

Rosie could tell from the sound of Isobel's wobbling voice that she needed some moral support. She put her glasses on and then tried to casually appear from the kitchen clutching a mug of what was now very cold tea. 'Hi guys,' she said cheerily, putting her cup down and going over to hug Bella. 'We thought you were camping, love? Mind you, I don't blame you for dodging that. Why on earth anyone wants to sleep in a tent is beyond me. Especially with the midges.' Rosie looked at the man. He looked vaguely familiar. He was rather handsome too.

'I'm sorry. I don't think we have met. My name is Rosie,' she said reaching over and pumping Luke's hand energetically. But as her eyes roamed over Luke, her whole body froze. Rosie couldn't believe who she was seeing. He wasn't just vaguely familiar; he was actually very familiar. Not only *that* but he was old enough to be Bella's father. *Oh, God.* Was this some kind of daddy issue thing and she was now going for mature men and father-type replacements? Was this why she had come to the island? To tell her mum that she had shacked up with an older man. *Jeezo.* But why *this* man in particular? Isobel would flip in a minute when the penny dropped and she didn't even dare to think about what Granny Margaret would say when she found out. And why hadn't Isobel even realised who this guy was? 'Erm, is this some kind of joke or something?' She looked over at Isobel in disbelief. 'Don't you know who this is, Isobel?' Then she turned to Bella. 'Are you going to tell us what on earth is going on?'

CHAPTER SIXTEEN

Bella noticed the switch in Rosie's manner straight away. She was always the warmest and most welcoming person in the room. Now the atmosphere was distinctly chilly and Rosie stood, her arms crossed defensively in front of her, glaring at Luke.

'What's going on, Bella?' Rosie said, her voice icy.

Isobel was now looking at both of them completely bemused.

What was wrong with everyone? Why were they acting so weirdly? Bella wished the ground would open up and swallow her. Especially as Rosie was now throwing daggers at Luke. Bella wanted to be anywhere but here. Despite everything that had happened today, she knew this was a big mistake. *Huge.*

'Has anyone ever told you that you look awfully like Luke Giles?' asked Rosie tersely. There was a moment's silence as the penny dropped and she and Isobel looked at each other. Then Isobel screwed up her face and squealed. 'Bloody hell, you *are* Luke Giles! What the hell are you doing here?'

There was a long and very awkward pause. Bella watched as Luke carefully studied her mum's face and waited for a flicker of recognition from him. *Anything* at all. There was nothing. Then he turned and held out his hand to Rosie. This time Bella could see something in his eyes.

'Nice to meet you,' he said, then frowned.

'Actually, we have met before,' said Rosie, picking up her mug.

He blushed and looked a bit embarrassed. Then he looked back at Rosie. 'You do look kind of familiar,' said Luke.

'That's because we have met before.'

And then Bella became completely confused.

'Bella, please tell me you're not going *out* with this man?' said Rosie incredulously.

'No!' she shouted.

'Then *what* are you doing with my daughter?' Isobel challenged Luke. 'Why are you here? Can't you find a woman nearer your own age?' She started to pace, which was never a good sign. 'This is completely outrageous. I mean, you might be famous but *seriously*?'

Oh, good gawd, thought Bella. What was wrong with her mum and Rosie? They were behaving like a pair of morons. 'Have you two been on the wine or something?' She glanced through the doors out to the garden and clocked the empty wine glasses and the ice bucket. She frowned at them both and shook her head in disappointment. This day was getting worse by the second. This was all she needed. A showdown with her tipsy mother and Rosie.

'Tsk,' said Isobel, shaking her head and ignoring Bella. 'Look at that *Titanic* fella who is always hanging around with the young girls. You don't want to become one of *those* famous guys who only dates women under the age of twenty-five. That's just sad and *very* desperate. I mean, is that really what you want, Bella? To be hanging around some old guy with a paunch while you frolic on a yacht? It's a *Daily Mail* story just waiting to be written . . .'

Luke widened his eyes in horror and was seemingly patting his stomach to check for the said paunch. Bella glared at her mum. 'Don't be ridiculous. Or so rude. That is just disgusting. We're not *dating*, Mum. I had to do this because you have refused to tell me the truth all these years.'

'Bella, what are you talking about?' demanded Isobel.

Bella sighed and stamped her feet in frustration. 'For years I have been asking you who my dad is and you refuse to tell me,' she said.

'That's not entirely true,' said Isobel, tears smarting in her eyes. 'You know I said he was a one-night stand in Glasgow . . .'

'You lied!' shouted Bella angrily.

Isobel looked ashen-faced and Bella momentarily felt awful. She was *never* normally short-tempered with her mum. But Bella was now on a roll. 'I found your diary in that box from Gran's house . . . when she was moving, she asked you to take some of your stuff back? It's full of old papers and photos and your journal from travelling in Australia.'

Isobel shook her head in disbelief. 'I don't understand what you're talking about. A journal? I didn't keep a journal.'

Bella looked across at Rosie hoping for some help. But Rosie was staring strangely at Luke.

Isobel sighed. 'Look Bella, can you just get to the point and tell me what this is all about?'

'I want to know if it's true,' said Bella flatly. She was tired now and the adrenaline from earlier which had kept her going all day had now seeped out of her. 'Is it true that Luke is my dad? In your journal you wrote that you were off to meet him again at some bay. You'd been having a fling with him in Sydney when he was on tour.'

Rosie clattered her mug down on the coffee table. 'Oh no,' she gasped and her cheeks turned red. 'I always wondered what I'd done with my diary. I thought I had chucked it away. I must have left it at your house.' She turned to Isobel sheepishly. 'And your mum put it in that box with the other stuff. I am totally mortified.'

Just then Bella looked between her mum and Rosie as she put two and two together again and finally worked out what had happened. Then she glanced at Luke who was staring at Rosie.

'I *thought* I recognised you,' said Luke.

'Yes,' said Rosie with an embarrassed chuckle. 'Once upon a time, we knew each other fairly well.'

'The Q bar in Sydney . . .' his voice trailed off.

'Yes, that was the place. We were supposed to meet up there but you didn't appear.'

Bella looked over at Luke in shock. He did at least look shamefaced.

'We left Sydney a day early. I called and left a message at the bar.'

Rosie shrugged. 'I never got the message. I just assumed you'd done a runner.' She waved her hand dismissively. 'Anyway, it's all water under the bridge now. That was a lifetime ago. It's just very odd seeing you again now.'

'So does that mean you're not my dad?' whispered Bella, feeling very dejected. Her heart sank as the disappointment washed over her.

'He is most definitely not your dad,' said Isobel, gently. 'Nothing ever happened between us.' She glanced over at Luke and shrugged.

There was a heavy silence and Bella gulped. 'I'm so sorry,' she said, her voice wobbling. 'What a complete mess I've made of all of this.'

'Oh, Bella,' said Isobel.

Rosie, who was obviously lost in a distant memory, cleared her throat. 'Your mum is right, darling. Luke is *definitely* not your father.'

There was another heavy pause before anyone spoke. Bella was the first to break the silence. 'I'm sorry, Luke. I am so sorry about all of this. What a mess.'

Luke patted her on the shoulder and at that moment, Bella wished that Luke *was* her father. He was actually really nice. Especially as he had been so kind to her today and had come over here with him on a crazy whim. She groaned, feeling completely mortified at the mess she had created by jumping to the wrong conclusions.

She watched as her mum and Rosie continued to look at each other. Something passed between them which made Bella feel uneasy. They definitely knew more than they were letting on. At least if Luke was her dad, it would be a bit easier to make sense of than the complicated mess that was now starting to unravel. It was all too much and she sank down on the sofa and burst into tears.

CHAPTER SEVENTEEN

Throughout his life, Luke had always been told he had the gift of the gab. Even at primary school he charmed the female teachers with his long eyelashes and cute dimpled smile. He had travelled the world, sold millions of records and had a successful career as an actor. He was best known for the role he played in a successful police series on Sky TV. Yet now as he sat in this quaint cottage on this island off the coast of Scotland, which he was physically unable to leave as there were no more ferries tonight, he didn't have a clue what to say. Or what to do. The usual plaudits and pleasantries that would roll off the tip of his tongue seemed glib and inauthentic. He felt desperately sorry for Bella who looked so vulnerable and lost as she sat with tears sliding down her cheeks. He had spotted a box of tissues on the coffee table and passed them to her. He also felt bad for her mum too. He had no idea what the real story was about the identity of Bella's father but he could tell from the stricken look on Isobel's face that there was more to it than him being a one-night stand. He had learned through experience that life was messy and complicated and he was sure she hadn't withheld the details from her daughter on a whim. There must have been a good reason for it. He just hoped that it wasn't an awful reason. He shuddered. That didn't even bear thinking about. Right now, he knew that for their sake he needed to give them some space. Especially as meeting Rosie had now completely unnerved him.

'Right,' said Rosie. 'I'm going to make some tea. I think we need a cuppa or maybe something stronger?'

Luke put his hand up and shook his head. 'If you don't mind, I will leave you to it. I think you could do with some space to talk.' He turned to Bella. 'I am sorry that this has been so upsetting for you and you didn't get the answers you wanted.'

Bella choked back a sob. 'You must think I am completely bonkers.'

Luke shook his head and tried to keep his voice light. 'There is nothing to say sorry for Bella. You've not done anything wrong . . . other than to mix up a few of the facts.' He shrugged. 'We've all done that plenty of times.' He could feel Isobel staring at him. 'For what it's worth, you did me a huge favour.'

She looked at him confused. 'How?'

'Look, I needed an exit strategy to get away from the golf fiasco and from my life in London and so you brought me here which is perfect.'

She frowned.

'I've got some work to do — a book to write — and I've managed to get a cottage for the summer. Nobody knows I'm here, well other than you and your mum and, um, Rosie. So I can just keep my head down and get on with it. My agent will be delighted if I can get the book to her on time.'

Bella didn't look convinced but at least she had stopped crying.

'Now, I'll get out your hair and let you talk with your mum.' He took his phone out his pocket. 'Mm. The reception doesn't look that great.' He rubbed his hand over his jaw and looked at Isobel. 'Do you think you could do me a favour please?'

'What?' said Isobel curiously.

'Can you call me an Uber or a Bolt?'

To his astonishment, Isobel burst out laughing and Rosie then joined in. Soon Bella was also chuckling with amusement.

'Did I say something funny?' he said drily, at a loss as to why his question was so amusing.

'Oh dear,' said Rosie. 'You can maybe get an Uber in Glasgow or Edinburgh. But you're on a Scottish island now. You've absolutely no chance. You can't even get Deliveroo. And, just so you know, there's no Amazon Prime delivery either.'

'Ah, right,' he said, feeling foolish. He was too used to the conveniences of life in a big city. 'I'm clearly too much of a city boy.' He shook his head.

'Your best bet is the local bus . . . or taxi,' said Rosie, kindly. 'But I don't fancy your chances tonight . . . however, if you don't mind my old banger, I can give you a lift there. Where is the cottage you've rented?'

At that moment he didn't care if he had to ride as a pillion passenger on her motorbike. He just wanted to get out of there and leave the women in peace to talk. 'If you're sure,' he said, 'then I would very much appreciate that. It's in Kilmory.'

'But Rosie, you and mum have been drinking. You can't drive if you've been on the booze.' Bella pointed outside to the ice bucket and glasses.

Rosie shook her head. 'We only had a couple of sips. So, it's fine, I am completely sober. No worries at all, Luke. I can drive you. That is as long as you don't mind my choices in music. I'm really getting back into New Kids on the Block. They've got a new album out and they're doing a tour and have got a residency in Las Vegas. *And* they're all well into their fifties and looking *very* good indeed.'

'*Ouch*,' said Isobel, 'just ignore her. She clearly was never a loyal fan if she can switch allegiances just like that.'

'Honestly, Rosie,' said Bella, who was now at least laughing even if it was in embarrassment.

Luke wasn't sure if it was a personal dig, but he decided to ignore her comments about the New Kids on the Block, the

American boyband who were, like the GFC, huge in the nineties. He would have *loved* to have done another album and a tour with the band, but his brother had put paid to that by shacking up with Cindy. Maybe he would write about it in his book.

'I'll promise to be on my best behaviour,' said Rosie, rolling her eyes. 'Honestly. I won't even sing along. Come on, let's get you organised.'

He caught Isobel shaking her head before she and Bella walked out to the car to transfer his stuff to Rosie's boot. He reached over and gave Bella a hug and kissed her on both cheeks. 'Look, I am sorry that this didn't work out as we hoped. But it will all be okay. Your mum seems really sound. Don't fall out with her about this. It's not worth it. Just trust that whatever she has done, she has done it for you.' He reached out to touch her gently on the cheek. Before he changed his mind, he reached into his pocket and pulled out a card which had his details on it. 'Just in case you want to get in touch, I'll be here for the next few weeks.'

Bella smiled gratefully. 'Thank you,' she said.

He bent down to pat Coisty who had come to find out what was going on. Rosie had started the ignition of her car and the music was loud with the song 'Kids' blaring out. She revved her foot against the accelerator.

Luke raised his eyes and laughed. 'Oh dear, wish me luck.'

'Yes, good luck with Rosie,' said Isobel. 'You will need it.' She put a hand on his arm. 'And thanks for looking after Bella. I'm sorry I jumped to the wrong conclusion.'

Luke looked over at Bella and then back to Isobel. 'You've done an amazing job raising her. She's a real tribute to you. You should be very proud of her. I know I would be if she *was* my daughter.'

Isobel blushed.

Luke gave them a wave, then opened the passenger door. 'Thanks for doing this,' he said to Rosie. 'I appreciate it.'

'It's all a bit surreal to say the least,' said Rosie. 'Let's just say that I'm doing it for old time's sake. Now, where did you say it is you're staying?' She reversed out the gravel drive and began driving down the narrow road which would take them back to the village.

Luke pulled out his phone and checked the directions. Then he groaned and looked up sheepishly. 'Um, the thing is the cottage is actually here in Kildonan not Kilmory. Sorry.'

'That's okay,' she said with a shrug. 'That should make it quite a simple drop off then. What's the name of the cottage?'

'Beach Cottage.'

'Are you actually having a laugh?' she said in shock.

'What do you mean?'

'Wait and see,' said Rosie. She turned the car and drove back towards the direction they had just come from.

He was confused. They had just come that way. Then he started laughing as he noticed the sign on the door.

'There it is,' he said, pointing at the beautiful traditional stone cottage which was on the single-track road with no through road which made it even more idyllic than he thought. The door had a slate sign on it with the words, Beach Cottage, etched onto it. Then he looked at the road and realised that the other cottage a bit further down was *Creel Cottage*. 'Ah,' he said, when he realised it was the house next door to Rosie's.

'It's a great spot,' she said, parking the car just beside the cottage and turning off the ignition. 'It's completely tucked away. You shouldn't get anyone bothering you here. And the neighbours are great. Quiet and keep themselves to themselves. Not at all crazy in any way.'

Luke laughed. There was something enchanting about Rosie especially the fact she was so self-deprecating. She made a refreshing change from the women who had been throwing themselves at him since his marriage breakdown. She was so authentic and normal. No wonder he had been attracted to her when they were younger. If only he could remember the details.

'So much for my wishful thinking that the cottage would be empty for the summer.' She shook her head in bemusement. 'And now *you're* here. You couldn't actually make this up.'

They both got out the car and Luke walked over to the key-safe by the front door, painted in a pale lichen shade, and lined up the dial with the code. The box opened and he retrieved the key, opening the front door. 'Here, let me get that,' he said to Rosie who was unpacking his bag and golf clubs from the boot.

'Are you sure about this?' she said again doubtfully, looking around. 'It's very quiet here. Island life is a bit different. Will you not be bored? Especially when you're used to living the high life in London. There really isn't so much to do here in comparison.'

Luke shook his head. 'It's perfect. It is quiet, not to mention the stunning scenery and that's all I need. And thanks for giving me the lift round. I *really* appreciate it.'

He smiled at her and she blushed.

'No problem at all,' she said nonchalantly. 'Well, I will leave you to it. And, remember, if you need to borrow a cup of sugar or anything else when you are here, then you only need to knock on the door.'

He regarded her for a moment as she stood looking at him pensively. She was rather beautiful and the way she kept tucking her hair behind her ears was quite endearing. 'Um, well I suppose the only thing I need to ask is . . . well, I'd be really grateful if you could keep it to yourself that I am here.' *Which was so not what I was thinking. Why did I just say that?* He could have kicked himself, especially when he saw how unimpressed she looked.

'Of course,' she said curtly. 'Don't worry. Your secret is safe with me.' She tapped her finger to her mouth and whispered, 'Sssh.'

'Thanks,' he said. 'You've been so kind to me. Especially when I turned up out the blue.' He paused. 'I just hope that Bella is okay. She's a good kid.'

Rosie grimaced. 'Mm, we shall see. Watch this space. I've a feeling there is more to come. But I'm sure it will all be okay. That's as long as Isobel hasn't dropped any huge clangers while I have been out.' She pulled her bag tighter on her shoulder. 'Right, I'd best be off. See you later. Enjoy!' Giving him a wave, she jumped into the car and drove the few metres to park in the drive of her own cottage.

Luke took his things into the little house and dumped them in the bright hallway. *What a day.* He walked through to the welcoming lounge which had windows overlooking the sea. Immediately he relaxed. He had a feeling he was going to enjoy staying here regardless of the strange chain of events that had brought him to Arran.

CHAPTER EIGHTEEN

The next morning, Rosie clipped Coisty's lead onto his collar and they left the cottage to make their way down the lane to the beach for their usual walk. There was no sign of life at Beach Cottage. She still couldn't believe Luke Giles was staying next door. Her fling from all those years ago. At the time, she thought she was head over heels in love with him when it was actually just lust. Although her younger self did think they had a genuine connection. But it was easy to imagine these things, she told herself, when you were young and having a brief fling with a pop star who probably had a girl, or several, in every town. Rosie had managed to move on very quickly afterwards with an Australian hunk called Brad. There were a few more flings after Brad and then she met Dermot, who she had thought was *the* one. She hadn't thought about Luke for years. Rosie wasn't on social media and didn't read magazines, unless she was at the hairdressers and even then, she preferred the gardening magazines. But when she saw him again she recognised him because he still looked gorgeous. It was Isobel who had told her last night that he had turned his hand to acting and had been in a successful police procedural series on Sky TV.

Coisty trotted alongside her at quite a pace and Rosie took in deep breaths of salty air. She didn't think she would ever tire of that fresh smell which invigorated her every morning. They didn't pass a soul and when they reached the sandy shore, she let Coisty run free. His tail was in full helicopter wagging mode a sign that he was particularly excited by life and he ran along stopping to push his nose into the ground and smell new scents.

As she wandered along behind him, her mind drifted between thoughts of last night's drama and her plans for that morning. Isobel and Bella were still fast asleep when she left and she wondered if she should give them some space to talk things through. She could definitely find tasks to keep her busy. She wanted to finish the weeding at the bottom of the garden and then mow the lawn. There was just a small patch of grass outside and she had cut it back last week. But the good weather and the rainfall during the past few nights meant it had quickly sprouted again. She loved the look of a manicured lawn and her dad had been very particular about making sure it was neat and tidy. Then she laughed as she realised, she was talking to herself again. Normally she was surrounded by people at work — in the classroom and staff room — and would see Dermot at home and then friends at the weekend. It had felt a bit weird to only have Coisty to talk to lately and podcasts or the radio to listen to. Then she found her thoughts wandering again, this time to her mum's old recipe book. She had been flicking through it and planned to make her traditional flapjacks at some point while Isobel was here. She missed having someone to cook for, so it would be nice to take care of Isobel for a change.

Looking at the ground at her feet, she saw a glint of blue glass in the sand. Bending down, she picked it up, smoothing the grains of sand away with her thumb. She had enjoyed collecting bits of sea-glass since moving here and had amassed a clean poo bag full of it. She unzipped her crossover bag, pulled out the small plastic bag and dropped the blue glass in with the other bits of what were mainly white and green shards. Then she whistled for Coisty. But when she looked up, she realised he was nowhere to be seen. He did quite often follow his nose and she wondered if he had got the scent of a rabbit or a dead bird and was now happily rolling all over it. As she scanned the beach ahead, she still couldn't see him. Where was he? Her relaxed smile vanished as she started to panic.

'Coisty,' she called. 'Coisty. Come and get a treat.' But the beach was deserted and no matter how many times she called his name and offered him a piece of cheese or sausage, the little dog was nowhere to be seen. She started to up her pace and lightly jogged over to the pile of rocks at the far end of the beach. As she neared them, she sighed in relief when she saw him lying on his back with his feet in the air. A man was crouched down over him, tickling his stomach. 'Coisty, there you are.' Coisty wagged his tail and looked beyond her as though he had no idea who she was.

'Hey there, good morning.'

Rosie sighed. Of course, the man had to be Luke. As cute as Coisty was, she had to remember that not everyone liked dogs. 'Oh, hi there,' she said as casually as she could manage. 'I'm sorry. I hope he wasn't bothering you. As you can tell his recall is not very good. Naughty boy.' She shook her head.

'Is that me or the dog?' joked Luke.

Rosie's cheeks flushed and she felt herself fumble with Coisty's lead. He jumped up and shook himself then promptly sat down again next to Luke. *He was outrageous.* Rosie was aware that Luke was gazing at her and she wondered if she had a piece of twig or something in her hair. She looked at him questioningly as she tried to subtly rake her hand through her hair in the hope of freeing any vegetation. 'Lovely morning, isn't it?'

'It's beautiful,' he said, smiling at her and his dark eyes crinkled in the corners.

Luke was dressed in jeans and a long-sleeved t-shirt which clung to his muscles. She felt something inside her shift and her legs actually started to feel a bit wobbly. She glanced again at his well-defined arms. He looked very strong and *capable*. Up close she couldn't help admiring his features. He had a few lines on his forehead and he looked very natural, so wasn't a filler kind of man, which was a relief. In fact, he had grown into a really good-looking man which was unusual for popstars who had been teenage pin-ups. Usually, they showed clear signs of their misspent youth, or had so much work done, they no longer looked real.

'This is a great spot,' he said, interrupting her train of thought.

'Yes, it is,' she said, realising she was still gazing at him. She bent down to stroke Coisty's head just as Luke bent down to pat him and their hands touched. Rosie almost gasped at the sensation.

'Coisty's an interesting name,' he said, his voice gruff.

'Um, yes, bit of a story there. I named him after Ally McCoist. The footballer,' she said as way of explanation.

Luke burst out laughing. 'You're kidding, right?'

'Nope, I'm really not. Okay, well anyway, enjoy your walk,' she said quickly, standing up and feeling her cheeks colour again. What was wrong with her and *why* did he keep looking at her that way? Her dog's name wasn't that weird, was it? Or did she have snot hanging from her nostrils or something? She brushed her nose with the back of her hand, suddenly feeling very awkward and a bit shaky. 'Bye for now. Come on, Coisty.'

'See you later,' he said. His smile seemed to push his cheeks up to his eyes and light up his whole face.

Rosie managed a sort of grin back, which felt more like a gurn and, turning away, she tugged at the lead so Coisty would follow. Why had she turned into a mushy mess? Clearly the first interaction she had with a man who wasn't her husband had thrown her into a spin. Yet he wasn't just any old bloke, a voice in her head reminded her. He was a man she hadn't thought about for over twenty years and his sudden reappearance had stirred up memories. With every memory the nerves in her body tingled, as though on fire. She walked away and made herself focus on the horizon ahead for as long as she could. Then she briefly looked back over her shoulder. But Luke had disappeared.

CHAPTER NINETEEN

Bella opened her eyes and then closed them again for a moment as she realised where she was. And why she was there. Then it all came back to her. *Nightmare*. What a disaster yesterday had been. She was in Ben's room, in Rosie's cottage on Arran. Bella rolled onto her side, pulled the duvet further up and placed her hands under her head in a prayer like position. Then she found herself looking straight at a picture of a group of guys that sat on the bedside table. As she looked properly at it, she realised that it was Ben and his friends. At least, she assumed that was who it was. It had been years since they had seen each other and she barely recognised him. He was standing on a ski slope, wearing bright blue trousers and a matching jacket. A pair of sunglasses were perched on his head and he was grinning at the camera. She picked it up and studied the image more closely. It was definitely Ben. His dimples were the giveaway. It was odd to think how close they were growing up yet now they were practically strangers.

Bella was older than Ben by one year and, she realised with slight guilt, she had enjoyed bossing him around when they were younger. When they hit the awkward teenage years, and she had viewed him as an extremely annoying *boy*, they had drifted apart. Especially as he lived in Edinburgh and had his own friends. She had her own social circle in Glasgow and certainly didn't want to be forced to hang out with a gangly teenager. So it had then tended to just be their mums who got together which was, she now realised, a bit of a shame.

As she looked back at the photo, she realised he was now *very* grown up. He was tall and broad and had chiselled features and her eyes lingered on the picture for a few extra moments. He was the type of guy who would usually make her heartbeat faster. If she hadn't known it was Ben she would have certainly been tempted. Why was she even thinking about stuff like this anyway? She had more important matters to deal with. Like yesterday's mess.

Groaning, she lay there for a while longer, trying her hardest to go back to sleep. But it was no use. Even though she was exhausted, she was also wide awake and knew she would have to get up and see her mum at some point. She had to face up to it. Bella pulled on yesterday's clothes and plodded downstairs where she found her mum sitting, nursing a cup of coffee at the kitchen table.

'Hello you,' said Isobel, smiling cautiously.

'Hi, Mum,' she said with a sigh. Dropping a kiss on her mum's head she said, 'I'm such a muppet. *What* was I thinking?'

Isobel stood up and pulled her in close for a hug. 'It's alright, sweetie. It was an easy enough mistake to make. I've no idea how Rosie's diary ended up in that box. But there you go. You now probably know far more than you would like to about Rosie in her twenties . . . but I suppose the silver lining in all of this is that you have helped Luke out.'

'What do you mean?'

'Well, it sounds like you did him a favour by bringing him to Arran.'

Bella smiled. 'Yes, I suppose so. And it was worth it to see the look on Rosie's face. That was priceless. Who would have thought she had a fling with Luke Giles. You were both quite wild back in the day, eh?'

'Definitely Rosie, not so much me,' said Isobel. She hesitated briefly as she looked at her daughter. 'You are the best thing that ever happened to me, Bella. And I'm sorry that I haven't been able to give you the answers you want.'

Bella sat down at the table and rested her chin on both hands. 'It's okay. You've told me all you know, Mum . . . anyway, I suppose I should think about heading back home.'

'Och, there's no rush,' said Isobel. 'Not if you were going to be away camping anyway. Stay on for a bit if you want. The room is there anyway and there's plenty of space. Ash won't be here until next week.'

'Ash is definitely coming over?' said Bella, yawning. 'I thought it was all a bit up in the air?'

'Yes, well, you know Ash. It's all a bit last minute.' Isobel smiled fondly. Ash was always flitting off to exotic locations and had always been charmingly unreliable. 'There's some kind of conference on at one of the universities in Glasgow — I don't know all the details — and Ash was asked to step in and cover a speech for a colleague who had to cancel.'

'Ah, great,' said Bella. 'I bet you can't wait. It's been ages since you all got together.'

Her mum nodded at her. 'I know, to think we haven't seen each other since before lockdown.'

'Hey sleepyheads,' said Rosie as she came into the kitchen with Coisty. 'You two are up early. I thought you would be shattered and having a lie in.'

'I'm sorry, Rosie, about yesterday,' said Bella sheepishly.

Rosie shook her head. 'Nothing to be sorry for. It's easy to put two and two together and get six. Anyway, thanks to you, Bella, my dog walks have suddenly become a *whole* lot more interesting.'

'What do you mean?' said Bella, raising an eyebrow.

'We bumped into Luke. Or I should say that Coisty threw himself at the man.'

'Is that why you're all flushed?' asked Isobel with a raised eyebrow.

Rosie shrugged at Isobel and grinned.

Bella chuckled as she looked at Rosie's glowing face which was either down to the sea air or the giddiness of being in close proximity to someone with a lot of sex appeal. Even though he was old enough to be her dad, she could see why Rosie was attracted to him. For an older guy, he was very charismatic. A bit like George Clooney who, in her eyes, was ancient but still had *it*. 'I don't blame you,' Bella said. 'He is a nice guy. Obviously far too old for me but some nice talent for you and Mum to appreciate. I thought he looked a bit like an older version of that guy from *Outlander*.'

Rosie looked blankly at her. 'What's that?'

'Mum is *always* watching it.'

'It's that programme I keep telling you to watch,' said Isobel, chuckling at Rosie. 'That one and *Virgin River*. That would keep you very entertained for a while, if you catch my drift.'

'Oh Isobel, honestly. You know I'm not that bothered about TV.'

'Clearly. Anyway, back to the main man, Luke. I suppose you could compare him to a fine wine,' said Isobel thoughtfully, 'in that he has definitely improved with age.'

Isobel had been single since last year since her last boyfriend turned out to be a numpty. It was a reminder that it was easier to be single. Over the years, she had always kept any boyfriends at arm's length, claiming she liked her space too much.

Bella realised she was lucky that it had always been her and her mum who had lived together. She would have hated it if there had been a succession of different men living with them over the years which was something that some of her friends had had to put up with. But she did at times wonder if her mum was lonely, even though she had never given any indication that she was at all.

'But maybe,' said Isobel suggestively, 'he is the island hunk you've been waiting for.'

Rosie laughed as she walked over to the coffee machine and made herself a drink. 'Well, yes, he is still rather easy on the eye. Especially after all these years.'

Isobel rolled her eyes dramatically and fanned her face.

'I, for one, think it is lucky we have always had different taste in men, Isobel, otherwise it could have been messy.'

'What about Ash?' said Bella thoughtfully.

'Yes, fortunately Ash has always had different tastes too otherwise it could have all got very complicated. Can you imagine? Apparently, the latest man is quite the catch. We've been told he looks very like one of the Hemsworth brothers.'

'Oh,' said Bella, perking up at a name she recognised. 'Which one?'

'No idea,' said Rosie, waving her hand. 'Although I've no idea whether we get to meet him or not. You know Ash. As vague as ever about everything, including whether the new bloke is joining us. From a selfish point of view, it would be nice if we could just have Ash to ourselves. We all have *lots* of catching up to do. Now, no pressure you two, but if there's anything you fancy doing today, let me know. I am going into the garden for a while.'

'That will help you get rid of all that pent up frustration,' said Isobel, winking at her.

'Bella, dear, would you like a coffee?' Rosie completely ignored the comment.

'No thanks. I'll put the kettle on and make tea, if that's okay?'

'Of course,' said Rosie. 'Just make yourself at home and I'll be in the garden. There's plenty of clean towels in the wicker basket in the bathroom so help yourself if you want to have a shower.' Then she disappeared outside, Coisty trotting behind.

'Why don't you have a shower first, love, and then we can make a plan?'

Bella nodded. She would wash and get dressed then think about checking ferry availability for the next few days.

A schedule always made her feel better. It gave her something to focus on and helped her feel more in control. As she started to walk up the stairs, she could hear her mobile ring in the bedroom. Running to get to it, she snatched it up and saw that it was the beauty salon calling.

'Hello,' she said, breathlessly worrying that she'd got her rota wrong and hoping that they weren't expecting her there today.

'Hey Bella,' said her boss, Georgie. Her voice was subdued and Bella frowned.

'Sorry to call you like this hon, but . . . look there's no easy way of saying this, Bella. We are having to close.'

'Close? What do you mean?' she said in confusion. The salon was usually shut on Sundays and Mondays and she wondered if Georgie meant it was closing early today or something. Even though it was still early in the day. Maybe there had been a leak or the heating had broken down and she had forgotten that Bella was on holiday.

'We are shutting the shop for good. It'll not come as a surprise, love, but things have been brutal this past year. We just can't keep going on like this. And the council are going to start charging for street parking. It's the final straw.' Georgie's voice wobbled and she sounded as though she was close to tears. 'We are having to let everyone go.'

Bella felt as though she had been punched in the stomach. 'Oh Georgie, I am so sorry. I can come in and help you finish up with clients though.'

She sniffed. 'Aw, thanks Bella. You are a wee gem. But when I say we're closing, I mean, we are actually closed.'

'What, now?' Bella shut her eyes in disbelief.

'Aye,' said Georgie, sighing. 'I'm having to let everyone go. With immediate effect. I'll make sure you're paid what you're owed and I'll give you a brilliant reference. I'm so sorry, Bella.'

'Okay, I'm sorry too.' Bella managed to mumble before ending the call.

CHAPTER TWENTY

Over the next few days, Rosie and Isobel explored the island together and made the most of the sunny weather. Both had been quite happy to walk and talk and then stop for coffees and scones. Bella had been sleeping in late, whereas Rosie and Isobel were both early risers. Rosie had initially tried to persuade Bella to go with them and to get some fresh air. But Bella had insisted that she was happy to have some slower starts to the day and that she didn't want to crash their holiday any more than she already had.

However, this afternoon, Rosie had insisted that Bella and her mum went to the café in Lamlash together. It wasn't that she didn't want to join them but she was keen to have some time to put the groceries away and catch up with some gardening.

She had waved them off saying there was plenty of weeding in the garden needing her attention and made them promise to return with a giant slab of chocolate cake for her. As she heard their car crunch over the gravel and drive down the lane, she grabbed the keys for the shed and wandered out into the garden to get ready for an hour or two of digging. Putting in her earbuds, she selected a Gabby Logan podcast, pressed play and was soon absorbed in digging out weeds and hoeing the flower bed while listening to Gabby interview Clare Balding.

While she worked, her mind wandered to what was happening in Beach Cottage next door. She hadn't seen Luke since that first morning though she had also deliberately varied her route. She had not been expecting herself to react in such a physical way when she had seen him. And certainly not after all these years. He was a fling from the ancient past and that was where he should stay. *This is what happens when your husband leaves you for a younger model. You start imagining all sorts and go into a fantasy world and hark back to the past. You need to give yourself a reality check,* she told herself.

Standing up to stretch her back, she pulled off the gloves and laid them on the grass. Coisty immediately picked one up and went haring around the garden with it, keen to play. Rosie laughed at him and went inside to make some fresh coffee. She spooned the grains into the paper filter in the coffee machine and filled it with water. Then she reached for a mug from the cupboard and flicked the machine on. It would take several minutes to percolate so she walked down to the bottom of the garden and stood, with her hands on her hips, as she decided what to do next. Either finish weeding the flower beds or prune the climbers which were now stretching well over into the neighbouring garden. She opted for more weeding and, as she satisfyingly pulled them out at the root, she half wondered about trying to make that spot into a vegetable patch. With the number of dandelions that also seemed to spring up across the lawn, which were apparently good for the grass, she knew she should try and go all mother nature and make tea or something with them.

She was parched. It was definitely coffee time. The sun was getting hot and as she stood up, she suddenly felt as though she was being watched. She turned round slowly and saw Luke looking over the fence from next door, which made her think he must be standing on something, unless he'd suddenly become a giant. He waved and looked as though he was speaking, but she couldn't hear him. She pulled out her ear pods and smiled. His eyes lit up, which was a bit disconcerting, and he beamed at her.

'Hello again,' he said. 'I'm sorry I didn't mean to startle you. I knocked at the front door and nobody answered and then I heard you in the garden. I just wondered if you could maybe lend me a little drop of milk, please for my coffee? I completely forgot to buy some.'

Her mouth dropped open. 'Milk?' she said, confused. 'You would like some milk?'

'Yes, please, if it's not too much trouble. I need to go to the shops and get some bits and pieces. I didn't realise . . . anyway it doesn't matter. I don't want to put you out.' He looked slightly sheepish.

Rosie sprung into action. 'Of course. Just give me a minute.' Then feeling very emboldened, which was way out of character for her, she made a snap offer. 'In fact, why don't you pop over. I have just made a pot of coffee and I'm about to take a break.'

He sighed deeply. 'I would love that. Thank you.'

Rosie gestured to the cottage. 'Just come to the front door and I'll let you in.'

CHAPTER TWENTY-ONE

When Luke reached the front door of Creel Cottage, he felt a bit discombobulated. On a typical weekday, if he wasn't on location and he hadn't been for a while now as the latest series he'd starred in had come to an end, he had a routine of checking emails, dealing with admin and meeting up with friends for coffee or dinner, or a game of golf or squash when he was in one of his healthy phases. Being here on this island, on his own, was liberating but he was also a bit lonely. He hadn't realised just how much he enjoyed the company of others and wasn't particularly good at being alone with his thoughts. The more he tried to focus on writing down some words — after all, that was the reason he was here — the more he got fidgety and distracted. He had been here several days now, yet had barely written a few hundred words.

'Hello,' said Rosie as she swung open the door and ushered him in.

'It's been a while,' he said jokingly and then inwardly cringed. A few days on his own had clearly turned him into an imbecile. He followed her through to the kitchen. Although the cottages looked almost identical from the outside their interiors were completely different. Beach Cottage might have been very high spec with lots of luxuries and mod cons but Creel Cottage was much homelier. The kitchen units were made from worn pine and the flagstone tiles looked as though they had been there for decades. He immediately felt welcome here. It was a space that was inviting and cosy and as he looked out through the French doors that opened on to the garden, he couldn't help but admire it. 'Wow, what a beautiful garden. Completely different to next door, which is all paving and decking.'

Rosie shrugged. 'I suppose that is easier maintenance, though, for a holiday home.'

'True,' he said with a nod. 'It is a very special spot. Especially with those sea views. But your garden is something else.'

'My dad was a keen gardener so I must give all the credit to him.' She paused and looked as though she was considering whether to elaborate. 'This was my parents' home for many years. They both passed away and, well, they left the cottage to me.'

'I'm sorry to hear that,' he said gently. 'It must be comforting to feel a bit of a connection to them through the house.'

Rosie nodded. 'Yes, it is. Anyway, please do come outside. I don't know about you but I am desperate for my caffeine fix.' She gestured outside and picked up a tray which had two mugs of coffee, a small pot of sugar, a jug of milk and a plate of shortbread.

Coisty, who was sunning himself on the patio, opened his eyes then wagged his tail lazily. Rosie laughed. 'You've lost your touch. He can't even be bothered to get up and greet you.'

Luke laughed and bent down to pat him. 'He is very cute, aren't you, boy?' Sitting down at the bistro table, he gratefully accepted the coffee from Rosie. She also encouraged him to try the shortbread.

'It's my mum's old recipe,' she explained.

He bit into the crumbly, buttery biscuit and chewed. 'Wow, it's delicious,' he said. 'I think it's the nicest shortbread I've ever had.'

'Homemade is always better, I think,' she said, her cheeks pink, evidently encouraged by his response. 'I'm trying out a lot of recipes from her old book that I found. It's been fun and even nicer to share them with friends.'

Luke took a sip of coffee. 'How is Bella doing? I haven't seen her. Did she end up going back to Glasgow?'

'No,' said Rosie, a little perplexed, and shaking her head. 'She's been in a bit of a tizz these past few days. She's lost her job in Glasgow. She's a beauty therapist and she got a call to say the salon was closing with immediate effect.'

Luke put his mug down on the table. 'Oh dear. Poor Bella. That will have come as a shock . . . honestly, I do feel for kids these days. Everything feels so much harder for them than it was in our day.'

Rosie sighed. 'I totally agree. Being young feels like a lifetime ago. But at least we had fun and we weren't always on edge wondering if our jobs were safe like kids are these days. Everything seems to be short-term and contracts. There doesn't seem to be much stability. It's no wonder they get a bit scunnered.'

He raised an eyebrow. 'Scunnered?'

She laughed and nodded. 'Scunnered. It means pissed off.'

Luke found himself lost for words which was most unusual. He was normally good at being a smooth talker but there was something about Rosie that unsettled him, albeit in a nice way. He got the sense that she was a bit nervous, not obviously so, but he was used to reading people and their body language. The way she was swinging her foot quickly was a bit of a giveaway. And just at that moment their eyes met and it was as though they were remembering a memory of something that had happened between them. Even though Luke was still trying to locate those specific memories he still felt a connection and he couldn't peel his eyes off Rosie. He could definitely feel a spark of *something* between them.

'Have you got kids?' asked Rosie hurriedly, breaking the moment, and reaching for the coffee pot to fill his mug up.

'Yes, two boys. Scottie is twenty-three and Ralph is twenty-two. They're both travelling together in South America right now. Seems they are having the time of their lives. How about you?'

'I've got a son. Ben. He's twenty-four . . . and he's also travelling. Though on the opposite side of the world. He's in Indonesia right now. So, you must have settled down and had kids not long after that world tour then?'

Luke nodded as he thought back to a very different stage in his life. What he didn't want to admit was that his marriage to Cindy had been a whirlwind affair after she had fallen pregnant. He thought he was doing the right thing by marrying her but it had actually turned out to be one of his better decisions as he had loved her deeply throughout their marriage. He loved their sons and he loved family life. It was just a shame that Cindy had fallen for his brother.

'Funny to look back to your younger days, isn't it? I know I feel like a different person now. You have kids and then it all feels like a complete blur,' she said, biting her lip. 'And then they grow up and have their own lives to lead. And we are left wondering what just happened. But it sounds like our kids are having a good time at the moment, living their best lives.' Although Rosie smiled, he could tell there was a sadness behind her eyes.

'And you? Are you living your best life?' he asked tenderly. He held his breath as he waited for her to answer. He couldn't help flickering his gaze over to her hand to check whether she was wearing a wedding ring. She was not.

'I'm fairly content,' she said slowly. 'I love living here on Arran in this house. I have Coisty. I love my job at the school — I teach English — and I have great friends . . . how about you? What's made you come and hide yourself away on Arran for the summer?'

Luke realised she was changing the subject and deflecting the attention away from herself and he didn't want to make her feel uncomfortable by probing too deeply. 'Well, believe it or not, I thought it would be a good idea to hide here as I have a book to write. And I thought the cottage would be an ideal solution. But I have to admit it's harder than I thought.' He knew full well he should really finish up his coffee and head back to try and actually get some words written. But sitting in the sunshine with a beautiful neighbour was far more appealing.

Rosie looked curious. 'What's the book you're writing?'

He coughed nervously and cleared his throat. 'It's my memoir. And my agent is going ballistic as I should have sent her some of it already. But when I sit down my mind goes blank. I'm actually at the point of wondering if I should pull out of the book deal altogether. I really don't think my life is all that interesting.'

Rosie burst out laughing, her eyes sparkling. 'I would beg to differ and so would thousands of others. I would say you've lived a more interesting life than your average punter. You must have loads to say. Maybe you're just taking the wrong approach.'

He leaned in towards her, elbows on his knees and his hands steepled together. 'Do you think so?'

She nodded. 'Yes. It's all there, isn't it? Inside your head. You must have millions of stories to write about. What we need to try and do is tease the stories and details out.' She looked pensive for a moment.

Luke was transfixed. Especially at the mention of *we*. *We need to try* . . . Was she talking figuratively or literally?

'Look,' she said, as though reading his mind. 'If you want me to help you I can . . . that's if . . . I'm not being too forward. I'm just used to working with kids who don't think they have much to say but of course they do. We all do. The kids just need some structure and encouragement and it sounds like you do too. But obviously tell me if I'm being too keen. I always get very enthusiastic at the thought of a project.'

Luke sat up straight, his heart racing. Would this work? Could this work? The truth was his options were limited and if he didn't get his finger out soon then there definitely wouldn't be a book. And that was why he was here. 'Are you really sure you don't mind?'

'Not at all,' she said firmly. 'I'm happy to help and give you some pointers.'

'Well, in that case, you're on,' he said, feeling more excited about anything than he had in weeks.

'I'll be back in a minute,' she said, jumping up and running inside.

Luke now felt energised and enthusiastic about the project instead of the mounting dread that had been chipping away at him for weeks. He watched as Rosie walked outside, now carrying a notepad and pen, and walked briskly over to the table. She sat down alongside him and quickly made some notes on a large piece of paper. Her face was a picture of concentration as she wrote quickly. Then when she looked up and saw him watching her, she blushed.

'Okay,' she said, ripping the paper from the pad. 'There you go.'

'What's this?' he said, taking the sheet from her.

'That is your *homework*.'

She said it firmly but kindly and as he looked at her notes and back up at her face, he knew she meant business. 'No time like the present,' she said popping the dirty mugs and plate on the tray. 'That's your breaktime over.'

'You want me to do this now?' he said timidly, really hoping he could just have another five minutes with her. He was so enjoying the company.

'Indeed. Set the timer on your watch or your phone for half an hour. It will help you concentrate.' She stood up.

'I better do as I'm told then. Thank you, Rosie.' Gosh, he wasn't used to anyone being so forthright with him and he had to admit he quite liked it.

'You are welcome. And, just so you know, I'm a hard taskmaster. And I expect results from my students.' She laughed, clearly relaxed in her teacher role. 'If you just focus on that for now and I will check in with you tomorrow. Then we can chat about what comes next.'

Luke couldn't believe he was actually feeling a flutter in his stomach at the way she was talking to him. He gave himself a shake. The last thing he needed to do right now was fall for his teacher, even though she was beautiful.

'Do you want to give me your number and I can drop you a message?' she suggested. 'Unless you'd rather I randomly knocked on your door?'

He grinned. 'Let's swap numbers and keep in touch that way.' He pulled out his phone and handed it to her so she could add her details. Then he quickly called her phone so she would have his number on hers.

As she saw him out, he was so tempted to hug her but that would be totally inappropriate — wouldn't it? He didn't want to scupper this before they'd even started. Instead, he smiled and thanked her for coffee and walked across the driveway to go next door. He felt hugely relieved and realised he had a spring in his step and was whistling cheerily. He couldn't remember when he had last felt so optimistic.

CHAPTER TWENTY-TWO

Bella decided that hanging out with her mum and Rosie had actually been a lot of fun. It had been good to see her mum switch off from the worries of work and enjoy time with Rosie. They always slipped into a comfortable banter with each other which came from knowing each other for so long. They were more like sisters than friends as they both had a habit of finishing each other's sentences and weren't afraid to let either know if they were being irritating.

Bella did feel a bit guilty that her arrival had somewhat changed the dynamic of her mum's holiday. She had started to cook dinner for them all regularly so that Isobel could focus on spending time with Rosie, which was the reason she was there, after all. Bella had also started taking Coisty out for long walks to give Rosie a break from her usual routine — though walking the cute dog was a pleasure and had helped Bella think about things and get some clarity back in her life.

Rosie had told them both that she had been really appreciative of the way they were looking after her. However, tonight, despite Bella's protests, she insisted that it was her turn to make dinner for them all.

'So, are you two having a fling again then?' asked Isobel, when she had got over the shock of Rosie's admission.

'Don't be daft. How does me helping with his book all of a sudden mean that we are having a *thing*? Honestly, Isobel, you and your filthy mind. I'm just trying to be neighbourly.'

'*Neighbourly?*' said Isobel drily. 'If that's what you want to call it, Rosie, so be it. I'd call it something else. Especially as you grin like a Cheshire cat whenever his name is mentioned. Anyway, if you are being so neighbourly then why don't you invite him round for dinner with us? It looks like you're feeding an army anyway,' she said, tipping her head in the direction of the huge chicken casserole that Rosie had prepared and was about to put in the oven.

'Fine,' she had said brusquely. 'I'll do just that. Great idea.' She picked up her phone to send him a text.

'What, you've got his number in your phone? When did that happen?' Isobel was incredulous.

Rosie screwed up her face in annoyance. 'That's what people do these days. They swap numbers.' Bella watched as Rosie then put her phone back down and smiled sweetly at Isobel. 'But do you know what, Isobel? I think I will just go and invite him the old-fashioned way.' Then she walked out the kitchen and out the front door.

'Blimey, she's not hanging about,' said Isobel.

Bella chuckled. 'What are you two like?'

'Oh, sweetheart, I can't tell you how good it is to hear you laugh again. And Rosie for that matter too. She has had a shit few months. She's so much like her old self. Or I should say her younger self.'

Bella shrugged. 'I know. But what else is there to do, Mum? We just need to get on with things the best we can. I mean, I've had a few days of moping around but I need to start job hunting. I'll go upstairs in a minute and sit at Ben's desk and get on with seeing if I can find any other openings close to home.'

Isobel looked at her thoughtfully. 'Okay, but don't put yourself under pressure, love. I can help you out if need be.'

'Thanks Mum, and I know you will. But I'm a big girl now. I need to sort this out myself.'

Isobel sighed. 'I am so proud of you. And something else will come along. I know it will.'

Just then the door slammed and Rosie ran back into the kitchen. 'Righto, that's us all sorted. Lay an extra space for dinner.'

Bella noticed she had a sparkle in her eyes.

'Someone's got a spring in their step,' said Isobel. 'I'm surprised you've not brought him back with you to get things *underway* early.'

Rosie scoffed at her. 'He's got an assignment to finish before he gets his dinner.'

'Oh, Rosie. Really? I think you're enjoying bossing the guy around. I almost feel sorry for the man.'

At that moment, Rosie's phone rang. It was Ben on FaceTime. 'Ben,' squealed Rosie.

Bella couldn't help smiling as it was exactly the same reaction her mum had anytime she called her. They were both easily pleased.

'It's so good to see you. And that beach looks stunning. Will you look at that blue sky behind you,' said Rosie.

'Hey, Mum,' said Ben. 'How are you? Is everything okay?'

'Yes, dear, everything is more than okay. I've got Isobel and Bella here . . .' she threw a warning look at Isobel.

'Hi, Ben,' trilled Isobel. 'Glad you're sunning yourself. Are you still in Bali or is it Thailand? I'm losing track of your exotic travels.'

'Hey, Isobel, in Bali just now. Who knows where next?'

'And have you got a special lady in your life?' she asked.

Bella cringed knowing that her mum was about to start grilling him for details.

'Maybe,' he had said with a laugh.

'Is Mabel back on then?' asked Rosie.

'Mm,' he said in a very non-committal way.

Bella listened with interest as her mum and Rosie stared at the phone. Mabel? *Interesting.* Then Rosie thrust the phone at her.

'Say hi to Bella, Ben,' she insisted in that embarrassing way that mums did, regardless of how old you were.

Bella squinted as she looked at the phone and saw Ben sitting on a bench with a tropical scene behind him.

'Hey, Bella, how are you?'

His sunglasses were perched on top of his head and she couldn't help but notice his *very* impressive pecs. He clearly was a guy who worked out. 'Hi, Ben,' she managed to say shyly when she realised he was waiting for her to say something. 'Long time no speak.' *Long time no speak.* What was she on? Who said stuff like that? She wasn't *forty.*

'Good to see you and so weird to see you with Mum. How come you're there?'

'Oh . . . a long story but I thought I would pop over and see them both quickly. And I'm still here. I'm sure they'll be trying to get rid of me soon,' she said, wondering why she was spouting so much random chat at Ben who she used to play cars and dolls with. 'I'm sleeping in your room,' she added hastily.

He grinned and she had to steady herself, surprised at her reaction to seeing him and hearing his voice. 'Lucky you. I'm sure it's like a shrine.'

Bella laughed. 'You could say that.'

'Eh, less of the cheek. I heard that, Ben.'

But Rosie was smiling fondly at her son's comments.

'Um, well it's good to see you, Ben. I better pass you back over to your mum. You know what they're like.'

'Aye,' said Rosie. 'This will be costing a fortune,' she said.

'It's fine Mum, it doesn't cost anything. Remember, I told you?'

Rosie shook her head. 'So you did . . .'

Bella watched as Rosie took the phone outside to the garden.

'I'll just get the table sorted for dinner,' said Isobel. 'Make myself useful. I wonder if I should light some candles too and give the place a wee hint of romance. Maybe play *Careless Whisper* in the background?'

Bella rolled her eyes. 'I think that would make it a tad awkward, Mum. Anyway, I might just, er, go and have a look for a job while I'm waiting then if that's okay. Unless you want me to help?'

'On you go, lovey. I'll give you a shout when it's ready.'

'Thanks, Mum,' she said, and then scampered up the stairs to Ben's room before her mum noticed that she was blushing. She plonked herself down on the bed and realised she felt a little bit wobbly. As though she had butterflies in her stomach. What was that all about?

She looked around the room. She knew Ben had never really lived here properly and the room was just classed as his on the rare times he was back in the country. Aside from the photo by the bed there weren't huge amounts of personal touches. Then as she glanced around, she saw something familiar sitting on the guest chair in the corner of the room. It was *Teddy*. She gasped and then ran over and picked the soft toy up. He was rather threadbare now, but still as soft and floppy as ever. She sniffed his head and was taken back to a time of life when she was a wee girl and she and Ben had played tea parties with their toys. Teddy was a regular visitor as was her toy, Piggy. Teddy and Piggy had been as inseparable as she and Ben once had. She put him down and pulled herself back to the present. That had been then, and this was now. Life had moved on massively and Ben was now on the other side of the world living his best life on the beach. But there was nothing to stop her sending him a wee reminder of the old days, was there?

Before she changed her mind, she quickly snapped the toy and scrolled for his details in Instagram. Then she sent him a picture with the caption *Remember this guy?*

Ben responded immediately. *Teddy! I miss him!*

I'll look after him. Promise. Bella smiled as she pressed send.
Where's Piggy?
Home alone in Glasgow. Having a party.
Ben sent back a text with three laughing emojis.
Bella laughed then gave herself a shake. Honestly, being around her mum and Rosie was clearly affecting her. Her next most pressing task was not to think about guys but to try and find herself a new job.

CHAPTER TWENTY-THREE

'Guess what,' said Isobel a few mornings later as she and Rosie walked Coisty along the beach in Kildonan.

'What?' said Rosie. 'Tell me more?'

'I think my wee mum has come up trumps with a possible job for Bella.'

Isobel had been a bit agitated that morning and Rosie wondered if she was finding the cottage claustrophobic with the three of them staying there. Or if she was just in panic mode about Bella's employment prospects. Fortunately, Bella hadn't raised the issue of her dad again. It seemed other issues had superseded that. For now.

Rosie and Isobel were walking side by side, keeping an eye on Coisty to make sure he didn't roll in anything smelly or dead.

'Well . . . you know her man friend, Bill? His daughter, Beth, is a reporter on the paper here and apparently knows everyone and everything.'

'You didn't tell her about Luke, did you?' said Rosie, taking a sharp intake of breath.

'No, don't fret,' said Isobel, shaking her head. 'I managed to keep schtoom. I mean, I love my mum but you know as well as me that little snippet of information would stay a secret for about three seconds and then the whole of Scotland would know where he was . . .'

Rosie placed a hand on her chest and smiled in relief. She knew Margaret meant well but she could be a bit of a loose cannon when it came to confidential information.

'Beth had phoned to speak to her dad who told her Mum was upset about Bella losing her job. Then she said that she knew the big hotel in Brodick was looking for a beauty therapist. And the position also has live-in accommodation which is brilliant.'

Rosie frowned. 'Yes, but do you think that's what Bella would want? I mean, it's one thing to come here for a visit, it's different to actually live and work here.'

Isobel tutted at her. 'You made it work though. And Ben enjoyed working here over the summer, didn't he?'

'I know, I suppose so, but our circumstances are quite different. I'm much older than her and I was ready to settle here. She's young and at a different stage of her life. Ben was just here for the summer and then took off.'

Isobel threw up her hands in exasperation. 'I know but she doesn't have a job at all right now, does she? Maybe it's the change that she needs.'

'But she might want to go back to Glasgow though to try and look for work there,' suggested Rosie.

'Och, I know, but being in Glasgow hasn't exactly worked out for her, has it?' said Isobel testily. 'She's lost one job and the other job she has working at the bars is totally erratic. If she applies for this job and gets it then it might just give her something to focus on. She always functions much better if she's got a routine. Otherwise, I'm worried she will get bored and have too much time to think about things . . . she doesn't have to worry about finding a place to stay here and then it might tide her over until she decides whether to go travelling or not.'

Rosie nodded thoughtfully, noticing that Isobel's brisk walk had slowed down to a trudge. 'That's true,' she said, looking at her. There was something about Isobel's expression that made her stop. 'You're looking awfully worried. She's young and resilient. She'll find another job soon. Are you sure this isn't about something else?'

Isobel shrugged. 'Ignore me, it's just this awful anxiety I have. I was lying in bed last night, worrying that she might never get a job and would be unemployed forever and stuck living with me.'

'So you were catastrophising things again then?' said Rosie gently.

Isobel nodded. 'You know me too well. I'm just overthinking a lot of stuff right now.'

'Coisty,' yelled Rosie and sprinted over to him as she saw him sizing up a dead bird lying on the pebbles ahead. She managed to grab his collar just before he threw himself onto it and did his own little dead bird dance. 'Phew,' she said to him. 'I didn't fancy having to shampoo you again. You are such a mingin' wee dog at times.' He looked up at her and barked. Clipping his lead onto his collar, she walked back towards Isobel. 'I suppose all you can do is suggest it to Bella and be led by her. The blessing is the timing of all of this has been quite good.' Then she noticed Isobel's confused face. 'I don't mean actually losing her job. I just mean the fact that she has been here with you when it happened. At least you can support her.' She was hit by a sudden pang of sadness when she thought about Ben. He looked happy, though, whenever she spoke to him and that was all she could wish for.

Isobel must have read her mind as she patted Rosie's arm. 'I know. I'm so aware of how much you must miss your boy. But he's having a great time and you should be proud. You raised him to be independent and confident enough to go off and explore the world. At least he didn't take after his dad.'

Rosie chuckled. 'Very true. Anyway, did you see that Ash has updated the WhatsApp chat?' she said, quick to change the conversation and steer it away from the topic of Dermot.

Isobel nodded. 'Yes. I was starting to wonder if this reunion would actually happen. The plans have been constantly changing.' She shook her head fondly. 'What is Ash like? I can't quite believe that by the middle of next week the gang will be reunited.'

'Indeed,' Rosie said, exchanging a glance with her friend. 'There's a lot to catch up on.'

They walked in a companiable silence for a moment before she spoke again. 'Tell me when you are next seeing your new best friend and neighbour?'

Rosie felt her spirits lift at the mention of Luke. 'We are making good progress with his writing so far. He's a *very* good student.' She giggled. 'But he finds it hard to focus. He seems to relax more when he can just chat and tell me about things, as though I were an old friend.'

Isobel winked. 'I bet he does,' she said with a dirty laugh. 'Though to be fair, he is good company. When he was round for dinner the other night he just seemed like a normal bloke.'

'As opposed to what?' said Rosie.

'Like, you wouldn't think he was a celebrity, would you?'

Rosie shrugged. 'I'm not sure he thinks of himself like that either. He's just a guy. I think we all get a bit obsessed these days about labelling people. But he is very unassuming. If you were meeting him for the first time then you would have no idea about his background, would you?'

Isobel nodded. 'Aye, I suppose not. He's certainly very down to earth for someone who was such a heartthrob.'

'Anyway,' said Rosie. 'I've suggested we go for a walk tomorrow to the library in the forest.'

'Is that a euphemism?' she said, with a wicked grin.

'No. It's a place, Isobel. And you and Bella are also invited to come along.'

'I don't know . . . I think we might feel like we're interrupting your date.'

'Isobel will you stop that. It's not a date. I'm just trying to help him out. Sometimes it's better just to walk and talk about things rather than be stuck in front of a computer.'

'Why are you grinning then? I know you, Rosie, and I know when you've got that dreamy look in your eyes.'

She sighed and momentarily wondered if she had ever looked dreamy when she was with Dermot.

'Seriously,' said Isobel, 'whatever it is that you're *doing* just enjoy it as it is agreeing with you. It's about time you had some fun.'

Should she be having fun with another man just now? She wasn't sure she would ever be ready for a new man in her life. Especially someone like Luke.

CHAPTER TWENTY-FOUR

'Is there anything that Granny Margaret can't do?' Bella asked her mum later that day. 'I mean, surely she could have worked for MI5 with all the questions she asks. She also has the argumentative skills of a top lawyer *and* now she has turned recruitment consultant.'

Isobel burst out laughing. 'I know, she is a force to be reckoned with. She'll be on *The Voice* next.'

Bella had bitten the bullet and, thanks to her gran's tip, she had called the spa at the hotel and said she heard they were looking for a therapist and she was available to start immediately. They had called her in for an interview and Bella, who decided she had nothing to lose, was confident and breezy and able to answer all the questions without clamming up. She smiled as she thought about her answer to the final question, *what do you love most about your job?* Bella had replied that she loved making a difference to people in such a short space of time. 'I love how different people are when they leave compared to how they are when they arrive and they literally have the weight of the world on their shoulders. It is a real privilege to hold that space for people and to give them a wee bit of pampering which can make a massive positive difference to their day. I love it when people leave feeling lighter and leave their tension behind.' The words were spoken from her heart and the spa manager, Chantelle, had beamed at her.

'Well, Bella,' she said, 'that was a really good interview. I can see why you are good at what you do. You clearly love your job.'

Bella hadn't needed to feign any enthusiasm at all as she realised just how much she loved the work she did. All the stresses at her old salon had taken away the enjoyment of the job as everyone had been so on edge and worried about whether they would stay open or not. With hindsight, it seemed ironic that a place of supposed wellness had actually made the staff so on edge. 'I do,' she said, nodding her head. She hadn't actually realised how much she wanted the job until she was sitting there in the interview. The hotel spa was impressive with several treatment rooms and the leisure facilities for guests made it extra special too. The décor was fresh and light with the walls painted in pale shades of lime which was very calming.

'I will need to check your references,' said Chantelle. 'But if they check out, which I'm sure they will do, then we can get the ball rolling.'

Bella knew that Georgie would give her a good reference so that wouldn't be a problem.

'And you said you can start immediately?' said Chantelle.

'Yes, I can. I might have to nip back to Glasgow to get some of my stuff. But I can be flexible about that.'

'And you know that live-in accommodation comes with the role if you need it? It's something we're really pleased to be able to do. And it means we are more attractive as an employer.'

Bella couldn't believe her luck. It felt as though the planets were aligned and everything was falling into place. 'Thank you,' she said, almost in disbelief. 'That would be great.'

Chantelle reached for her hand and shook it warmly. 'I will be in touch later today.' She glanced at her watch and then her notes. 'Is this the best number to call you on?'

'Yes,' said Bella.

'Right, Bella, thanks for coming in and I will phone you as soon as I can.'

Now, as she sat in Rosie's garden with her mum, she kept frantically checking her phone. She didn't want to miss Chantelle's call.

'If they offer you the job, will you need to start straight away?' asked her mum.

'I did say that I would nip back to Glasgow to get some stuff. Is that okay? I arrived here with very little.' Her trip to Troon felt like months ago rather than just over a week ago and she had managed by borrowing some of her mum's clothes. 'If I go home and get my stuff sorted and move into my new place, the room is then free for Ash and the new man and I'm not in the way.'

'You wouldn't be in the way,' scoffed her mum. 'Anyway, who knows what's happening. Ash may well come alone.'

'I've already gate-crashed your holiday with Rosie . . . I don't want to overstay my welcome. But I will *definitely* be back in time to see Ash. I wouldn't miss that for the world.'

Isobel was about to say something when Bella's phone started to buzz. She jumped up and answered. 'Hello,' she said, her stomach fluttering with nerves.

'Hi, Bella. It's me, Chantelle. I'm so pleased to say that your reference is all good and I can offer you the job.'

Bella grinned at her mum and silently punched the air. 'That's great news. Thank you so much. I can't wait to start.'

'Would Monday work for you, Bella? That gives you the weekend to get sorted and then if you come in on Monday morning for nine o'clock, we can sort out your uniform and all the paperwork then. Oh, and if you want to access your accommodation on Sunday that's fine. I will just send you an email about that now. You know where to go and someone will let you in.'

'Thank you, Chantelle. I am so looking forward to getting started.'

'Me too,' said Chantelle and laughed. 'I'll see you Monday.'

'Bye,' sang Bella, and ended the call. She ran to her mum and hugged her tightly.

'This is such great news,' said Isobel. 'What a great experience. And you know Rosie isn't too far away if you need her.'

Bella beamed. 'Thanks Mum. Er . . . I have one more favour to ask though,' she said, trying to keep her tone light.

Isobel raised an eyebrow. 'I wonder what that could be . . . you'd like to borrow the car to go back to Glasgow?'

She nodded sheepishly. 'Is that okay? It just makes it easier for me to go and get all my stuff.'

Isobel reached up and ruffled her hair. 'Of course it is.'

'Hey,' said Rosie, walking through the front door with Coisty. She looked at them, puzzled. 'Have I missed something?'

'Oh, Rosie, guess what? I've got myself a job at the hotel spa round in Brodick.'

'Amazing news. I'm so pleased for you Bella.' Rosie gave her a big hug.

'Aye well, she has lots to do. She's got to head back home to get some stuff. Isn't that right, Bella?'

Bella's mind was racing and she didn't know what to do first. Run upstairs and grab her bag or try and sort the ferry. As though reading her mind, Rosie took charge.

'You'd better get cracking then. Go and gather your stuff and me and your mum will see if we can get you on the next ferry.'

Bella chuckled. 'You two are the best. And this job will be the best. It feels like things are finally looking up.'

CHAPTER TWENTY-FIVE

With Bella's sudden departure for the mainland, Rosie was trying to do her best to persuade Isobel to come on the walk with her and Luke. They were sitting on the squishy sofa both still in their pyjamas and enjoying an early cup of tea.

'No danger,' Isobel said. 'I'm not being the third wheel.'

'Will you be quiet,' said Rosie. 'It's not like that.'

'Rosie, if you're trying to tell me to button it, then you should know better than now that I won't. All I'm saying is that I am not up for playing gooseberry. Especially on a romantic walk through the woods. Which is, by the way, the perfect place to have your wicked way with him.'

Rosie winced.

'Honestly, I'll be quite happy having some time to myself. Especially after everything that has happened since I arrived. I could do with some solo time. I've already had a look at the buses and I'm going to go into Brodick to do some shopping. There are a few wee gift shops I want to check out and I want to go to Home Farm to get some of that cheese and maybe some new perfume too.'

'But I feel awful,' wailed Rosie. 'You're supposed to be here to see me and I've dumped you for a random bloke.'

Isobel shrugged. 'It doesn't matter at all. We weren't expecting Bella to arrive and to bring an unexpected guest . . . and then we weren't planning on her making such a hasty exit. It's not quite been the holiday either of us expected. And that's okay. Keeps us on our toes. Anyway, the reason I wanted to come and see you was to cheer my supposedly broken-hearted friend up. But it would seem someone else is doing a *more effective* job. And that makes me happy.'

Rosie threw a cushion at her and snorted. 'Will you stop that! We are just friends. In fact, not even that. I'm his teacher and he is my student.'

Isobel smirked. 'If that's what you want to call him.'

'Listen, about when Ash comes . . .' said Rosie.

'Stop trying to change the conversation,' said Isobel, who had evidently read her thoughts. 'I know what you're going to say.'

'Do you?' Rosie had tried to broach the subject a few times during the week already and Isobel had either changed the topic of conversation or Bella had walked into the room.

Isobel nodded grimly. 'Yes. I know it's something that I need to deal with. I'm not convinced that will be the end of it for Bella. But you're right. I think it's worth discussing when the three of us are together.'

'I think that's a good idea.' said Rosie glancing over at Coisty who was sitting on the rug staring at Isobel. 'But I also think that you're overanalysing things and worrying too much. It will all fizzle out. Especially when Bella starts her new job. She will forget all about it.'

'Mm,' said Isobel non-committedly and patted Coisty's head. He had now jumped up beside her on the sofa and sat as close to her as he could. Isobel's fitness watch buzzed. 'That's my sign to move, Coisty. I've been sitting down for too long.' She stood up, stretching.

Coisty slinked over to sit next to Rosie, who knew that the conversation was over for now. 'Right boy, come on, we'd better go and get ready for our walk too.'

'I'm already looking forward to our debrief later,' said Isobel with a wink.

Rosie shook her head in exasperation. 'Well, you will most likely be disappointed.'

***

A couple of hours later, Rosie and Luke were making their way through the forest and up towards the falls of Eas Mor. It was a walk that Rosie hadn't done for ages and she thought that Luke might like to explore and see it. Especially as there was a café there too. She hadn't told Luke where they were headed as she wanted to surprise him. Her only instructions had been to wear comfy shoes as they would be walking for a while. When he indicated that might be a problem as he only had his smart trainers and golf shoes, she had rummaged in the hall cupboard and loaned him a pair of Ben's. As they made their way through the lower forest walk, with Coisty running ahead in his element with the smorgasbord of new smells, Rosie inhaled the scent of pine.

Luke was wearing navy shorts and a grey t-shirt, with a sweatshirt tied round his waist. He took off his baseball cap and ran his hands through his hair, shaking his head in awe. Rosie couldn't help but smile at his appreciation of being outdoors.

'Yes, it's the simple things in life that are the best,' she said with a sigh.

'Are you going to tell me where we are headed then?' he asked with a quizzical smile.

'Nope. You'll soon see, when you spot the sign,' she said, and jerked her thumb in the direction ahead. 'Come on. Let's keep going.'

'It's just as well I trust you,' he said. 'It's not everyone who would feel safe being led deep into the forest like this.'

Rosie grinned. 'True. Who knows where I might take you. Come on,' she said sternly. 'Let's keep moving.'

'You're quite militant,' said Luke with a chuckle. 'I'm sure you'd give that Tartan Wanderer guy a run for his money.'

Rosie was puzzled for a minute as she wondered who he was talking about. The Tartan Wanderer? 'Ah, you mean Logan?'

'Is that his name? Yes, I saw some of his leaflets in the cottage and I burst out laughing when I saw he was known as the Tartan Wanderer. What a brilliant name.'

Rosie nodded. 'Yes. I don't think I'm quite in his league as a tour guide,' she said. 'Logan is here for the serious walking tours and I believe he is quite popular with the ladies who follow him on Instagram.'

'Yes, I checked him out,' said Luke. 'I can see why he would be popular. His posts are great. He's quite the actor.'

'Are you jealous?' she asked jokingly. 'Yes, I have heard his Instagram posts are very entertaining. Though I haven't seen them. But I've heard he is actually very down to earth.' She was standing close to Luke now and gave him a small nudge.

'Are you saying that I'm not?' he said, his eyes wide.

She pursed her lips and shrugged. He was very easy to wind up. 'Mm, I've not quite made up my mind yet.'

He feigned a look of outrage and, as they continued to walk, Rosie and Luke chatted like old friends. He was very easy company and a great storyteller. Especially when it came to some of the escapades that he and his band got up to while touring.

'You have so many great tales to tell, Luke. You should put that in the book too. You've probably got several volumes of stuff there.'

He shrugged. 'I don't know about that. It's just life, well, my life, and I find it tricky to know what people will be interested in. It's fine when I'm verbalising stuff, like this to you. That's when I think maybe I have got some good stories to share. It's just when I sit down to write it that I seem to clam up.'

'Have you thought about just recording yourself telling them and then transcribing them afterwards? Just pretend you're talking to someone or leaving a very long voicemail.'

He considered this and nodded. 'That's a good idea. I hadn't thought about that. But I will try it. Thank you.'

Rosie gave a self-conscious smile. He was doing that thing of staring at her again which she was finding unnerving. 'Which do you prefer?' she hurriedly asked. 'The singing and touring or the acting?' But just then Rosie's phone started to buzz. She pulled it from her pocket and frowned when she realised it was Dermot. Ignoring the call, she switched it off and tucked it away in her small backpack.

'Is everything okay?' said Luke, concerned.

'Fine, fine,' she said, brushing off his comment and glancing ahead through the trees. 'Sorry. What were we saying there?' Rosie was annoyed that seeing Dermot's name had thrown her and she couldn't help wondering what he was calling about now. Surely, he wasn't going to start up about getting the cottage valued again. She wanted to scream with frustration and she hoped Luke wouldn't detect the shift in her mood.

'I was saying that you're really easy to talk to, Rosie. It just feels like the words flow when I'm telling you the stories. You're a good listener.'

Rosie blushed and shook her head vehemently, wishing she could accept his comment graciously. But she was struggling to think any gracious thoughts right now. All she could think of was ways in which she could dispose of her ex-husband. But the way Luke held her gaze was certainly helping to sooth her anger.

'I'm happy to listen, Rosie, if it would help to talk?' he said gently.

Rosie was about to brush him off again but paused. He had a sincere look in his eyes and, well, maybe telling him might actually be helpful. 'That was my soon-to-be ex-husband calling,' she said tentatively. 'It tends to trigger me when I see his name appear on the screen.'

Luke nodded at her but didn't say anything.

'He wants me to sell the cottage which I'm absolutely *not* doing. He decided to walk out and it was his choice to take up with another woman...' Rosie's voice wobbled slightly as the enormity of what Dermot had done hit her again.

Luke's eyes were focused on Rosie and he gave her a kind smile. 'I am so sorry, Rosie.'

She shrugged. 'It's okay... splitting was the right thing to do. I now realise that our marriage had been over for a while. It just still all came as a shock and I just can't believe the cheek of him suggesting I should sell Creel Cottage. I mean, it belonged to *my parents*.' A tear trickled down her cheek and Luke reached forward and gently wiped it away. At which point Coisty came bounding up to her and sat barking for a treat. *Honestly*, she thought, *it was like having a toddler at times*. He had a way of ruining the moment which was probably just as well. 'Honestly Coisty, what are you like?' She shook her head and shrugged apologetically to Luke. 'Anyway, we are here.' She pointed to the sign at the small car park they had arrived in.

'Oh, I know where you're taking me,' he said as they crossed the road to the start of the trail. 'You're going to take me to the library in the woods?'

'You already know about it?' asked Rosie, feeling a bit deflated.

He must have realised how disappointed she looked because he lay a hand on her wrist and she almost jumped at the spark she felt. He shrugged apologetically. 'Another leaflet in the cottage,' he said, cringing. 'But there is no way I would have come up here alone, Rosie. I'm a bit out of my comfort zone just now. So, thank you for bringing me.' He flashed her a grateful smile.

The rain had suddenly begun falling like a sheer mist and they both put their hoodies back on and pulled up their hoods as they started ascending the track towards the falls. The only sound to be heard was their shoes crunching on the carpet of pine needles and leaves underfoot. Rosie was glad that Luke was happy to walk in companiable silence at times and didn't feel awkward when there were lulls in their conversation. Especially as some of the climb was quite steep in places. She watched Luke as he glanced around in awe of the scenery.

'It does feel like we are in the middle of nowhere,' he said in a low voice as they stopped to glance at the waterfall. Coisty was running ahead and then back to check they were coming. The trail had an assortment of beautiful wood carvings and they stopped to admire their intricate details.

'Look,' he said, pointing over. 'It's like something from a fairy tale. It's magical. Far better than what it looks like in the leaflet,' he said softly. Luke had now walked towards the small cabin which was covered in moss and grass.

She followed him over. 'Shall we go inside?' She looked up at the sky, pointing at the blue patch in the distance. Inside the hut, the walls were covered with hundreds of pieces of paper which visitors had pinned up. A mixture of words, stories, pictures and poetry. ''It's so peaceful,' she murmured quietly. Luke was now standing very close and she felt him brush against her and she felt her legs turn to jelly.

'Thank you, Rosie,' he said. 'I will never forget this. It's incredible.'

Rosie wasn't sure whether he was talking about the library or this moment and she felt as though invisible threads were drawing them closer. She sighed, longing to rest her head against him for a moment. Then she cringed at herself. *Was she having some kind of midlife crisis after her marriage split?* She'd forgotten what it felt like to be held and her heart was racing so quickly that she was sure he must hear its thud. Then, when she raised her eyes to look at him, he looked as though he was about to bend forward to kiss her. But when she heard a shout of 'we made it', they sprang apart as three walkers started to make their way through the door and into the library. The moment was lost.

'Let's write a Haiku,' suggested Rosie quickly.

'A what?' said Luke.

'It's a really short poem, with three lines, the first one has five syllables, the second line has seven syllables and the third has five syllables.'

'Okay,' said Luke dubiously. 'I'll watch and learn from you.'

Rosie picked up a pencil, chewed it in thought for a moment and then started to write.

The wee library
Tucked away in the forest
A place to reflect

Luke grinned and nodded. He picked up a pencil and leaned over a piece of paper.

Deep in the forest
Is a library of words
Now I need coffee

'Brilliant,' said Rosie. 'You're a poet. Just like that. And what's even better is there's a café at the bottom.' She started to edge towards the door. 'Looks like the rain has gone off.' She laughed and said, 'Last one down buys the coffee.' Then she raced off leaving Luke to catch up.

CHAPTER TWENTY-SIX

Luke was grinning from ear to ear when he got back to Beach Cottage. He paced the kitchen, the lounge and then the garden. He felt as though he had been drinking strong coffee all afternoon and his thoughts were scattered and flying in lots of different directions. He made himself stand still as he planted his feet firmly on the grass and took a breath in a bid to gather himself. He loved spending time with Rosie, just the two of them, outdoors and walking and talking. He couldn't remember when he'd last enjoyed himself so much and had such a laugh. Feeling deliriously happy was something he hadn't experienced for a very long time. He had been so close to pulling her towards him and kissing her properly in the library. Then they were interrupted. Which was perhaps not a bad thing as he wasn't sure he could stop kissing her once he started.

When they had arrived back at the cottages, they stood for a moment and then Rosie had turned to him, her eyes bright, and he had hoped she was going to invite him in. Perhaps they could take up from where they were about to start.

'Would you like to come in for a drink or another coffee?' he said. Really what he wanted to do was to reach forward and gather her in his arms. But then she shook her head. He'd panicked that he had completely misread the situation. Maybe she was just being friendly and he'd overstepped the mark. He inwardly groaned.

'Not to sound like a nag or anything . . . but, you are going to go into that cottage and get to work. You've already had your coffee break for the day. Set that timer and plan a reward for getting the words done. A beer or a cup of tea. Anything that will make you just write,' she had said firmly.

He sighed. That wasn't exactly what he'd been hoping to hear. He was finding it difficult to drag his eyes away from her even though he knew she meant business. In the short time that he had spent with Rosie, he knew she was kind and gentle but also had a steely side to her too. And the more time he spent with Rosie, the more the memories had started to come back of their time together in Sydney. The way her eyes sparkled when she teased him about doing his homework reminded him of the Rosie back then. She had always been first on the dance floor and would twirl around laughing and beckoning him to join her. Although life of late might have dampened her enthusiasm slightly, he could still see flashes of the old Rosie in the way she twirled around the beach with Coisty and grinned whenever Isobel cracked a joke. She had been similar then too which was why he had fallen for her.

'Righto,' he said, in mock fear, slightly disappointed that their time today was coming to an end. But much as he wanted to hang out longer with Rosie, he knew she was right. He needed to remind himself he was here for one reason only and that was to write his blooming book. The last thing he needed was to become emotionally involved with someone. She was in a vulnerable place, too, after her marriage breakdown and he was glad she felt able to open up to him when they were on their walk. Her husband was clearly a twit.

As they got out the car, she shut the door and blew him a kiss. 'Off you go. I'll check in on you tomorrow,' she said, more softly now. 'And thanks for today, Luke. I really enjoyed your company. And the coffee and cake . . .' She looked as though she was about to say something else then thought the better of it. 'Remember, I want you to have made progress. Or else.' She wagged her finger at him, and her gaze seemed to linger for a moment, before she turned and crunched across the gravel to the front door of Creel Cottage.

He had burst out laughing and turned on his heel and done as he was told.

Now as he stood in the garden, he knew that he needed to follow her advice. Being with Rosie was intoxicating but what he needed to do now was focus. Luke allowed himself one more smile, then, glancing at his watch he saw it was just after five o'clock. He would work for a couple of hours and then his reward would be some dinner and a cold beer. It was handy having the small village shop which he had managed to buy some essential supplies from. At some point he could do with heading to one of the larger villages for a bigger shop, but for now he would make do.

***

Four hours later, Luke was still sitting at the oak kitchen table with his laptop open. He leaned back in his chair and yawned, then stretched his arms above his head. Now he knew what Rosie was talking about when she said he needed to get into the zone and just write. He had been concentrating so intensely that he had lost all track of time. But he had written loads. He picked up his phone and pinged her a quick text.

I got in the zone! Loads of writing done. Fancy a beer in the garden to celebrate?

Then he deleted it without sending it, feeling a bit foolish and self-absorbed. She still had her friend, Isobel, there visiting and he had already taken up loads of her time already. He walked to the fridge and took out a bottle of beer and took it outside trying to keep his eyes averted from next door. He didn't want her to think he was being totally dependent and weird.

CHAPTER TWENTY-SEVEN

The next morning, Rosie woke up with a jolt when she heard a loud knock at the door, followed by Coisty's barks. She sat up bleary-eyed and jumped out of bed when she saw the time. She must have slept in. Then her phone buzzed with a message. She could see it was from Luke and her heart skipped a beat. She stood up, slightly dazed and momentarily wondered whether to check her phone or answer the door. But when she heard the knocking again, she pulled on her dressing gown, shoved her phone in her pocket and rushed downstairs. As she swung the door open, she rubbed her eyes. Her jaw almost hit the ground when she saw who was standing there.

'Hey, Mum,' said Ben, grinning at her.

Rosie gasped loudly and then promptly burst into tears. Ben grabbed and hugged her tightly. She couldn't believe her boy was here and she clutched him tightly. Rosie let herself shed a few more tears then gave herself a shake. The last thing she wanted to do was go to pieces. She needed to pull herself together. It wasn't fair on Ben. Stepping back and keeping her arms on his, she said, 'But how . . . what are you doing here?'

'I was just passing and thought I would pop in and say hello,' he said jokingly.

'Am I dreaming? You're supposed to be in Bali?' He was wearing shorts, trainers and a light jacket. His face was tanned by the sun and his hair was streaked with blonde. He did *not* look like a local.

'Not anymore, Mum. I really am here on Arran with you.' He reached forward to give her another hug. Coisty, who had managed to sneak round the ajar front door, jumped up and pawed his legs excitedly. 'Hey, Coisty. How are you, boy?' Coisty barked and wagged his tail as Ben bent down to scratch his ears.

Millions of questions raced through her head but she couldn't articulate any of them. It didn't matter. The main thing was that Ben was here now for however long and she was going to make the most of it.

'Come on in,' she said, opening the door. 'I see you've travelled light.' She chuckled as he easily swung his rucksack on his shoulder and walked into the house.

'I have my world on my back,' he said. 'Though I might have to do some washing, if that's okay, Mum?'

'Of course it is,' she said with a shake of her head. 'Just leave it by the machine and I will get it sorted. Now, what can I get you? Are you starving? Do you want a cup of tea?'

'Yes, please, a cup of tea would be great. And I wouldn't say no to a wee snack, Mum.'

Rosie watched as Ben kicked off his shoes in the hallway then hung his coat on a peg next to the door.

Isobel appeared at the top of the stairs looking very bleary-eyed. 'Am I dreaming or did I hear Ben's voice?'

Rosie laughed. 'He's here. He's really here.' She wiped away a tear of joy that had trickled down her cheek.

Isobel ran down the stairs. 'Och, Ben. What a lovely surprise,' she said, hugging him. 'Look at how much you've grown.'

Ben grinned. 'Good to see you too, Isobel. Thought I'd surprise my mum. Looks like I woke both of you up.'

'Aye, changed days, Ben. It's our turn to lie in bed till noon.' Isobel chuckled.

Rosie was still in shock. She had to reach over and grab his arm to make sure it was *really* him.

'I'll go and shower and get organised and leave you two to catch up for a bit,' said Isobel diplomatically.

Rose smiled gratefully at her as she disappeared upstairs. 'Come on through, sweetie,' she said, linking her arm through his as they walked into the kitchen. 'You know where everything is. Make yourself at home.'

'I'll just go and wash my hands,' he said.

As she waited for the kettle to boil, she remembered her phone and the message from Luke. Pulling it out her pocket, she opened the message and read it. Even though she was already smiling at Ben's surprise appearance, she felt her grin grow even wider.

'Just go and relax next door and I'll bring this through,' Rosie said as she made two mugs of tea and sliced some tea loaf. She followed him into the living room, where he was slumped on the sofa. Coisty jumped up next to him. She sat opposite, still unable to believe that he was actually *here*. She waited a few minutes until he had taken a few sips of tea and eaten several pieces of tea loaf on the plate. 'You're hungry?' she teased.

'Nah, not really. I got something on the ferry.'

Rosie chuckled as she watched him demolish the final piece of cake on the plate. 'I don't understand. When did you decide to come back and why didn't you tell me?'

He raised an eyebrow and shrugged. 'I had been thinking about it for a while, Mum. Then I saw a flight and decided to go for it.'

'Dare I ask how long you're back for? And if everything is okay, love?'

Ben chewed thoughtfully as he studied his mum's face. 'I'm not too sure how long. That just depends . . . how are you, Mum? Really how are things?'

Rosie pulled a face. 'I'm fine, love. I've had a good summer with Isobel here and Bella, though that was all *quite* eventful to begin with.'

'How come?' said Ben, putting his mug of tea down on the small table next to him.

'I'll fill you in later,' she said, not wanting to get drawn into that right at this moment. 'And Ash is coming soon.'

'I know. Bella told me. I half wondered if we might bump into each other on the plane.'

Rosie chuckled. 'I didn't realise you and Bella were in touch.'

'Um, yes, just a bit. A few messages on Instagram and stuff, you know? It will be nice to see her, once I'm over the jet lag.' He gave a sudden yawn. 'But don't say anything, I want it to be a surprise.'

'Got you. I will brief Isobel. In the meantime, I think you could do with a nap. Just head up to your room, love.'

'Thanks, Mum,' he said with another yawn. 'I think I will.'

She stood up and hugged him again. 'This is the best surprise ever,' she said happily. 'It's so nice to have you back.'

CHAPTER TWENTY-EIGHT

Later that night, Bella was sitting outside at the beach bar which was about twenty minutes from work along the Fisherman's Walk, a raised wooden walkway which took her along the beach. She couldn't quite believe that she was in Scotland as she gazed at the bright blue sky and shimmering water that stretched out in front of her. She'd kicked off her trainers and was digging her feet into the cool, crumbly sand. She took a few shots with her phone and made a mental note to share them on Instagram later. She had no idea the beach bar existed until Chantelle had mentioned it to her at work.

'It's a bit of a hidden gem,' she'd said. 'If you're not sure where to go to then it is quite easy to miss.'

Bella was grateful that Chantelle had offered to take her one night after work. As she had finished up for the day, Chantelle had placed a hand on her arm. 'If you're free tonight, let me show you Brodick's coolest bar.'

Now that she was here, it did indeed feel like the world's most amazing bar. She could have been on a Greek island or a Caribbean beach albeit without the soaring temperatures. Yet it was warm enough to sit with her cotton dress on and shoes off and feel quite comfortable.

'What did I tell you?' said Chantelle arriving back at the table, from the beach house bar, with two pale green cocktails which looked very refreshing.

'I know, you were right. It's out of this world,' said Bella. 'I had no idea it was here. It's absolutely stunning. You must come here all the time. Not bad for your local bar, eh?'

Chantelle sighed and took a sip of her drink through a straw. 'That lemon balm that's in there is divine,' she said, smacking her lips together. 'I don't actually come enough. You know what it's like, there's always other stuff to do like laundry and shopping and life admin. It's good you're here as it's reminded me that we have amazing stuff on our doorstep but it's easy to get waylaid with the routine.'

Bella took a sip of her drink. 'It's delicious and *very* drinkable,' she said. 'I know what you mean. I guess this is all quite a novelty for me at the moment with being new here. It's so different to life in Glasgow.'

'No ties to keep you there then?' asked Chantelle.

'Nope. I am single, which is the best way to be.' Bella already knew that Chantelle lived with her partner who had recently moved to the island from Ayr on the mainland.

'Well, a change can be a good thing, Bella,' said Chantelle, drawing her from her thoughts. 'And from the feedback I've heard from guests, they seem to be really happy with your treatments. Especially your reflexology technique. So I for one am glad you're part of the team.'

'Aw, thanks,' said Bella. 'I love it. I really do. It's a great place to work and I'm glad I'm being kept busy.' She had only been there for a few days but so far, so good. The great thing about starting her new job so quickly meant that she didn't have time to analyse whether she was doing the right thing. She realised that the move to Arran and this new job was all about her and nobody else which actually felt rather good. And as they chatted, Bella realised that her shoulders were no longer hunched. She actually felt relaxed for the first time in ages. There had been so much tension at her old work, everyone walking on eggshells, that she hadn't noticed just how on edge she had been. Maybe it was the sea air, or having a boss who was relaxed and not always worried like Georgie had been, but she really did feel like she was on holiday. Wasn't there a saying that if you enjoyed what you did you would never work another day in your life? As she gazed at the water gently lapping the shore and listened to the chatter and laughter around her, she felt as though she had found the job of her dreams.

***

Later that night as she lay on her bed in her room in the staff quarters, she posted the pictures from the beach bar on her social media. Within minutes her phone pinged with a message from Ben. They'd been messaging quite a bit since she had sent the picture of Teddy which had triggered a lot of reminiscing. It had clearly brought back happy memories for him too. It was as though they were kids again, easily exchanging banter and having a bit of a laugh.

Looks quite nice, he messaged. *Are you actually in Bali??*

She typed a laughing emoji. *Looks very tropical, doesn't it? Who would have thought the Firth of Clyde could look so inviting?*

I can't believe I didn't know about that place when I was there last summer.

Insider knowledge, typed Bella, who grinned as they continued to chat.

You'll need to take me there one day.

She smiled when she read his reply. Then quickly sent another of her own. *You're on.*

Bella had previously told him that it was nice seeing his mum and that she seemed to be doing well. She didn't think it was appropriate, though, to tell him about his mum's fledgling romance with Luke. She didn't want to worry Ben, as she knew he was protective of his mum, especially after what his dad had done. Bella had mentioned that she was sorry about what had happened with his parents and that she hoped he was okay.

Thanks for asking, Bella. Lots of people don't. They have just like totally avoided the subject. Which makes me feel even worse.

Bella was glad that she had addressed it rather than trying to pretend it hadn't happened. They'd always been frank with each other growing up and she was glad they could still be honest with each other. Although she wasn't yet ready to tell him the real story behind her sudden arrival on Arran last week with Luke. Where to even begin?

Yawning and then looking at the clock by her bed, she realised she would need to get some sleep. It was later than she thought and she was glad that she and Chantelle had only had one cocktail at the beach. Though she was very tempted to stay and have more. But the last thing she needed was to have a hangover in her first week into the job. *Well*, she typed, *some of us need our beauty sleep. I'd better get to bed.*

I think you must be referring to me. You look okay to me.

Bella felt her heart skip a beat. Was he *flirting?* Then she reminded herself that he had a girlfriend.

Very smooth, I can see your chat is still as good as ever. Speak tomorrow!

He sent back a laughing emoji and she quickly locked her phone and then switched off her lamp. She closed her eyes and was soon dreaming about being at the beach with a cocktail in her hand, the gentle sound of waves rolling into shore and the feel of warm sand beneath her feet.

CHAPTER TWENTY-NINE

The next day Rosie and Isobel were up early to walk Coisty. Then Rosie had a rummage in the freezer to see what she needed to buy at the shops later. Now Ben was back, she knew she would have to cook some proper meals. He was always hungry and had already emptied the fridge in the short time that he had been here. He had spent most of yesterday sleeping and catching up with jet lag. She was pleased to have him home, for however long he chose to stay.

Glancing at the clock, she realised she had better wake Ben up if she was to get him to Brodick on time. Last night, over dinner, he had told them that he planned to stay around for a while and had a meeting about some work at the distillery in Brodick. He had contacted Fergus in case there was anything going at the outdoor centre. Fergus couldn't help but said his friend James, who managed the distillery, had a vacancy. Ben said Fergus had been sworn to secrecy about his return, which explained why he hadn't stopped to talk to her at Cèic last week. 'He would have been worried about putting his foot in it,' said Ben with a grin.

Now, she looked around for Coisty who had vanished. Rosie smiled and shook her head. She knew exactly where he would be. If there was a warm body to curl up next to then he would be right next to it. He hadn't left Ben's side since he arrived back home. Rosie ran up the stairs two at a time. Ben's bedroom door was lying wide open thanks to Coisty who must have jumped up and forced it open with his two front paws. As suspected, Coisty was there and he put his chin on Ben's side and opened his eyes as if to say, 'What is it?'

Rosie reached over to gently shake Ben awake. 'Ben, love. It's time you got up, if we are to get you to Brodick on time.'

'Okay. Two minutes,' he said groggily. 'I was planning to take the bus. I don't want to be a hassle.'

'Don't be daft. I'll take you round. Isobel and I need to go and get some shopping anyway. Do you fancy eggs and toast for breakfast?'

Ben nodded. 'Thank you. I'll be right down.'

An hour later, they pulled in at the distillery in Brodick. 'Hope it goes well,' she said, glad that he had some smartish clothes from the wardrobe at the cottage. He wore a pair of black jeans and a white polo-shirt. Ben had always been a shorts and t-shirt kind of boy and wasn't in the least bit concerned about his appearance. But he'd at least combed his hair and made the effort. She caught her breath not quite believing that her little boy was now definitely a young man.

'Thanks, Mum,' he said, giving her a kiss on the cheek.

'Go in there and smash it,' said Isobel with a laugh.

Ben rolled his eyes. 'Okay.'

'We'll go and do the food shop. Text me when you're done and we'll treat you to a coffee?'

'Um, okay. That sounds good. Though I was going to see if Bella was around too. I wanted to surprise her.'

'Just as well I haven't said anything then,' said Isobel with a laugh. 'Don't worry, your mum briefed me to keep schtoom. Leave it with me. She doesn't start her shift until later. Let me see what I can do.'

He grinned. 'Right. Thank you. Hopefully I won't be long.'

'Good luck,' she called as he closed the door.

CHAPTER THIRTY

Earlier that morning, Bella's alarm woke her with its rude screech. She sat up, rubbing her eyes and yawned. Then, when she realised she didn't start work until two, she lay back down again. She should have switched the alarm off last night. There was no rush for her to pull on her uniform and race over to the spa. She let herself doze for a while longer and then eventually stretched her arms above her head and sat up as she thought about her plans for the day.

Work had been really busy since she started and she was loving it. She had made it clear she was happy to take on extra shifts when needed, knowing that things would soon quieten down after the busy summer rush. It also meant she would be able to take some time off, hopefully, over her birthday next month. Glancing out the window, she could see that it was a bright day and she had been planning to explore Brodick a bit more and perhaps take the bus round to the café in Lamlash. She had been longing to go back to the place she had been to briefly with her mum, especially as she and Rosie kept raving about their homemade cakes.

An hour later, Bella walked along the promenade in Brodick, breathing in the fresh and salty air. She passed a few familiar faces from the spa and waved when she saw Becky from work with her mum, Kirsty, and her Aunt Amy on the other side of the road. When she saw the large black and white Caledonian MacBrayne ferry berthed at the terminal, she knew the bus would be leaving soon for Lamlash, so she made the decision to jump on it and go round to the next village to treat herself to breakfast at Cèic. As the bus turned left, to follow the road to Lamlash, she gasped when she saw what she thought was Rosie's car passing by. She squinted to look and waved when she realised it *was* Rosie with someone else, most probably Luke, sitting in the passenger seat. She could just about make out her mum in the back seat. She quickly sent her a text.

Just going to Lamlash for a wander and was on bus leaving Brodick as I saw you driving past. Let me know if you have time to meet for a coffee? Could meet you at Cèic xx

A few minutes later, she felt her phone vibrate.

Great! We have a few errands to do in Brodick. Will text when near. Mum xx

Bella read the reply from her mum and smiled. She was more than happy to stroll around Lamlash for a while until it was time to go to the café as it was such a beautiful morning. It would be nice to get outside and get some fresh air and explore. Whenever she passed through Lamlash, she was very taken with its pretty cottages which overlooked the sheltered bay. She was also intrigued by the Holy Isle which Rosie had told her was owned by Tibetan monks who ran retreats at the lighthouse there. Although she had visited Cèic with her mum, she didn't appreciate what a stunning spot it was as her mind had been elsewhere worrying about being unemployed.

She pottered around some of the gift shops making a point of going into *The Wee Trove* that her gran and Mum had told her about. Her gran had gifted her some beautiful earrings from there at Christmas and she wore them all the time. She made a point of telling the owner, Thea, how much she loved them. Then, when she noticed the time, she realised she should head over to Cèic. She stopped to take a quick selfie with the beach in the background and then quickly sent a message to her gran. Although they had spoken a couple of times since Bella had started her new job, Bella felt a pang of guilt that she hadn't spoken to her as much as usual.

When she saw an empty table outside the café, she decided to grab it. Sitting down, she sent a text to her mum to let her know she was outside waiting. Then she placed her phone on the table and closed her eyes for a moment, to allow the sunshine to bathe her face.

'Bella,' called Isobel, in a sing-song voice.

Bella opened her eyes and looked up. She jumped up smiling and gave her mum and then Rosie a hug. 'Hello,' she said merrily. 'Oh, I thought you might have brought Luke?' Then Bella noticed Rosie's knowing smile over her shoulder and turned round to see who she was smiling at.

'Ben,' said Bella, shocked. 'Ben,' she repeated, this time a bit more incredulously. 'What are you doing here?'

'Hey, Bella,' said Ben, beaming. 'Surprise, eh?' He reached over to hug her.

She hugged him tightly and then took a step back to look at him. 'It certainly is. When did you get here? Why . . . how?' She was breathless as she looked at him and could feel herself blushing.

'You two sit down and have a quick debrief,' said Rosie in an excited voice. 'Your mum and I will go and get the coffees. Just the usual? And don't worry we will get scones too.'

Bella and Ben managed a nod before Rosie and Isobel disappeared inside the café. Ben sat down on the chair next to her. 'I still can't believe you're here.' Her heart was now racing and she felt slightly giddy with excitement, which she could pretend was down to her not eating breakfast. However, Ben really did look as good in the flesh as he did in his pictures, which had more to do with it. His piercing blue eyes lingered on her face and she felt her body stiffen when his arm brushed hers. 'This is wild.' She shook her head, unable to pull her eyes from his face. 'I don't know what to say.'

Ben raised an eyebrow. 'That's a first. You've usually got plenty to say about things . . .'

She nudged him and tutted. 'Right, hang on a minute and start from the beginning. What has happened and when did you get back?'

Ben gave her a potted version of wanting to come home to see his mum. 'She's doing surprisingly well,' said Ben, sitting back in his chair, 'which is great but . . . she looks fantastic and seems really happy so perhaps the single life is suiting her.'

Ah right, thought Bella. Rosie obviously hadn't told him about Luke yet so she reminded herself not to put her foot in it. Just then, Rosie and Isobel arrived back at the table.

'Cano will bring the stuff out in a minute,' Rosie said.

'Isn't this amazing to have you both here like this?' said Isobel, chatting quickly. 'Who would have thought you would both be on Arran like this and working nearby?'

Bella felt as though her jaw was about to hit the ground for the second time in ten minutes. 'Working?' she said to Ben in surprise.

He looked sheepish. 'That was going to be my next piece of news. I've been offered a job round at the distillery in Brodick. They're short-staffed and I can start straightaway.' He glanced over at his mum. 'James also said that if I want, I can use his flat. He lives with his girlfriend now and it's empty apart from when his friend is over doing walking tours. Is that okay?'

Bella watched Rosie's face. Did she notice a look of relief pass over it?

'Yes, of course, that's great, Ben. Makes sense for you to be nearer work and there's more happening for you young things in Brodick.' She looked up and thanked Cano for bringing out their coffees and scones. 'I'm just going to go inside and get some napkins,' she said. 'Back in a moment.'

Ben frowned. 'That went better than expected. I thought she would be wanting me at Creel Cottage with her.'

Bella looked at her mum as she raised an eyebrow and they both quickly took a sip of coffee.

'Um, well, I'm sure it will all work out, what with Ash arriving soon as well.'

'Of course,' said Ben, steepling his hands together. 'Things might have been a bit cosy anyway if I had stayed. I'm not sure Ash would be happy to share a room with any of us. Or vice versa.'

Isobel grinned. 'I know. Ash tends to be a tad messy.'

'By the way. I don't want you to think I'm being a total stalker or anything like that – with the job in Brodick.' He shrugged. 'It's just that I spent all my savings on the flight home and I need to save up now before I go back.'

This piqued Bella's interest. 'Don't be daft. I am just still fairly gobsmacked that you are here at all. But won't your friends miss you?' She did of course mean *Mabel* in particular.

'Nah,' he said, taking a sip of his coffee. 'They're all away now anyway. People are always moving. It's fine.' He looked at her meaningfully. 'It's good to be back.'

She smiled at him, feeling her cheeks flush again. Now she was starting to understand what her mum was talking about when she spoke about hot flushes and why they annoyed her so much.

'Here we are,' said Rosie, arriving back with a pile of napkins.

'Hey, there's Fergus,' said Ben pointing to the café entrance. 'Let me run over and say hello.'

Bella watched him as he lightly jogged over to a man who had just come out the café. They hugged.

'Oh God, Bella, you didn't say anything about Luke, did you? I will tell him, I just haven't had a chance and then I hoped you hadn't said anything.'

'Sorry, I completely put my foot in it when you arrived and I said I thought you were bringing Luke. I could tell you from your face that you hadn't mentioned him to Ben.'

'He didn't hear that don't worry. And no, not yet . . .'

Bella gave her a reassuring smile. 'No, don't worry. I didn't say a thing.'

'When are you going to tell him?' asked Isobel.

Rosie sighed loudly and her shoulders visibly slumped. 'I just wasn't quite expecting all of this. It's all been a bit of a surprise.'

She glanced over at Ben standing with Fergus, who then pulled something from his pocket, handed Ben his coffee cup and started to run. *That was strange*, thought Bella.

'I don't mean to be so secretive but, well, I suppose I will have to talk to him soon,' said Rosie.

'Talk to me about what?' said Ben, arriving back at the table.

'Um, about what you said to Fergus to make him dash off like that,' said Bella hastily. 'Did he not rate your chat?'

Ben grinned. 'Ah, that was his pager. He got a shout. He's a volunteer with the lifeboat crew.'

'I hope it isn't anything too serious,' she said.

He shrugged and picked up his coffee. 'Time will tell. He just has to drop everything when it goes off. I got used to drinking a lot of his coffees when I worked with him last summer at the outdoor centre. It always used to happen just when he had been in to buy his flat white.'

Bella chuckled, relieved that Ben was now more focused on eating his scone than what she and their mums had been talking about. She looked at Rosie who threw her a grateful look.

CHAPTER THIRTY-ONE

With the excitement of Ben's sudden arrival home, Rosie hadn't seen Luke since their walk together in the woods but she had exchanged a few texts with him and he assured her he was churning out the words. That made her happy. She had told him that Ben had arrived back and would be working and living in Brodick. It was probably best he was keeping a low profile and that they did have some space from each other anyway. The last thing she wanted to do was distract him. However, today she had asked him if he would like to chum her and Rosie to Lamlash. Ash was due to arrive later that day and they needed to get some shopping in. Luke had texted her back saying he would love to come.

'What if anyone recognises you?' said Isobel as they got out the car beside the Co-op.

He shrugged. 'I don't think anyone will. I'm just a regular guy. It's amazing how you can go about your business if you stay low key and don't make a big deal of things', he said.

'I suppose that's true,' said Isobel. 'I once saw that big hunk from *Game of Thrones* in Boots in Buchanan Galleries. I didn't know it was him. It was just some bloke trying to decide which brand of toothpaste to buy. I just wondered why the assistant was paying special attention to the dental section. I asked her where the floss was and she glared at me. It was only when the chap walked away, with the tooth whitening variety by the way, that she told me who he was. I would have been none the wiser.'

Rosie had no idea who Isobel was referring to and shrugged. She glanced at Luke unable to think of him as just a *regular guy*. It was a bit cooler today and he wore his jeans, a sweatshirt and had pulled his beanie hat on. 'Saves me worrying about my hair,' he had said earlier when Isobel had made a comment and asked him if he was going busking. She was becoming more and more like her mother every day. As far as Rosie was concerned his hair was perfect.

'Right, what's the plan?' said Isobel. 'Get the shopping done and have a wander? Or get the shopping done and then have a coffee?'

'Shopping and coffee,' said Rosie and Luke in unison.

Isobel smirked. 'You're both so *in tune* with each other.'

Rosie looked sheepishly at Luke then glared at Isobel. 'Come on. And Isobel, just remember it's your turn to buy the coffees.'

'No bother at all,' she said, completely unfazed.

Rosie had made a list of things to buy for Ash's stay. She planned to make a spicy sausage pasta that night and then do a barbeque tomorrow as the weather looked set to be fair. Then, after that, if Ash decided to stay longer, they could eat out. It didn't take Rosie and Isobel long to gather all the necessary ingredients and then drop them off at the car. Luke was waiting on a nearby bench which overlooked the sea.

'I love this place,' he said. 'It's like a painting.' He pointed over to the island. 'That's the Holy Isle?'

'Yes,' said Rosie, opening the car and putting the shopping in the boot. 'You can go over and visit it. Or volunteer there. I think they're always looking for people to help in the kitchen and the garden. I would imagine that is another good place to escape to.'

'Have you been over?' asked Isobel curiously.

'Yes, I did a mindfulness course there last year.'

'Did you?' said Isobel. 'You kept that quiet.'

'Because you would accuse me of going all woo-woo,' said Rosie, shaking her head at her friend. 'I know how sceptical you can be. But actually, it was great.'

'I'm sure it was,' said Luke. 'Mindfulness can be really great. I know it's helped me with stuff.'

Rosie gave him a small smile. 'Anyway, they have a website in case you want to find out more.'

He nodded thoughtfully.

Isobel clapped her hands together. 'Right, let's go and get some coffee at Cèic. What would everyone like?' Isobel took their orders and walked ahead then disappeared inside the café.

Rosie and Luke took their time to wander over and then decided they would sit outside.

'You're a bit quieter today, Rosie. Is everything okay?' said Luke, touching her on the elbow.

Rosie felt her arm tingle at his touch and she was glad she had her sunglasses on as he was right. She *did* feel out of sorts. And not just because of his current proximity to her. She knew that Ash's arrival would completely shift the dynamic in the cottage and Isobel was already starting to behave strangely, which she tended to do when she was nervous. It would, of course, all settle down after Ash had been there for a day or so. It was always like this. 'Yes, just thinking about Ash arriving and all that needs to be done.' She flicked her hand dismissively. 'It will be fine . . . it's just been ages since we were all together and it can sometimes take us a while to readjust to being in each other's company. Ash can sometimes be a bit full on, you know.' Rosie could already hear what Ash would have to say about Luke which made her feel a bit edgy.

Luke nodded thoughtfully. 'I can understand that,' he said, and then his mobile started to ring. 'Sorry, I had better take this,' he said apologetically as he looked at the caller's number. He stood up and walked away to take the call. 'Hey there,' he said softly into the phone.

Rosie watched him as he leant against a wall a few metres away. He rubbed his hand over his jaw, which she noticed he did when he was stressed. She wondered who he was talking to. From the way he answered the call, it sounded as though it was a woman. Not that it was any of her business, but she couldn't help being curious. She also felt a stab of envy at the thought of Luke and another woman which was not how she wanted to feel at all.

'Here I am,' said Isobel in her sing-song voice which was kept for when she was feeling anxious. 'They will bring them right out and I wasn't sure whether to get cake or scones and figured it was morning so too early for cake so I got a variety of scones. Lemon and blueberry, fruit and plain. I thought we could share them. And I got butter and jam. I wasn't sure who wanted what. You know what my mum is like with the butter and jam and how she was never allowed both when she was young because of rations. And so having both is a real treat.' Then she suddenly sat down seemingly exhausted with her verbal offload.

Rosie reached over and patted her arm knowingly. It was all she needed to do. There was no need for words. They knew each well enough to know what was going on. Just noticing was enough. 'That all sounds great. I'm sure it will all be fine,' she said soothingly. She moved her gaze back to Luke, who was still on his mobile and now pacing around.

'Who's lover boy on the phone to?' said Isobel flippantly.

'I have no idea and he is *not* my lover boy,' said Rosie.

'Well, he should be,' said Isobel. 'You both look at each other with absolute *longing*. It is quite fascinating to watch. The sexual tension is outrageous.'

Rosie sighed as Cano arrived with their drinks and scones on a tray. Luke was still on the phone but he gave Rosie a small nod to indicate he had noticed and would be with them soon. His eyes were now fixed on Rosie and she blushed and looked away.

'See what I mean,' said Isobel.

Rosie shook her head but couldn't stop grinning.

'Sorry about that,' he said with an apologetic smile as he strode towards them and sat down at the table.

'Everything okay?' asked Isobel quickly.

'Mm, yes. Just work stuff, you know.'

Rosie and Isobel waited, expecting him to elaborate but when he didn't, they changed the subject. Isobel was very good at filling silences and started talking at great length about a series on Netflix she had been watching. Now it was Rosie's turn to notice that Luke wasn't quite himself. He nodded politely as Isobel talked, but Rosie noticed a real shift in his energy since he had taken the call and he was definitely distracted. She tried to catch his eye but his mind was clearly elsewhere — as was Isobel's, who was chattering nineteen to the dozen, even though Rosie and Luke weren't very engaged with what she was saying. She didn't seem to realise her words were going over their heads. Rosie grimaced. It didn't matter that they were all in this beautiful location together at this moment. None of them were present and all of their minds were elsewhere. Rosie took a bite of scone and chewed thoughtfully. It was a reminder that you couldn't escape your problems no matter how hard you tried.

Their walk in the forest seemed a distant dream. She had been reliving it ever since and now thought she had completely imagined their connection. Especially as Luke was now being a bit offhand. Who had he been speaking to on the phone just there? Because whoever it was had completely ruined his mood. Isobel had drained her coffee in record time and the caffeine was making her extra fidgety.

'Right,' she boomed. 'Would anyone like another coffee?'

'Thanks, but no,' said Luke glumly, glancing up at the sky which had fittingly turned grey.

The wind had also picked up and dark clouds had rolled in from nowhere. Rosie took off her sunglasses and groaned. It looked as though it was about to start raining. 'I think we had better make a dash for it,' she said. 'It looks like there is about to be a downpour any minute now.'

The café staff were clearing away cups and plates from the other tables and Rosie, Luke and Isobel were the only people left sitting outside.

'Come on,' said Luke, gathering the things on the tray and handing it to Cano who had just come outside to help. 'Thank you,' he said to Cano. Then turned to Rosie and Isobel and called, 'Let's make a dash for it.'

They just made it to Rosie's car before huge fat raindrops started to pelt down.

'Yuck,' said Isobel. 'Summer in Scotland. Just brilliant. Fabulous sunshine one minute, pishing rain the next.'

'Doesn't matter,' said Luke. 'At least we managed to have coffee and delicious scones before it started. Thanks, Isobel. I must get it next time.'

'I'll hold you to it,' said Isobel.

The atmosphere in the car was sombre as they drove back to Kildonan and Rosie couldn't help thinking that the weather matched everyone's gloomy mood. Everyone seemed lost in their thoughts and as the windscreen wipers screeched as fast as they could to keep up with the rainfall, she couldn't help thinking that the miserable weather had set the tone for the rest of the day. She just hoped the ferry that Ash was on wasn't cancelled.

CHAPTER THIRTY-TWO

Bella still couldn't quite get over the fact that Ben was actually here on the island. After their surprise reunion at Cèic, Isobel and Rosie had suggested that she help him move his things over to the flat in Brodick.

'If you two take the car over, that means you are back in time for your shift starting, Bella,' said Isobel, in full organisational mode.

'By the time you get back to the cottage,' said Rosie to Ben, 'I will have your laundry sorted and some meals made for your freezer and can drop you back off.'

Bella laughed as she saw Ben's eyes widen. 'I wouldn't argue with either of them.'

'You are outnumbered, Ben. It's better if you just do as you are told,' said Isobel, drily.

'Okay. Whatever you say.'

James had asked Ben if he could start working at the distillery that night as they were short-staffed and holding a wedding. He was more than happy to help.

Bella and Ben had slipped into an easy banter together as they had ferried his belongings, and a pile of cleaning products that Rosie had insisted they take, to the upstairs flat which was handily placed for the distillery.

'This is ideal, isn't it?' she said, looking around at the sparse but clean flat.

'Yes, it will be nice to have some space again. I have slept in too many different beds these last few months.'

Bella had raised an eyebrow and given him a knowing look which had made him blush.

'I didn't mean like that,' he insisted.

'Whatever you say,' she said, smiling.

'Let's catch up properly when we next have some time off together?' said Ben suddenly.

'Great. Though I suspect you are going to be full on for a bit if you're just starting. You know Ash is arriving soon?'

'Yeah, Mum mentioned that already.'

Bella had glanced at her watch and groaned when she realised the time. 'I really need to run,' she said. 'Chantelle won't be happy if I'm late.'

'Come on, I'll run you round to the hotel,' said Ben. 'May as well make the most of Mum's car while I have it.'

Bella was glad she would have a few more minutes with him and as he drove around the bay she couldn't help but notice the blonde hairs on his tanned and very muscular arms. She gave herself a shake. 'Just in here is great,' she said, signalling to the small road where the staff accommodation was situated. 'Thanks, Ben. I hope tonight goes well at work and we can catch up properly soon?' She unclipped the seatbelt and felt herself tremble slightly when he put his hand on her arm.

'Thanks for your help today, Bella. It's great to see you.' He reached over and kissed her on the cheek and she could smell the scent of his shampoo.

'See you soon,' she'd said, blushing, as she got out the car. He'd grinned at her and driven off.

Now Bella had a couple of days off work and was on the bus making her way round to Kildonan where she would stay for the night. The rain had started falling that morning and had been constant ever since. It was such a contrast to the other evening when she had been at the beach bar. But she reminded herself that it didn't matter what the weather was like. Tonight's excitement was that Ash was finally here and she didn't care whether it rained, snowed or hailed. She was almost giddy with excitement at the thought of seeing Ash, who she loved to bits.

As the bus meandered its way to the south of the island, she looked out the window letting her thoughts drift. She thought about how much she was enjoying work and how lovely the team were. She'd made friends with one of the lifeguards at the pool, Becky, who was back from university in Dundee for the summer. They had made plans to go out later that week and Becky had also invited her to try out her aunt's yoga class at the village hall. Bella closed her eyes and thought about Ben. Again. He had messaged her a few times saying work was great but crazily busy.

The journey to Rosie's cottage took around half an hour and although she had texted her mum to let her know she was on her way, she hadn't received a reply which was unusual. Her mum's phone was normally always with her. Although maybe she'd just got completely distracted with the excitement of Ash being back and didn't realise Bella had been in touch.

By the time Bella got off the bus and made the walk to Creel Cottage she was completely drenched. She knocked the door quickly, hoping someone would let her in and fast.

'Oh, Bella,' said Rosie, eventually opening the door. 'There you are. I am so sorry I should have offered to get you from the bus stop at the very least. Come on in out the rain.'

Bella stepped across the threshold. 'That's okay. I did text Mum to let her know I was on my way.' She frowned at Rosie who seemed distracted. Normally she made a fuss of any visitors who came to the cottage. But she was looking towards the living room and Coisty was nowhere to be seen either.

'Is everything okay?' asked Bella.

Rosie hesitated before answering. 'Yes, sorry we just got caught up talking,' she said levelly. 'Here, let's get your wet stuff off. I'll hang it in the airing cupboard to dry. Shall I get you something dry to change into?'

'That's okay,' said Bella, now wondering why her mum and Ash hadn't come to the door to greet her too. 'I've got my pyjamas with me. I'll just take my jeans off and put them on just now.'

'Good idea,' said Rosie brightly. 'You do that and come through and I'll let them know you're here.'

A pained look flickered across Rosie's face and Bella wondered what had happened. Is that why Ben was worried about her? Had he sensed something wasn't right with his mum? Maybe she was ill? Or it was something to do with Dermot? Bella went into the downstairs loo to change and then pulled out her phone to check whether her text to her mum had actually been delivered. It had, which was so strange. Then she noticed a message from Ben. Did he know what was going on with his mum now and was letting her know?

Hey Bella, hope you have a nice time with the oldies. Bet it will be fab seeing Ash. Say hi to everyone from me. Bx

Bella grinned when she saw the kiss. She replied with a heart. Then realised she really wished he was there for moral support and she quickly typed a message. *Wish you were here x* Something was definitely amiss and Ben was the only other person who would understand. He always got the in-jokes and their mums' funny ways. She washed her hands and quickly pulled them through her hair, which had turned to frizz in the rain. Then she unlocked the door, dumped her bags into the hall and walked towards the living room where she could hear voices. Except it wasn't the low murmur of excited chatter from friends who had been reunited after years of being apart she could hear. The voices were raised and they sounded as though there was a bit of a *tense* discussion going on. Bella's excitement about seeing Ash quickly faded. Maybe joining them at this very minute wasn't the best idea. No wonder Rosie had looked so strained when she had answered the door. Bella's timing obviously hadn't been ideal. Her hand hovered above the door handle.

'We did what we thought best at the time,' said Rosie pleadingly.

'I know we did,' said Ash. 'But none of this was planned, was it? But it's all worked out okay over the years, hasn't it? I thought we had agreed this *was* all for the best?'

'Well, yes, and it has been,' said her mum tensely. 'But it's been much easier for you. You've been away the other side of the world all this time. It's been *me* who has been dealing with all the questions. I absolutely hate all the lies. It's eating me up inside and even more so this past couple of weeks. I can't do this anymore. We need to put an end to all this.'

There was a silence and Bella waited for someone to talk.

Ash spoke first. 'What do you mean?'

'I mean, I think we should just come clean.'

'But are you sure Isobel? Because if we do then there is no going back,' said Ash.

Bella took a sharp breath. What were they talking about?

'Yes, I am sure. I haven't thought of much else lately.' Her mum again. 'It's time we told her. We need to talk to Bella and tell her the truth.' Bella was on high alert when she heard her name being mentioned. Why were they arguing about her?

'Look, I will respect your decision and support you. Of course I will. I . . . I just don't get why we need to do it right now.'

'Because . . . as I have already told you,' said her mum now speaking extremely slowly but loudly, a tell-tale sign she was close to losing the rag, 'she has been asking lots of questions about where she came from. She even went and confronted Luke Giles, for God's sake. And I have had enough of all of this. That was the final straw. I always said there would be a time when we would need to tell her the truth. And I know for a fact that the time is right now. I just can't lie anymore. It's not fair on Bella or on any of us.'

'I know, I do understand that,' said Ash, with a loud sigh. 'I just wasn't expecting us to be having this kind of reunion. I guess I would have liked to have a bit more time to mentally prepare.'

'Mentally prepare?' shrieked her mum. 'God, you can be a total eejit at times. Will you listen to yourself. You've had plenty of time to get your head round all of this.'

Bella stood frozen in the hallway unsure whether to move. This wasn't how it was supposed to be. They were all meant to be excited to be reunited again and drinking glasses of fizz together. Shouldn't they be gathered around the table eating Rosie's famous spicy sausage pasta and catching up on what everyone had been doing since they had last been in the same room together? Having a massive fallout should not be on the agenda.

'Hey,' said Rosie, more softly. 'Ssh. Come on, Bella might hear you. This isn't the way to do it. In fact, I wonder where she is. She's been in the loo for ages.'

Just then Bella swung the door open and stood surveying the scene in front of her. Ash was white-faced and standing by the wood-burning stove, her mum's face was streaked with tears and Rosie sat on the sofa with Coisty tucked in tightly beside her. He managed a feeble wag of his tail, clearly aware that something wasn't right in the house.

'Bella,' gasped her mum, rushing over to her and giving her a hug.

Bella was tense in her mum's arms and she took a step back. She could feel the blood rushing to her head and she bit her bottom lip as she tried to keep the tears at bay. 'Does anyone want to tell me what this is all about? Why are you all shouting at each other?'

Her mum crossed her arms and stared pointedly at Ash, who now walked to Bella and pulled her into a hug. 'It is so good to see you, darling.'

Then all of the jagged jigsaw pieces of Bella's life started to slowly slot together as she realised what they were arguing about. She untangled herself from Ash's arms and surveyed the scene. It didn't take a genius to figure out what the missing piece was. Bella couldn't quite believe she hadn't fathomed it until now. Yet it all made perfect sense. The answer had been right in front of her all along. Nobody spoke and the only sound she could hear was the tick of the grandfather clock in the corner. Bella stared at her mum and then she turned and looked at Ash.

'Is it true?' she said in a whisper as she looked again at her mum for confirmation and then back again towards Ash.

A pained-looking Ash took a step towards her.

Bella held up her hand as though to say halt. 'Is it true, Ash? Are *you* my dad?'

CHAPTER THIRTY-THREE

Rosie watched as Ash slowly nodded his head. There was disbelief and shock then, finally, recognition in Bella's eyes. Ash stepped towards Bella and wrapped his arms around her in a tight embrace. Isobel sat down on the sofa, her head in her hands. This was not the scene any of them had envisaged when they had found out Isobel was pregnant all these years ago or when she had eventually confessed who the father was.

Bella looked over at Rosie, her face a picture of utter confusion. Which was no wonder. Bella had known Ash for all of her life and as far as she was concerned, he was the cool and crazy uncle who lived on the other side of the world.

'But I don't understand,' said Bella in disbelief, as she untangled herself from his arms. 'You're gay . . .'

Ash reached for her hand and gently led her over to the sofa to sit her next to her mum. Then he got Rosie's little foot stool and positioned it opposite them. He leaned in towards them both and clasped his hands together.

Rosie felt as though she shouldn't necessarily be there while they chatted. But it felt too disruptive to leave the room and she knew that Bella may also want to speak to her about it too. After all, she had known about Ash and been part of the secret. She just wished Isobel had told her at the time, when she had discovered she was pregnant in Sydney. Instead, she had claimed she was homesick and flown back to Glasgow. Rosie hadn't found out the truth until much later.

'I'm sorry for all of this, Bella,' said Ash. 'And regardless of what you may have heard out there in the hallway, I want you to know that I am glad that you know the truth now.'

'I still don't understand how it happened though,' said Bella, gazing around the room in shock.

Isobel dabbed her face with a tissue, a pained expression on her face.

Bella studied her mum's face curiously and Rosie watched Ash give Isobel a quizzical look as though to say *will you tell her, or will I?* But Rosie knew that Isobel would want to be the one to tell Bella what had happened.

Isobel reached her hand over and squeezed Bella's tightly. She took a steadying breath and started to speak. 'Well, you know that Rosie and I were travelling in Australia and that Ash then joined us when we were in Sydney.'

Bella glanced across the room at Rosie, who gave her a reassuring smile, wishing she could wave a wand and make everything okay for Bella. She hated seeing her in distress.

'We were both out one night catching up — Rosie was out with Luke. We had too much to drink. We were younger and those were the days when we didn't think much about the consequences. It just happened. And I'm so glad that it did, Bella. I wouldn't change the past for a minute.'

'I'd had lots of girlfriends,' continued Ash. 'And a few boyfriends that I'd kept quiet. But deep down, I knew I was gay and I was still trying to figure it out. It was hard. My parents were super strict and not exactly open-minded, so would not have approved at all. It might be hard for you to appreciate, especially as your mum is so relaxed about stuff, but my parents were the polar opposite. My upbringing had been so oppressive and there was such a stigma around being gay. I felt that layer of guilt every single day. I just couldn't shake the feeling that if I stayed there then I could never find the true me.' He paused. 'Leaving Glasgow was like a *massive* weight being lifted off my shoulders. Moving to Australia was the best thing I could have done for my own sanity. I didn't feel like I fitted in anywhere. Especially not in Glasgow. I hoped that by moving across the world and getting away from my parents and the small world I'd been brought up in, I would have some headspace and things would work out for me . . . which they have,' he added hastily. 'But at the time I had just arrived in Australia, I was overly excited, I was over the moon to see your mum and Rosie and that particular night in question, we had both had a lot to drink.'

Bella's eyes were fixed on Ash, who looked apprehensive.

Ash bit his lip. 'It was really hard,' he said. 'But I had to do it. Admitting to myself that it was okay to be me and that I needed to accept myself for the real me was just part of the journey. It was a long time ago and I guess we were all different people back then.'

Rosie found herself thinking about Luke again. Ash was right. It was easy to forget they were all younger once with hopes and dreams and different ideas of how their lives would unfold. There was no way that any of them could have predicted their worlds from that short time in Sydney colliding again like this.

'It was just one of those things,' said Isobel softly. 'But it was meant to be, Bella.'

'Your mum is right. I might have been trying to deny my true feelings. I was so worried about coming out and I did sleep with a lot of women, in the hope that it would make my feelings disappear. But, of course, it didn't.' His voice was choked with emotion. 'And I am glad it happened that night, otherwise there would be no you. And that is something I can't even begin to imagine.'

Bella wiped away a tear that had rolled down her cheek and Isobel reached for her hand. 'Ash left the next day to go to Queensland. He had a new life to start there. Rosie and I stayed in Sydney for a few more weeks as we wanted to spend Christmas and New Year there. That's when I started feeling sick and I took a test and found out I was pregnant.'

Rosie still felt guilty when she thought back to that time and that she hadn't noticed what was going on with Isobel. She had been so wrapped up in her own little world, although she knew now that it would have made little difference. Isobel's mind was made up, and she was definitely going home.

'And when did you find out about me?' Bella asked Ash quietly.

'Not until just before you were born,' said Ash.

'I hadn't told a soul about who the dad was. Not even your gran. I just said that I'd got pregnant after a one-night stand at The Tunnel, a nightclub in Glasgow, and I didn't know who the father was. And do you know something? I had always wanted to be a mum. I just hadn't met anyone I wanted to settle down with. I still haven't,' said Isobel with a brittle laugh. 'But there was no way I wasn't going to go ahead with the pregnancy. By the time you were due, Rosie was home and I told her the truth. I didn't know who else to turn to. Ash had always wanted to travel and make the most of being single. Rosie and I were so happy to finally see him happy and being his true self away from Glasgow. I didn't want to tell him as I knew he would come back to do right by me and I didn't want that for him. So, I didn't tell him until just before you were born.'

'Your mum phoned me and told me the week before you were born,' he said, his eyes misting over.

'You've got Rosie to thank for that,' said Isobel. 'She thought Ash had a right to know. I didn't know what to do. I was so overwhelmed and worried about doing the right thing.'

'And what did you say when she told you?' asked Bella, fascinated.

'I didn't know what to say. It was such a shock. When your mum told me, it was the last thing I expected to hear. I had finally started to be *myself* in Queensland without worrying about what anyone thought of me. Your mum told me *not* to come back, as we couldn't be a family, and that she wouldn't want me to give up on being my true self. She reminded me that I'd had to travel to the other side of the world to gain some independence and distance from my parents.' He looked at Bella and shook his head in sorrow. 'I was in my first proper relationship and everything was going well. I was being *me*. But I agonised on what to do, Bella. I felt like I had already let you down.'

Isobel shook her head. 'You didn't ever let Bella down, Ash. It was such a difficult position to be in and it was my idea to keep it between the three of us. If your parents had found out, the pressure on you and the fall out for not coming back to us would have been awful.'

Ash grimaced. 'I was never able to tell them I was gay. So, you see, all of that meant that I couldn't be a proper dad to you. Not in any kind of conventional way. But I promised Isobel that I would always be part of your life. No matter what. I vowed that I would be an amazing uncle and I would help support you. Always and no matter what. And as soon as I saw you, I fell in love, Bella. And that hasn't changed and never will. I love you from the bottom of my heart and I am so proud to be your dad. I'm just so sorry that you are hearing all of this now. We thought we were doing the right thing.'

Rosie felt the tears slide down her face, as she watched the emotional scene unfold in front of her. She had never seen Ash speak so tenderly or sincerely to anyone. He had always been kind and caring, and lots of fun, but never as openly emotional as this. She watched as Bella's face crumpled and she dissolved in tears. Then Ash moved to the sofa beside her and he and Isobel held her tightly while they all cried. Rosie stifled her tears as much as she could and then buried her face in Coisty's curls.

CHAPTER THIRTY-FOUR

Luke was up early and walking along the beach, lost in his thoughts. He knew Rosie was aware something had happened as his mood had been sombre after taking the call from his agent, Linda, at the café in Lamlash yesterday. In a way he was grateful for the sudden rainfall as it meant they could get back to Kildonan and he could lock himself away again, claiming he had to write. And that had been true. He had written a heartfelt tribute to Linda and was planning to dedicate his book to her. If it hadn't been for her tenacious attitude, she wouldn't have got him the book deal in the first place. He had a lot to thank her for.

Although yesterday's rain had passed and the sun had come out again, the morning air was cool and he inhaled huge gulps of it. He wanted to make the most of the seaweed infused air while he could. Before too long, he would be back in congested London which he was not looking forward to in the slightest. He narrowed his eyes as he saw a woman walking towards him and then realised that it was Bella. 'You're up early,' he said to her and smiled warmly. He had grown fond of her these past few weeks.

'I couldn't sleep,' she said with a shiver.

'Ah, you must be back for the big reunion then?' said Luke, now realising why she was in Kildonan this morning and not Brodick. It was then Luke noticed how pale she looked and the dark circles beneath her eyes. She seemed exhausted and when she shivered again, he immediately took off his jacket and handed it to her. 'Here, put that on. It's not as warm as it looks, is it?'

She gingerly took it from him. 'Are you sure?'

'Of course. I've got lots of layers on,' he said, 'you need it more than me. It's not quite t-shirt weather, is it?'

Bella pulled on his jacket and zipped it up to her neck. 'Nope.'

'Do you mind if I walk with you?' he said.

She shrugged. 'Sure.'

Luke frowned as they walked side by side. He kept giving her sideways glances expecting her to say something, but it was as though she had lost the power of speech. 'Any reason you couldn't sleep?' he asked gently.

Bella didn't answer immediately. But he knew if he walked with the silence for a few moments then she may start to talk. He could see her chewing her top lip as she thought about it and Luke just kept walking alongside her. The sound of the waves lapping the pebbles was mesmerising and a few minutes had passed before she started to speak.

'Man trouble,' she said slowly.

'Ah, okay,' said Luke, desperately wondering what he could say that might be of help.

'I found out who my dad is last night . . . ' she said quietly.

'Oh,' said Luke, trying to keep his voice level. 'That must have been a shock?'

She nodded. 'I still can't believe that my mum kept it such a secret for so long . . . although I can now understand why. It kind of blew my mind.'

'Mm,' said Luke non-committedly. 'And how do you feel now you know the truth?'

She shrugged and then stopped to pick up a pebble. Luke stayed by her side and watched the seals basking on the rocks. 'Aren't they incredible?' said Luke, when he realised she hadn't answered.

'Mm,' she murmured, before dropping the stone back onto the beach. 'I don't really know. I'm probably still in a bit of a daze. At first, I thought it was you, but it wasn't, and now . . . it was just a bit unexpected,' she said. 'Though it also kind of makes sense.'

Luke nodded. 'And does knowing who it is change things for you?'

'I don't think so,' she said as she started walking again. 'I mean, they both explained why they had agreed to keep it a secret. It was all a bit complicated back then. I get why it was all kept hush-hush.'

Luke didn't want to probe by asking who *they* were but he assumed Rosie and Ash were also part of the secret given that they were all together last night. Instead of asking her more questions, he just stayed silent and they kept walking a circular route which eventually took them back to the cottages.

'How about a cuppa?' said Luke, pointing at Beach Cottage. 'You look like you could do with warming up a bit.'

Bella didn't need any persuasion and she followed Luke inside the house, kicking her shoes off by the door. He led her to the living room where she sat on the chair by the window and curled her legs up underneath her.

'I'll just put the kettle on,' he said, and passed her a throw which she tucked around her legs. In the kitchen, he quickly sent Rosie a text to let her know Bella was with him in case they were about to send out a search party. His mobile buzzed immediately and he looked at it to read her reply.

Thanks Luke. Yes, there was a panic when we realised she was gone. We were about to go and look for her. Sorry to drag you into this. I hope she is okay. And you too.

He typed out a reply. *She is here and will be fine. I am just making her some tea and then she will be back. Please tell Isobel that she is okay and I will look after her.* X

He had pressed send before he realised he'd added a X. Whoops.

Okay. Thanks so much. We appreciate this. Rosie xx

'It's not every day you find out who your dad is,' said Luke, setting down a cup of tea on the small table next to Bella. He could see the vulnerability on her face and it was the same look he had seen in the bar at Troon that day, when she had confronted him.

She nodded. 'I guess not. Although it's not as much of a shock as I expected. It makes sense.'

Luke waited for her to elaborate.

She clasped her hands around the mug and looked at him. 'Ash is my dad.'

'Oh,' said Luke, trying not to look surprised. He was not expecting Bella to say that. 'I see. I just kind of assumed that Ash was a woman. Just shows you should never make assumptions or jump to conclusions.' He raised an eyebrow at her.

That made Bella chuckle and he was pleased to see a smile brighten up her face. 'I guess thinking he was a woman is an easy assumption to make. He was always part of the girl gang with Rosie and my mum. I suppose it was an even bigger shock as he is gay.'

Luke nodded solemnly. 'Does it change anything? In terms of the way you feel about him. I get the sense he is someone who has always been in your life. Is that right?'

Bella nodded. 'Yes, he has always been part of our family, just like Rosie has been. When I think of my childhood, I don't think I lacked in anything. I suppose it would have been nice to have a dad but plenty of kids in my class at school only had one parent and those who did have a dad often didn't like him anyway. My mum was always there for me and I had my gran. And when I think about it, Ash was always there too. He made the effort to visit when he came back to Scotland and would call a lot. And he never forgot my birthday or Christmas. When I think about it, I was really lucky that I didn't have a dad who I thought was a dick.'

Luke nodded kindly as he listened. He knew so many men who were absent fathers and had nothing to do with their kids. The fact that Ash was here right now and had been so involved and made time to visit her over the years, despite the distance, had to be a good thing for Bella. She had always had her dad in her life, but just didn't know. 'So, does knowing about the biological link with him change things now? Does it change the way you feel about him?'

She looked at him thoughtfully. 'Not at all. I've always felt connected to him. He's always been there for family stuff, like an uncle, and has made a lot of effort to be part of my life. I just always thought my dad had been some random one-off. That's what mum had always told me and I believed her until I found Rosie's journal.'

Luke felt his cheeks colour as he thought of Rosie and her secret diary of their tryst.

'As it turns out she wasn't being entirely untruthful. He *was* a one-night stand. But at least mum knew who he was. He wasn't just some random guy she had picked up in a nightclub. In a way that probably feels better. I can stop scanning random men's faces in crowds, wondering if they *might* be my dad. Or ambushing poor men like you and jumping to the wrong conclusion.' She gave him a sheepish smile. 'Now I feel like I know where I came from and where I belong. Does that make sense? Sorry, Luke, I am rambling.'

Luke nodded. 'Absolutely that makes sense and it's a lot to get your head around, Bella. It's good you're able to talk about it though. I think it's normal to want to know where you belong and who you belong to. But in the short time that I have known you it's always been clear that your mum is utterly devoted to you, as is Rosie.' He drank some tea. 'Life can change in an instant, Bella. And we never know what might happen,' he said, thinking about yesterday's call with Linda. 'I know it's a lot to process. But it sounds like your mum did the very best she could, especially as she knew she could never have a future together with Ash. It must also have been difficult when he was living in Australia.'

'And gay. Let's not forget that,' added Bella, rolling her eyes. 'You know, Ash has been the closest thing I've had to a dad over the years and the main older male figure in my life. I know I'm lucky to be able to say that about him, especially when I think about some of my friend's parents. My friend Lily's dad is an alcoholic, and look at Ben — his dad was an adulterer!'

Luke winced as he thought about his own sons and the fact their mother was also in that camp. Then he momentarily found his thoughts drifting again to Rosie.

'Ash has always been kind, considerate and funny,' continued Bella, 'and he's always been there for me. Perhaps not geographically but certainly at the end of the phone. How many people can say that about their dad?' She sat for a moment, lost in her own thoughts, then uncurled her feet and put the mug on the table. 'Thanks, Luke. That chat has really helped me figure stuff out. You should be a counsellor or something...'

Luke grinned at her. 'Mm, that may be a step too far.' But her whole demeanour had changed in the time that she had sat in the cottage. She looked lighter and less tense.

'You're right, though. I can't change the past and there's no point in blaming them for what they did. Who would have chosen to be in that position? Mum wasn't that much older than I am now. I can't even begin to imagine how she must have felt. Or what I would do if I was in her shoes. It must have been really hard for her.' She stood up and shrugged off Luke's jacket and handed it to him. 'Thank you, Luke. I'd better go next door and tell them to stop fretting.' And then her stomach rumbled loudly. She laughed. 'Whoops.'

'Can I get you some breakfast before you go,' he said. 'I can make eggs on toast?'

She shook her head and quickly hugged him. 'Thanks, but no, you're alright. Rosie said she would make pancakes this morning and I didn't eat any dinner last night. I felt too sick. But now I am famished.' She hurried to the door and pulled on her shoes. 'Wait, do you want to come as well? I'm sure Rosie would love to see you.'

Much as Luke would have loved to see Rosie, he knew it wasn't appropriate right now. They needed their space to talk all of this through. He reminded himself that his feelings for Rosie were growing more intense by the day and he was now in dangerous territory. Because Luke knew he would have to head back to London, sooner rather than later.

CHAPTER THIRTY-FIVE

After spending the next two days with her mum and Ash, Bella headed back to Brodick feeling much happier than she thought possible. The three of them had had a lot of heartfelt conversations and there had been much soul searching. However, Bella was now starting to accept the truth. Sure, she was still processing it all. It was a lot to get her head around. But it all made sense. She couldn't quite believe she finally knew who her dad was. After all these years.

She also realised that she couldn't wait to tell Ben. She had sent him a few messages to let him know that the oldies were all fine and that she had some news but she would give him a full debrief when she was back in Brodick and away from prying ears. He kept asking after his mum and whether she was okay and Bella reassured him that she was fine. She wondered if he had suspected anything about Luke. Although, she had no idea how he would know, unless Rosie had said anything to him, which she wouldn't imagine she had. Rosie's cottage was cosy but small, especially with the four of them staying there, and it was tricky to find a quiet spot to call him. The mobile reception on the beach wasn't great either, otherwise she would have tried to phone him from there. She was looking forward to catching up with him when she was back in the privacy of her staff room. Even better, she hoped they might be able to connect in person. Ben had asked to meet her during his break later.

Her mum offered to take her back to the hotel and Ash insisted on coming too. He was keen to spend every minute he could with her, as though he was making up for lost time. Bella had rather sternly pleaded with him not to start acting differently towards her. He had agreed but also insisted on staying on in Arran for a few more days. He wasn't due to go back to Australia for another two weeks. Instead of heading to the mainland as he'd originally planned, to catch up with friends in Edinburgh and London, he had postponed and booked into a guesthouse in Brodick. Isobel was going to take him there after they had dropped off Bella.

'Are you still heading home tomorrow, Mum?' she had asked when they pulled into the hotel car park.

Her mum looked tired, although it was no wonder. It had been an emotional time and not exactly the holiday she had planned for. More like a summer of secrets that you would expect to read about in a book.

'Yes, love,' she said. 'I'm off home for a rest. And I'm sure Rosie will be glad to have her house back to herself too.'

'And what about Gran?'

'What about her?'

'Does she know about Ash?'

Her mum shook her head. 'No, well, unless she is psychic. But I didn't tell her. Much as I love my mum, that would have complicated things even more. To be fair she seemed to accept what I said and never asked me about it again.'

Bella frowned. That was most unlike the gran that she knew and loved. 'And will you tell her? About Ash? I'm sure she will be fine about it all.'

Isobel yawned. 'Yes, I will. But I will choose my moment. I don't have the energy at the moment to share that nugget of news quite yet . . . I will bide my time.'

Bella couldn't stop herself from laughing. Her gran had recently told her that she considered herself to be very open-minded. 'Yes, I think that's wise, Mum. Although Gran did tell me the other day that she considers herself to be quite *woke*.'

Ash chuckled and her mum groaned. 'I was in the car with her and she was busy telling me what a progressive attitude she has. Meanwhile, she almost crashed the car as she flicked her finger and gestured at the other driver . . .'

'Oh, Gran! What is she like?' Bella laughed, and her eyes welled up with affection as she thought about her wee gran. Bella had thought a lot about her mum the past couple of days and how much she had sacrificed to bring her up as a solo parent. She thought about her gran and the amazing bond they had. Memories of getting together with Ash, Rosie and Ben on beach picnics in Troon and Gullane and visits to Edinburgh Zoo flitted through her head. Her mum and gran also used to bring her over to Brodick when she was a wee girl. She had so much to be grateful for.

Ash got out the car and gave her a hug. 'This looks like a nice place,' he said. 'Maybe I'll check out the spa and book in for a treatment while I'm here. A manicure or something like that.' He winked at her.

That was much more like the Ash she was used to and that put her at ease. 'Send me a text when you're settled and maybe we can make plans to have dinner tomorrow?' she suggested.

'Sounds like a plan. It's a shame I couldn't get booked into the hotel but I am quite looking forward to checking this guesthouse out. It looks very stylish.'

'What's it called?' said Isobel.

'It's Meadowbank Guesthouse. It's not far from here.'

'That name rings a bell. I'm sure we'll find it,' said her mum.

'I know the name of that place too,' said Bella. 'My friend at work lives there. Her parents run it.'

'I'll come and have a nosy and help you get all settled,' said Isobel.

'I'm sure poor Rosie is glad to be shot of us for a while. What a summer she's had!' said Ash. 'I feel like I've barely had a chance to ask her about Dermot and how she is bearing up.'

'I don't think her summer has been all bad,' said Isobel, giving Bella a wink.

'I saw that,' said Ash. 'What have I missed?'

Her mum gave him one of her looks. 'I'll fill you in later.'

Ash's eyes lit up at the thought of some news that didn't involve him.

Bella gave her "parents" a bright smile and then walked away. 'See you later,' she called.

'Ask Ben if he's free for dinner too?' Ash called after her.

She nodded and as she walked away, she let her shoulders slump. Bella was exhausted. It had been an intense couple of days and she was looking forward to her own space now, pulling on her pyjamas and just relaxing in her own bed tonight. But she also *had* to talk to Ben. He was not going to believe what had happened. As soon as she was back in the privacy of her own room, she texted him.

I'm back in Brodick. Are we still on for later when you get a break? X

She didn't have to wait long for his reply. *Definitely. Meet me by the distillery? I should be there in an hour. x*

CHAPTER THIRTY-SIX

Bella hadn't yet made it inside the distillery but had admired it from the outside every time she had passed. It was a stunning building which seemed to blend in with the surroundings. It was right on the beach and had floor-to-ceiling windows, with amazing views across the water. Becky, from work, had mentioned that her Aunt Emma had married there two years ago. Now, as she approached it, the sky was streaked with pink and she could understand why it was such a romantic spot.

She waved at Ben who was leaning against one of the benches outside. He was dressed in navy blue shorts and a pale blue polo shirt with the emblem of the distillery etched on the front pocket in gold thread. When he looked up, a grin spread across his face.

'Look at this,' she said, gesturing at the building. 'It's really impressive.'

'Have you not been in yet?'

She shook her head. 'Nope. Not yet. But now you're here, I will make it a priority to pop in sometime for a coffee. I'd like to have a proper look inside.'

He raked his hand through his hair and stood up straight. 'I can show you now if you want?'

'Nah. It's your break. Leave it till another time. How long have you got?' She was very aware of the fluttering of nerves that were gathering in her stomach, thanks to being in such close proximity. There was something about the uniform that seemed to make him even more handsome than ever.

'I've got half an hour. We could walk for a bit, if you want?'

Bella shrugged. 'Yes, that's fine with me.'

She had pulled on her jeans, trainers and a white vest top and her hair hung in wavy tresses over her shoulders. Now, she was wishing she'd made more of an effort. They started to wander along the promenade, listening to the squawking gulls.

'What's the news, then?'

Bella exhaled loudly. 'I know we don't have long so I'll need to give you the soundbite version. I found out who my father is, when I was in Kildonan.'

Ben raised an eyebrow expectantly. 'And?'

She shook her head, wondering where to even begin.

'It's okay, you don't need to tell me.' His voice was gentle.

Her throat thickened. 'It's okay. I want to.' She paused. 'My dad is Ash.'

He stopped in his tracks and spun round to look at her. 'No way.'

'I know. It was a shock to me too.' Bella turned to face him and frowned. Then she gestured for them to start walking again and explained what had happened and told him why their mums and Ash had kept it a secret all these years.

Ben listened intently as she talked, then finally exhaled loudly through his mouth. 'Seems crazy to think how different things were back then for Ash.'

'Yes, I felt so sad for him, when he explained it all.'

'How do you feel now?' Ben asked, his voice smooth and soothing.

'Okay. I mean, he's always been in my life, if you think about it. I'm actually glad it's him and not some random bloke that we haven't had any connection with.'

'Oh, Bella, that is a lot to hear. But I'm glad you're okay about it. And is he?'

She smiled. 'Yes. In fact, before I forget, he's invited you to dinner with us tomorrow. We're meeting at the pizza place.'

He tutted. 'I'm working but let me see if I can change my shift.' He pulled a face. 'It's just so busy and I have only just started. I'll try. If not, tell him he needs to come and say goodbye. He came in earlier with Mum and he hasn't changed a bit. Still the same old crazy Ash.' He laughed and then looked at his watch. 'Damn. I'm sorry, but I'd better head back.'

'Sure,' she said. 'I'll walk back with you. It's nice just to be able to finally tell you.' A wave of relief almost overcame her as she managed to say, 'Thanks for listening.'

He slung his arm around her shoulder. 'You don't need to thank me. We're friends. You can tell me anything.'

She was momentarily deflated when he referred to them as being friends but then huddled into him, grateful that he was there, and they walked quietly back towards the distillery. Too soon they arrived and Bella didn't want to let go of him, especially as she felt the warmth of his arm across her bare shoulders.

He untangled his arm and his eyes were full of compassion as he looked at her. 'I'm glad you know the truth and it's Ash.' He cleared his throat. 'Let's face it, he's a much better man than my dad.'

Bella reached over and patted his arm. 'I know. I'm sorry.' She wanted to tell him the rest of the story, about ambushing Luke and spiriting him across to Arran, thinking he was her dad. However, she would leave that for another time and another day. That might be better for when Rosie was ready to share her part of the story.

Ben leant down and kissed her on the cheek, lingering a second longer than a friendly kiss. 'Sorry, I'd better run. I'll message you later.'

'Bye, Ben.' She watched him jog back into the building and then turned to walk away, feeling the imprint of his lips on her cheek. She could scarcely believe that she was missing him already. She also felt slightly confused. Friends tended to just give each other a peck on the cheek, and that was definitely more than just a peck.

CHAPTER THIRTY-SEVEN

Rosie felt a small flicker of guilt for feeling so relieved to finally be home alone. She was still processing the fact that Ben was home, never mind everything else that had happened since then. She had gone round to the ferry terminal with Isobel that morning and Ash had also come to wave her off. He was enjoying his time at Meadowbank Guesthouse and, after they had said goodbye to Isobel, they had gone into the distillery for a coffee. Ben had been rushed off his feet and had managed to run across to give them both a hug. Then he had disappeared to help James with something.

Ash had only heard snippets about what had happened with Luke and what had led him to staying next door. After he had grilled Rosie about what was going on, to which she could truthfully reply that she and Luke were just friends, she turned the questions on Ash. It sounded like he had enjoyed having some time to himself to explore, and work on a journal paper he was late in submitting, and, of course, he had planned to meet up with Bella when she had finished working. He was taking her for one last dinner the following night before he left for the mainland.

After a couple of hours of stripping beds, doing several loads of laundry and pegging the sheets out on the washing line, Rosie allowed her thoughts to turn to Luke. All was quiet next door and she assumed that he was getting on with the book writing. He had been a brilliant support to Bella the other day and she hadn't yet had a chance to thank him properly. Once inside, her thumb hovered her phone as she wondered whether or not to get in touch. Then she told herself not to overthink things. Surely it was better to check in than not? She quickly typed out a message.

Hi, how are you? How is the writing going? Rosie xx

Normally he was quick to reply and so she waited to see if the three dots, a sign he was responding, would appear. But there was nothing. She checked her WhatsApp messages, in case Ben had been in touch. There weren't any messages from him either. She sighed in frustration at herself. This wouldn't do, she was becoming too needy, a sign that she needed to go out and do something to take her mind off things. Reaching for a glass from the cupboard by the sink, she turned on the tap and filled it. The water was cold and it was only when she swallowed it that she realised how thirsty she was. She drank another glass quickly and then filled up Coisty's bowl with fresh water too. When her phone started to ring, she snatched it up and then dropped it like a hot potato when she saw it was Dermot phoning. She felt her hackles rise and promptly switched it off.

Rosie knew there were plenty of tasks around the house that she could do to keep her busy. The living room needed a lick of paint and the kitchen cupboards needed to be emptied and scrubbed. She also had a huge stack of books to read which seemed to be growing by the day. Coisty was looking at her watchfully, waiting to see what she was going to do next. She picked up her current read and snuggled in the armchair by the window and he jumped up and squashed in beside her. But, however hard she tried, the words seemed to swim in front of her eyes and she just kept reading the same page over and over without taking anything in. Sighing, she slammed the book shut and put it on the coffee table. Rosie felt completely out of sorts. Dermot's call had really annoyed her. She didn't particularly want company, but then again she didn't really want to be in the cottage on her own either. She had already walked Coisty and didn't fancy another trek along the beach, even though it was usually her place to think. Even the thought of some light gardening, her usual go to, didn't appeal. It had been a cool morning but now the sun had finally burned through the clouds and was high in the sky.

Then she knew exactly what to do. She picked up the landline and quickly made a call. 'Maisie, it's just me, Rosie. How are you?'

'Fine, dearie,' she said.

'I thought I would pop over and see you, if that's okay?'

'Oh, I would love that. Are you coming now?'

'Yes, if that suits. I'll be with you in about twenty minutes,' said Rosie, twirling a lock of hair in her free hand.

'That's great. I will pop the kettle on for you coming. And I hope you're bringing wee Coisty?' asked Maisie hopefully.

'Of course,' said Rosie with a chuckle. 'I wouldn't dream of leaving him behind. Now, do you need me to bring you anything in. Any bits and pieces from the shops?'

'Not a thing, dear. Callum dropped my messages off earlier. Just bring yourself and that furry wee fella of yours.'

'Great. See you soon, Maisie.'

'Bye, dear,' said Maisie.

Rosie smiled at the thought of seeing Maisie, who was an old friend of her parents. She hadn't seen her for a few weeks and she knew that spending an hour with her was exactly what she needed. She quickly wrapped up some pieces of shortbread to take, grabbed a bottle of red wine from the rack — Maisie was very partial to red wine — and then she pulled on her shoes and grabbed the car keys. 'Come on, Coisty. Let's go and see Maisie.' He barked and wagged his tail.

* * *

A few hours later, Rosie drove back to Kildonan feeling much more relaxed and reassured about things after spending some time with Maisie. The drive back had given her a chance to think about what her friend had said. Maisie was ninety-two and showed no signs of slowing down, either physically or mentally. She had boundless energy and razor-sharp wit and always insisted that her good health was down to her daily dose of red wine. She had only recently given up golf, claiming she'd had enough of the game. Although privately Rosie thought it had more to do with her eyesight and not always being able to see where she had hit the ball. Her parents had been friends with Maisie and they had all played golf together at the club in Lamlash. She had been a kind friend to Rosie when they had died and told her that her door was always open if she ever wanted to talk. Rosie did feel a bit guilty that she had only seen Maisie once since Dermot had left and at the time she hadn't really wanted to go into too many details about it. But now she felt more at peace with it and she filled Maisie in on what had happened.

Maisie had sat in her batwing chair, looking immaculate as ever in lilac trousers and a white blouse embroidered with tiny daisies, listening carefully. 'Oh, aye,' she had said drily. 'Sounds like you've dodged a bullet with that one, Rosie.' She had pursed her lips together and reached down to scratch Coisty's ears. He had plonked himself right next to her as soon as they had arrived. 'Well, you know what they say,' she had said pointedly at Rosie. 'Onwards and upwards. Maybe it's time for you to get back in the race. You are single and ready to mingle.'

Rosie had almost spluttered her tea out at that point. Maisie sounded so like Isobel. When she had done a double take and looked again at Maisie, the older woman was the picture of innocence, though her eyes were twinkling in amusement. But she knew Maisie was kind of right. Not necessarily about jumping into bed with the first man she could get her hands on. But she knew she had to move on from Dermot and that meant sorting out all their affairs so she could get closure. She reluctantly realised she might have to actually speak to him in order for that to happen. So when she parked the car outside Creel Cottage, she decided just to take the bull by the horns and call him. But when she reached into her handbag for her phone, she realised it wasn't there. She quickly turned the bag upside down and emptied the entire contents onto the passenger seat. But all that she tipped out was her purse, house keys, some tissues, a packet of chewing gum, a small tin of lip balm, a few pound coins and a couple of crumpled receipts. She frowned and scratched her head. That was strange. Where had she left it? She turned to Coisty who was waiting patiently in the back to be freed from his harness. 'Wonder what I've done with my phone, Coisty.' He tipped his head to one side. 'It's okay, don't worry, I'm not really expecting you to answer me, Coisty. Crikey, what's happened to me?' she said with a chuckle. She then remembered that she had switched it off when Dermot had rung earlier, then flung it on the sofa in irritation. She must have forgotten to pick it up when she went out to see Maisie. She realised that she actually hadn't even missed it until that moment which felt quite freeing. Instead of going straight into the cottage she decided to take Coisty for a quick walk.

CHAPTER THIRTY-EIGHT

Luke sat on a bench overlooking Kildonan. Rosie had told him it had always been one of her dad's favourite spots and he could understand why. With a view of the islands of Pladda and Ailsa Craig, it was the perfect place to sit and think. On a clear day like today you could see the Ayrshire coast. He had noticed and loved the numerous benches which were thoughtfully placed all over the island. It told him how proud the locals were of their island and that they wanted to share its beauty with everyone. The benches were there as reminders to take a break and be still for a while. It was good advice and something he hoped he could hold onto when he returned to London. The thought of which was now preying heavily on his mind. Taking a moment to notice things and appreciate them was becoming increasingly important to Luke.

'Hey there,' said a voice.

He didn't need to turn round to see who it was.

'Mind if we join you?' said Rosie.

He patted the seat next to her and grinned. 'Of course not.'

Rosie sat next to him, close enough for their legs to touch. Coisty sat at their feet. Her eyes were sparkling and she was smiling. She somehow seemed lighter and freer. He wondered if something had happened.

'Look at that,' he said, pointing to islands ahead. 'Pladda and Ailsa Craig. Is that right?'

She nodded.

'Wow,' he said, 'and is there anything on them?'

Rosie shook her head. 'Not a lot other than birds and, of course, the lighthouse on Pladda. Though there was some chat about developing holiday lodges there too. But who knows.'

'It is really stunning,' said Luke thoughtfully.

'I think so,' said Rosie. 'And another random piece of information is that curling stones are made from the granite that is harvested from Ailsa Craig.'

'This is like having my own personal tourist guide,' murmured Luke, who was just glad that they could now relax in each other's company again after being a bit awkward at the start.

In that instance, he was transported back to a Sydney bar and she was laughing loudly at something he had said. Then he had leaned forward and kissed her. A memory floated through his mind of them lying together in his hotel room cocooned from the rest of the world. He gave her a sideways glance. If only he had known then what he knew now. How different might his life have been? He and Rosie obviously weren't meant to be together back then. They were too young and neither ready to settle down. But what if he *had* settled down with her? Or what if he had met someone else who wasn't Cindy? What would his life have been like if Rosie hadn't met her husband? But then that would have meant he wouldn't have his boys and Rosie wouldn't have Ben. He knew that neither of them would have been without their kids. Life had a way of unfolding as it should.

'What have you been up to?' said Rosie with a smile, nudging him.

'I was out walking. It helps me think,' said Luke, rubbing a hand over his jaw which was now covered in stubble.

'About?'

'About how much I love it here. How wonderful it has been to have space and not be surrounded by people. It made me realise how much I appreciate the countryside and the sea — and this.'

She looked at him. 'Who would have thought that a summer on Arran would have transformed you like this?'

Luke knew it wasn't just the place that had done that and he turned to look at her. 'How amazing it has been to reconnect with you after all these years. Do you remember the Q bar?'

Rosie nodded. It was the Sydney bar they had met in all those years ago. She nodded and looked at him curiously. 'Especially the sticky floor.'

He laughed and reached for her hand. 'All this time alone writing and walking and thinking means I have been doing a lot of soul searching, Rosie. And remembering things from way back.'

'What sort of things?' said Rosie gently.

'That night when we met at the bar. I'd never laid eyes on such a stunning girl.'

Rosie stared straight ahead, her cheeks burning red and he wondered if she was remembering it too.

'The thing is I did recognise you when I saw you here that night I arrived with Bella. But everything was so out of context. It just took me a while to piece things together.'

Rosie shrugged. 'That's okay.'

Luke took a deep breath then exhaled a long sigh. 'I guess what I'm trying to say is that I'm sorry. For being young and stupid and for disappearing. But most of all, I'm sorry for ever letting you go.'

'Well, I have to say that I do now see you in a different light.'

'Oh,' he said hopefully.

Rosie glanced at him. 'Yes, I no longer think you're the selfish and self-absorbed prick that you were in your twenties.'

'Ooft. I suppose I deserved that,' he said. 'And now?'

'Now, I see the real you. I feel like over the summer I've got to know the real Luke who is kind and compassionate and funny...'

Luke waited for her to finish. 'And...'

Rosie laughed. 'And you're not bad looking either, given your age.'

Luke felt a surge of excitement in his stomach and tried to shrug casually. 'You're not too bad yourself.'

As they sat together on the bench, holding hands, Luke realised there was nowhere else he would rather be right now. He wasn't exactly sure how Rosie might respond if he opened up in the way that she had. But at least they seemed to be on the same page. Then she leaned over to kiss his cheek and her grip on his hand tightened. His heart was racing with excitement as he wondered if he should kiss her properly. It felt as though he was a teenager again, unsure how to make his next move. He wished he didn't feel like this but he was stuck and had no idea what to do next.

'Well, I was not expecting you to be here and us to be having this conversation,' said Rosie finally. 'And I was just having a *Sliding Doors* moment as I walked up here. I was thinking how different my life might have been if I hadn't met Dermot. Hindsight's a wonderful thing, isn't it? But it doesn't matter. What's done is done and I for one wouldn't be without Ben. I do think life has a way of happening the way it should.'

He nodded thoughtfully. 'True,' he said softly. 'Life has a funny old way of working itself out.'

'That is exactly what a wise friend of mine told me earlier,' said Rosie. 'Whits Fur Ye'll No Go By Ye. That means, what's for you won't go past you.'

His breath caught in his throat as Rosie turned towards him and leaned in to kiss him. Her lips brushed very softly against his, hesitant at first and then more probing. This time Luke didn't hesitate to return her kiss. Eventually, they pulled apart and grinned. Rosie's cheeks were flushed and he traced the curve of her face with his hand. 'I think we should head back, don't you? Unless you want the neighbours to start talking.'

Rosie giggled and stood up, grabbing his hand. 'You are the neighbours.' She reached up on her tiptoes to kiss him again and he pulled her close.

'Still,' he said with a groan. 'I think we should take this inside. I don't want to be charged with engaging in lewd behaviour outside.'

Rosie sniggered. 'True. You don't want to get done with breach of the peace.' She grasped his hand and tugged Coisty's lead with the other and they walked briskly down the hill towards the cottages.

But as they approached Creel Cottage, he sensed a shift in Rosie's energy. She seemed nervous and fidgety and paused at the lavender filled wheelbarrow next to the front door. She scuffed her shoe against the gravel. Luke realised what was wrong and when he suggested that she come next door instead, a look of relief crossed her face.

'Thanks, Luke. It just feels a bit weird to be taking you back to mine, if you know what I mean . . .'

He reassured her with a nod then a lingering kiss.

'Let me just pop Coisty in,' she said, her cheeks still pink.

'Sure thing,' he said. 'Though only if you are sure . . .'

She answered him by kissing him firmly.

Luke had just opened the door at Beach Cottage when Rosie appeared behind him. She wrapped her arms around his waist as he walked into the hallway where they stood, awkward at first, until Luke turned round and gently put his hand behind her neck. He pulled Rosie towards him. Then he paused. 'Are you sure about this?' He traced a finger across her lips and then down her neck to her collarbone.

Rosie raised an eyebrow then cupped her hand around his. 'I most certainly am.'

CHAPTER THIRTY-NINE

The following morning Bella was scrolling through Instagram, and felt her chai seeds solidify in her mouth when she saw a post Ben had been tagged in. It looked as though Mabel from Bali was still very much on the scene if the many pictures she had posted were anything to go by. There were photos of them together in a crowded bar, grinning into the camera, lounging together against a palm tree with an orange sky behind them as the sun set in the distance, sipping cocktails on the beach *and* she had even taken a selfie of them in a swimming pool. Who even did stuff like that? Wasn't that a bit tacky? Bella knew that if she ever tried something like that, she would most definitely drop her phone in the pool. Ben clearly didn't think it was tacky though as he was grinning from ear to ear and had his arm draped around Mabel's shoulders in most of the pictures. The same way he had put his arm around her shoulders yesterday. Maybe he did that with all the girls? There were plenty more pictures — she had clearly done a massive photo dump and, according to the date, it was the day before Ben had arrived back on Arran — but Bella had seen all she ever needed or wanted to. The message from the pictures was very clear. They were very much an item and very *together*, despite

Ben claiming that she had moved on. Yeah, right. Perhaps she and Ben were just friends and Bella was reading too much into it. She dumped her breakfast in the food bin, rinsed her dish and then stomped over to the spa building ready to start her shift.

She must have been frowning as she walked into the spa entrance and Chantelle took one look at her and gently placed her hands on her shoulders and spun her back towards the door. 'You're a bit early, Bella, and I think it might be an idea for you to go outside and walk for five minutes and then come back and start your day again.'

Bella didn't think it was a good idea to argue with her new boss, and so she gave her a small nod, then turned on her heels and went back outside where she paced around the grounds of the hotel, staring at the grass at her feet. But she soon felt her heart rate start to slow down and when she saw Becky and her twin brother, Tom, in the distance she caught up with them and had a quick chat before they needed to be poolside. They made loose plans to meet at the beach bar later in the week and by the time she walked back to the spa most of the rage she felt had dissipated.

'Feeling better now?' said Chantelle.

She nodded sheepishly. 'Yes, I am. Thank you. And I'm sorry for arriving in a bad mood.'

'Everything okay?' Chantelle was now behind the desk and she glanced down at the screen.

Bella shrugged. 'Nope. I just saw something on Instagram that annoyed me. But I'm fine now.'

'You do know that you should never believe what you see on social media,' said Chantelle kindly. 'Do you want to tell me what's bothering you?'

Bella chewed her lip. 'I saw someone I like tagged with another woman. I thought he liked me, but clearly I've misread the situation.'

'Is this the guy that I've seen you with here? Because I can tell you that the way he looks at you tells me that there is no way he has a girlfriend elsewhere.' She gave her a knowing look.

Bella smiled shyly. 'Thanks Chantelle, and thanks for suggesting I go and get some air. And I am sorry. I don't normally arrive at work in a cross mood.'

Chantelle laughed. 'That's okay. I just didn't want you taking your frustration out on the clients. I know having a bit of strength can be good for doing Swedish and sports massages but your first client is a facial and it is one of our more senior clients. I'm not sure that she would have appreciated you pummelling her cheeks in a rage. It wouldn't do our reputation much good if people come for a relaxing facial treatment and leave with two black eyes and a bruised face.'

Bella laughed. Chantelle was right. And she knew that by the time she started the facial she would feel a lot better. Strangely, she always found work really calming and knew the time would fly by. She had a full day of appointments so there wouldn't be any time for her to think about Ben and Mabel at all. Anyway, she would much rather focus on what Chantelle thought. Did Ben really look at her in that way?

Despite her best attempts Bella still couldn't help wonder about Ben and Mabel and was intrigued to see a message from Ben when she switched her phone on after work. She was meeting Ash for a bite of dinner at the pizza place and Ben still hadn't confirmed whether he could come or not.

I am so sorry, Bella. I am having to work. Nobody could swap. Tell Ash to come and see me before he leaves! It was so good to see you yesterday. Thanks for telling me. I could do with some advice. Let me know when you're free? XX

She didn't reply. Bella was no longer in the mood to speak to Ben. Nor did she have time if she was to meet Ash in half an hour and still had to shower. She knew she was being a bit pathetic but the photos with Mabel had obviously a raw nerve.

***

'Is everything okay?' asked Ash when Bella arrived at the pizza place.

'Yes, fine,' she said, trying to sound breezy. She slid into the booth opposite.

'Are you sure?' he said gently.

Bella smiled tightly and ordered a beer from the waiter who had just arrived at the table.

'How is work going?'

'Really good,' said Bella. 'I'm learning lots and it's always busy. It makes a nice change from my old work.'

'Well, cheers,' said Ash, raising his bottle against Bella's beer which had just been placed in front of her.

'Cheers.'

'How about you? How has your day been?' she said, trying desperately to pull herself out of the funk she was in.

'Well, that guesthouse is just heavenly. I can see why it's so popular. The bed is so comfy it means I don't want to get up. Kirsty makes a mean Scottish breakfast. And there are wee boxes of shortbread in the room.' He leaned over to rummage in the pocket of his jacket which lay next to him on the seat. 'Here you are. I persuaded her to give me a box to give you.'

Bella smiled. 'Thanks, Ash, sorry, Dad . . .' she said awkwardly as he handed it to her.

'Bella, love, call me whatever you want. If Dad feels weird then Ashley or Ash is fine. Just be comfortable. This is going to take us both some getting used to.'

'Okay,' she said with a shrug. She had to admit she was finding the whole name thing and the etiquette of what to call him a bit of a struggle.

'Right, let's order food and then you can tell me what is really on your mind,' he said assertively. 'I'm going to have the Margherita pizza. How about you?'

'Pepperoni, please,' said Bella, feeling her stomach rumble and realising she hadn't eaten since the chai seeds at breakfast earlier.

After drinking her bottle of beer and hungrily tucking into the pizza, Bella relaxed.

'Did you ask Ben?'

'He couldn't make it. He's working but he said you must come by the distillery to see him before you leave.' She frowned.

Ash leaned forward. 'What's on your mind?'

She sighed. 'I don't know. It's just that I thought Ben and I had a connection and now I'm wondering if I've misread it completely. I met him yesterday and told him that you're my dad. He was really lovely about it and . . . I thought there was something between us.'

'What changed then?'

She told him about the pictures she'd seen on social media then swore him to secrecy. 'Don't you say a word to Mum or Rosie about it. Can you imagine?' She rolled her eyes in horror.

'Don't you worry. It will be our secret. Anyway,' he said with a naughty laugh, 'I think Rosie is otherwise engaged at the moment. Who would have thought? But having Luke back in her life is clearly agreeing with her.'

Bella nodded. 'Do you remember much of him at the time?'

He shook his head. 'No, she was quite mysterious about who she was off to meet. I do remember that. But we were all so young and self-absorbed with our own stuff going on. I'm just pleased she's happy and hope she's having some wild sex with the man. Let's face it, Dermot was always a bit dour.'

Bella couldn't help but chuckle.

'So, what are you going to do about Ben?' Ash wiped his mouth with a napkin and sat back.

'Not a lot. It seems even though he is *here* he is clearly still with Mabel.'

He regarded her for a minute. 'Do you know what?'

Bella shook her head. 'What?'

'At the risk of sounding like an old codger, I have a feeling that things will work out. You and Ben have always had a special connection and nothing will change that. I know you had a lapse there during the teenage years. But there's nothing to stop you from being friends again in the way that you were. If it's meant to be more than that then it will be.'

She sighed. 'You are right. I need to stop focusing on Mabel and just focus on the fact that Ben and I have rediscovered our friendship again.' She shook herself, realising how whiny she sounded. Especially about a bloke.

'Things aren't always as they seem Bella. Look at your Instagram posts. There are quite a few pictures of you with *Dudley Diddley* or whatever he was called.' Bella had previously filled Ash in on the demise of Dudley.

'He is long gone though!' said Bella in horror.

'Yes, but the fact he is still on your page could mean you still have the hots for him.'

'No,' she gasped. 'Not at all.'

'Well, I know that but others might not.'

Bella nodded thoughtfully. 'True. And a friend said something similar to me earlier about not believing everything on social media. And you are right, Ash. Which makes me think I had better delete the pictures of Dudley then! Anyway, sorry to moan about it all. I've bored you for long enough. Tell me about you and your plans for the rest of your time here.'

He leaned forward and rested his elbows on the table. 'Well,' he said. 'I've made a few changes to my schedule and I do need to leave tomorrow as planned. I'd better pop in and see Ben at the distillery before I get on the ferry or he'll never talk to me again.' He grinned. 'I've got meetings in London I need to go to. But I thought I would try and come back up and see you before I go back to Australia? I thought when your mum comes back for your birthday?' His eyes were twinkling then a worried look crossed his face. 'Only if that works for you Bella. I'm just aware that living on the other side of the world means I never get to actually see you on your birthday.'

'I would love that,' said Bella, touched. 'It would be great to see you again before you head back to Australia.' She felt a pang of sadness when she realised that she didn't know when she would see him again after this summer.

As though reading her mind, he reached across and clasped her hand. 'And we will of course need to make a plan for you to come and visit me in Oz. Maybe next year?'

Bella grinned feeling more upbeat than she did when she'd arrived at the restaurant earlier. 'That's a great idea.' It would give her something to focus on and a trip to visit Ash would do her the world of good.

CHAPTER FORTY

Over the next few days, Rosie and Luke were inseparable as they rekindled the passion from their earlier days together. When they weren't in bed, Luke was furiously typing away on his laptop, while Rosie read drafts of his manuscript and made suggestions for changes. Coisty had also settled quite happily into his new routine and didn't seem to mind that there was a new man on the scene who was taking up a lot of Rosie's attention.

Luke had been vague about when exactly he would need to go back to London and so Rosie stopped asking, deciding it was better to make the most of their time together while they could. She had suggested showing him a bit more of the island while he was there and they had managed to do an early morning hike up to Coire Fhionn Lochan, a mountain loch with a white gravel beach. But today, she was taking him round to Blackwaterfoot for a walk and to watch the sun set. She had packed a picnic and told him to bring his swimming stuff, just in case.

'The only problem is that I don't have any swimmers with me. I could skinny dip?' he said suggestively as he dipped his head to kiss her on the nape of her neck.

'You could, but if you do that, I will ditch you and pretend I don't know who the weird naked man in the sea is. I've got my reputation to protect,' she said half-jokingly. Rosie was actually quite glad she hadn't bumped into many of her students this summer. They must have all left the island and gone elsewhere for the summer break. Or perhaps she had just been lucky. But she knew she was glowing and she wouldn't be able to hide her feelings if she did happen to bump into anyone she knew while Luke was with her. 'I'll go and see if Ben has an old pair of shorts you can wear.'

'Not Speedos then?' he said in mock disappointment.

Rosie had given him a withering look and disappeared to find Ben's old board shorts.

When she pulled into the small car park near Shiskine golf club, it was fairly quiet which she felt pleased about. Most tourists and walkers would be on their way back home now or to their rented accommodation.

'We can either walk along to King's Caves first of all? Or swim?' The King's Caves were a series of seafront caves which were formed during an ice age and had views out to sea across the Kilbrannan Sound.

'Walk and then swim?' he suggested.

'Sounds good to me.' She had pointed to the trail ahead and they followed it with Coisty leading the way.

'I bet that's a nice golf course to play,' said Luke, glancing over at the nearby clubhouse.

'Yes, my parents used to play here. They loved it. It was one of their favourite courses.'

'Did you ever try it?'

Rosie nodded. 'Yes. I used to play quite a lot when I was younger; I was actually quite good,' she said shyly. 'And then sometimes when I came over to visit them, I would hit a few balls. But it takes a long time to play a round and I never seemed to have enough time. I was always rushing about trying to be a mum and work and be there for Dermot.'

'And now? Would you take it up again now you have more time?' said Luke.

Rosie shrugged. 'Perhaps,' she said eventually. 'I guess I've never thought about it until now. I do have a set of clubs but it's been yonks since I used them. How about you? That's why you ended up in Scotland in the first place, to play golf. Do you miss it?'

He laughed. 'I know, imagine that! And I have my clubs with me and I haven't touched them since I arrived. Mind you I have been otherwise engaged. But you have some lovely courses here. Maybe one of these days I will play them. You know it kind of saved me when my marriage broke down. I would take myself off to the golf course and play for hours. It gave me some time to think.'

Rosie glanced sideways at him. 'It must have been hard anyway without the other man being your brother.'

He nodded. 'It was a massive shock and felt like the ultimate betrayal. Cindy and I had our problems for a while and neither of us were particularly happy. I just didn't expect her to get together with my brother.'

'Have you been able to forgive him?'

He grimaced. 'I haven't had a proper conversation with him since I found out. He has been so contrite over it and has left voicemails and texts apologising. I know that neither of them set out to hurt me deliberately. But it did. Hugely. And I haven't been able to speak to him since then as I was afraid I might punch him. I know that says more about my male ego.'

'And now?' she said gently. 'How do you feel about it now?'

'They are seemingly happy together. And life is too short to hold grudges. Writing the book has definitely helped as it has made me realise if I want to move on with my life, I will need to forgive them both.'

There was no need to say anything and instead she squeezed his hand.

They walked along the trail which led down to the beach and didn't pass another soul. 'It's so quiet,' said Luke. 'Not that I'm complaining. But where has everyone gone?'

Rosie stopped and stretched her hands out in front of her. 'I made them all go home. Especially for you,' she said jokingly. 'I know you celebs like to have the VIP treatment.'

Luke laughed at her and grabbed her round the waist, planting a kiss on her lips. 'Well, I certainly feel like a very important person these days and that's all down to you.'

* * *

Two hours later, Rosie and Luke had stripped off and were swimming in the clear water marvelling at what a beautiful evening it was. With the stretch of golden sand, and the lapping water it did feel as though they were in their own exotic paradise.

'I will never forget this place,' said Luke. 'Thanks for this, Rosie. It's been such a special day.' He dried himself off with a towel and then sat down on the sand next to Rosie.

She reached for his hand. 'Thank you for reminding me how to smile again,' she said. 'And how to . . .' her voice trailed off as she realised that she was about to say love. Gawd, that was the last thing she needed to do and would truly spoil the moment.

'And?' he said inquisitively.

Fortunately, Coisty chose that moment to start digging and Luke was soon covered in sand.

'I'll just go and get the food from the car,' she said, jumping up and dusting herself down. She was getting a bit cold now that the sun was starting to dip and she pulled on her shorts and a warm hoodie.

'Okay, thanks,' said Luke. 'I'll keep an eye on Coisty and make sure he doesn't disappear down under.'

After collecting the picnic hamper from the car, she walked back to their spot on the beach and saw Luke on his phone. As she got closer, she realised his face looked serious. Rosie felt a sinking feeling in her stomach as he looked up at her and frowned. This did not bode well. When he finally ended the call, he looked at her with despair in his eyes. 'I'm so sorry, Rosie.'

'What,' she said, dropping the picnic bag onto the sand and feeling anxiety start to mount. 'What's happened?'

'It's my agent, Linda. She's been taken into hospital. I need to go and see her as soon as possible.'

Rosie opened her mouth. 'Oh,' was all she could stutter.

'I need to go back to London.'

Rosie didn't need to look at her watch to tell him that he couldn't leave the island tonight as the last ferry had left. Selfishly that meant she had one more night with him before their romantic time together came to an end. Then she felt guilty for even thinking that when his agent was clearly unwell.

He reached out and touched her face tenderly. 'Don't worry, I know I can't go anywhere right now,' he said. 'Let's just make the most of tonight.'

Rosie forced a smile, reminding herself that she had the past amazing week to remember and hold onto. She needed to be grateful for that. But inside she felt as though she was crumbling. She bit back the tears and leant against Luke and let him hold her.

CHAPTER FORTY-ONE

Since arriving back in London, Luke had constantly checked his phone for a message from Rosie. He felt awful that he had left so abruptly. But after receiving that call, he knew he had to go and see Linda. It had been a rash decision though and one that he was starting to regret. By the time he got back, she had been discharged from hospital and didn't appreciate him making such a fuss.

'I'm not dead quite yet,' she had said to him in her droll tone when she had opened her door to find him standing there with a huge bouquet of lilies.

'I was worried about you though. I know how much you underplay things and I wanted to see you for myself. Especially when I heard you were in hospital.'

She rolled her eyes at him and ushered him through the door. 'Coffee?' she said.

Luke watched her as she bustled around her kitchen as though everything was normal. But she did look more fragile than usual despite the brave face she was putting on. When she had called him to tell him she had been diagnosed with breast cancer he had automatically assumed the worst.

'I only called to tell you because I'll be starting treatment and so might not be as readily available as I usually am,' she said sternly. 'It's all okay, Luke, and treatable. I didn't mean to scare you and expect you to take the first flight home.'

'You didn't. Obviously you've been on my mind since you called to tell me. But it was Joyce who called to let me know you were in hospital.' Joyce was one of Linda's clients and also a close friend.

'Well, you know what a drama queen she is. It's no wonder she is so in demand,' said Linda drily.

Luke had then felt a bit foolish for leaving Arran so quickly. He'd clearly been away from city life for too long and it had affected his judgement. Being holed up in front of a computer had made him lose perspective. But he wanted to do the right thing. Linda had been such a support to him over the years and he would never have forgiven himself if something happened to her and he hadn't been there. But he had a longing to be back on Arran with Rosie.

'Tell me, how is the book going?' She raised an eyebrow and then deftly flicked on the coffee machine.

'Good. I am almost there.'

'Almost. What does that mean?'

'Um, that I am nearing the end. Kind of.' Which wasn't entirely false. He had managed to get most of his stories down on paper now and just had some reordering, editing and refining to do, as suggested by Rosie. He knew it wouldn't be long before he had the manuscript ready to share. He just needed a wee bit longer. What had happened to him? He was even thinking like a Scot now. It was clearly the Rosie, Bella and Isobel effect.

'I like what you've sent through to me so far. It has all been very entertaining. And I know the publishers are happy too. Though they might want you to add more spice.'

He looked at her quizzically. 'Spice?'

'Yes. A bit more detail about your earlier sexual exploits. Especially with the higher profile women who were in the public eye at the time. You know? So we can engage the reader and build a bit of mystery and sexual tension to keep them wanting to read on. It will also make a great serialisation for the press too.'

Luke shuddered. He really didn't want to go into detail about any of that stuff. God, that was the last thing he wanted to write about. 'I'm not writing the next *Fifty Shades*,' he said tersely. 'And anyway, a true gentleman never does tell.'

'Pah!' Linda laughed as she placed a coffee in front of him. 'Bollocks. Heaven forbid. I'm just saying be prepared to add in a little more *detail*. In my vast experience they may well ask. Publishers are *obsessed* with it. As are the readers who will be buying it. And if you want it to be serialised — and I'm thinking the *Daily Mail* — then their readers will absolutely want some of the sordid details.'

He took a sip of coffee and decided a swift change of subject was required. He really didn't want to be discussing his sex life with Linda. It didn't feel entirely appropriate. And he didn't want to think about readers wanting salacious details either. 'When does your treatment start? And how are you feeling, Linda?'

She waved her hand dismissively. 'Nice change of topic. It starts next week and I'm fine. Honestly. I was just admitted into hospital as I had an infection. It was a precaution. I'm fine and that's why I pay for expensive private health care. You don't get to my age and not face a few health issues unless you're super lucky. Even Elle Macpherson had her own health cancer scare and she was younger than I am now. I will be absolutely fine. I'm a fit old bird.' She cackled loudly.

Luke didn't like to point out that Linda was now well into her sixties and still smoked like a chimney and drank like a fish. 'That's a good attitude to have,' he said.

'But enough about me. Tell me about you and the Scottish island you've been hiding out on. What I want to know is how on earth you have managed to stay off everyone's radar? Have you just been sharing the place with a few farmers and sheep?'

Luke thought about Arran and how much he loved it. It had been extremely easy to stay off grid there. Although he had never been the type of person to court attention, unlike his brother who had always loved being famous. But over the years Luke had learned that if you quietly got on with things then you could lead a peaceful life. He thought about how tranquil the island was and how much he appreciated the quiet and the lack of sirens which constantly seemed to blare at all hours of the day in London. He thought of the views of the sea, his morning walks along the beach and trudging through the woods with Rosie. Ah, Rosie. And Bella, Isobel and Coisty. He had grown very fond of them all. He missed Beach Cottage, where he felt so relaxed and at home, and his writing routine and the garden at Creel Cottage and morning coffee breaks with Rosie. Most of all he missed Rosie and the way she threw her head back when she laughed. He missed the way she tucked her hair behind her ears and her dry sense of humour. And he thought about the times they had been together and how whenever they had touched, the sensation had sent tingles down his spine.

'Luke' said Linda knowingly. 'Have you got anything to tell me? Because you look as though you are daydreaming about someone rather nice if the huge smile on your face is anything to go by.'

He felt his cheeks redden.

'And you're blushing. Oh. My. God. Luke Giles, in all the years I have known you I don't think I have ever seen you blush. Not once. Tell me right now what is going on? What have you been up to? Are you in love?'

Luke considered his options knowing that he didn't have long to think. He lifted his cup and drank some of the coffee in a bid to buy him a few seconds.

Linda set down her coffee cup and stared at him. 'Luke, tell me more. I am *waiting*.'

Suddenly he felt self-conscious. He wasn't actually ready to share his thoughts and feelings about Rosie with anyone yet. Especially when he hadn't even shared them with her. He needed to talk to Rosie. He needed to tell her how he felt.'

'Luke. What's the big secret? Are you in love? Have you fallen in love over the summer?' Linda's eyes widened in excitement. 'Can you add this into your book? What a wonderful way to finish it off. A spicy romance on a Scottish island. I love it!'

He inwardly groaned and gave her a grim look. 'Sorry to disappoint you Linda, but no, I am not in love. That is unless you can fall in love with a place? In which case yes, I am in love with the island of Arran. It's gorgeous, enchanting and has completely got beneath my skin. And since I've left the place, it is all I can think about. I am obsessed. I am in love.'

Linda regarded him suspiciously for a moment. 'Well, my dear, if you want my advice, I would strongly suggest you get back there as soon as possible and finish the damn book. Especially now that you have seen for yourself that I am very much still alive and kicking.'

Luke was torn. 'But I want to be around in case you need me. That's why I'm here.'

'Pfft,' said Linda scathingly. 'You know I hate any kind of fuss. Though I do appreciate the flowers,' she said hastily. 'But if you want to help me then the best thing you can do is get back to the new love of your life. Because it has been absolutely ages since I've seen you looking this happy.'

Luke grinned and threw his arms around Linda. 'Well, okay, if you insist.'

'I do. I've already got Joyce fussing over me which is enough to tip me over the edge. I don't need both of you. Now skedaddle.'

CHAPTER FORTY-TWO

It had been several days since Luke had left and Rosie was sitting on the sofa at Creel Cottage enjoying a cup of tea. A smirr of rain was falling gently from the pale grey sky. She stared out the window, mesmerised by the way it drifted past like a delicate web of mist. Life had been so crazy lately that it felt good to take a pause and just be alone for a while. Luke actually being here these past couple of weeks had felt like a distant dream and with a pang of sorrow she realised how much she missed him. The morning that he had left she had longed to cling to him and plead with him not to go. Fortunately, she had managed to hold herself together. When she had dropped him at the ferry terminal, she had tried to keep the conversation as light as possible. 'You do know that you need to return for your golf clubs,' she had said, waggling her finger at him.

'Yes, Rosie,' he said. 'That's all I'm coming back for. Just my golf clubs.' He had taken her in his arms and kissed her tenderly. 'I will be back, Rosie. I promise.' She inhaled the scent of his citrus cologne and hoped it would remind her of him. She had already nabbed one of his t-shirts which she had been sleeping in. But she would keep that detail a secret. She had surprised herself at just how intoxicated she had been by him. He had given her a small wave and then turned to disappear into the terminal building. Rosie had composed herself for a few minutes and then decided that going to the distillery for a coffee would be a good distraction. She might even get a glimpse of Ben who had been working back-to-back shifts. She knew she would need to tell him about Luke at some point. However, trying to pin him down was proving tricky. When she had gone in, he was rushed off his feet as usual and it was hardly the time or place to have a deep and meaningful conversation. She quickly drank her coffee and, on her way out, he had rushed over to say bye and said he would call her soon.

Now, she took a moment to admire the garden which was a rainbow of colourful blooms thanks to her persistent work over the summer and she hoped her dad was proudly looking down at what she'd managed to do with it. The cottage felt so quiet with nobody there and she knew she should get used to it. Though she wasn't quite sure she would ever get over the empty nest phase of Ben being away. Coisty was tucked up on the sofa beside her and he quietly barked as he dreamt. She glanced at her watch knowing she should move soon though she was really very comfortable where she was and her eyes started to feel heavy. Before long, Rosie was soon fast asleep.

'Hi, Mum,' said Ben gently, giving her a little shake. Coisty was barking excitedly.

'Oh,' she said in surprise. 'I must have dozed off.'

'I let myself in with the spare key under the mat.'

'Is everything okay?'

He nodded pensively. 'I got the afternoon off at the last minute so I thought I would jump on the bus and come over. I did text you.'

Rosie fished around for her phone which was under a cushion. 'Do you fancy a cuppa?' She stood up and stretched.

'I'll make it for you.'

She followed him into the kitchen watching him curiously. 'How's work been?'

'Full on, but great,' he said. 'Sounds like it's been quite full on here too what with Ash and everything?'

Rosie nodded. 'Yes, I was waiting for the right time to fill you in.'

He smiled. 'It's okay, Bella already has.'

'And how is she?'

'She seems okay about it all and can understand now that she knows.'

Rosie sighed and reached into the cupboard to take out two mugs.

She knew from the way that he was biting his bottom lip, a sure sign of nerves, that something was on his mind. 'Is there something you want to tell me?' she said, trying to keep her voice as level as possible.

'Well, yes, I do have some news for you, Mum, but I'm not sure if you already know.'

'Oh. I'm intrigued now,' she said.

But then she realised that Ben wasn't smiling. In fact, his face was now masked with worry.

'What is it, dear? Is everything okay?' she said, taking her tea from the counter.

Ben leant forward and wrapped his hands around his mug and watched Rosie closely.

She gave him a rueful smile. 'What's wrong, Ben?' *Did he know about Luke?*

'Have you spoken to Dad recently?'

Rosie shook her head. 'Nope. He did try calling me the other day and I phoned him back but it went straight to voicemail. We have been communicating through lawyers. He wants me to sell the cottage so we can divide our assets. I told him to take a hike.'

Ben's eyes widened. 'Seriously?'

'Yes,' said Rosie, 'though none of this is for you to worry about.'

Ben looked at her sideways. 'So, you've not actually spoken to him in person?'

Rosie shook her head wondering what on earth Dermot had been up to now. It wasn't as though things could get any worse. Could they? She really didn't care what he was doing anymore. 'No, why?'

Ben smiled feebly. 'He said he would tell you. He promised.'

'Tell me what?' she said, curious to hear what the big mystery was.

'I'm so sorry, Mum. This is part of the reason I wanted to come home. I knew he wouldn't have the balls to tell you himself. And I've been really worried about you. I thought you would be really upset when you found out.'

'Found out what?' Rosie was now sitting upright on the sofa.

Ben gulped. 'That woman he is now shacked up with is pregnant.'

CHAPTER FORTY-THREE

Bella had woken in the middle of the night, which was unusual for her as she was normally a good sleeper and had adjusted surprisingly quickly to her new accommodation. Her colleagues all worked different shifts in the hotel covering housekeeping and the bar and restaurant so they were rarely, if ever, all in the shared block at the same time. It was the perfect solution for her right now. For a nominal amount of rent, which also covered bills, Wi-Fi and two meals a day, she could easily save the rest of her salary which was higher than it had been at her previous job. She was also grateful that she didn't have to work two jobs and she didn't miss the bar work she'd been doing in Glasgow at all. Ash had been right: things did have a way of working out. She made a mental note to send something to her gran to say thanks. If it hadn't been for her then she wouldn't have heard about the job or even considered it as a possibility.

She reached for her phone and saw that Ben had messaged her.

Hey, hope you're okay? Fancy catching up tomorrow? I've got the day off.

A flicker of guilt had been gnawing at her since the night he had texted her asking for some advice. She hadn't had a chance to talk to him about whatever was on his mind. That was because she was worried he might want girlfriend advice and that was something she didn't really want to help him with. She quickly composed a message and pressed send. *Yes. Definitely* x

As she lay there trying to get back to sleep, her thoughts drifted to the plan to visit Ash in Australia next year. She hadn't yet told her friends from Glasgow the truth about Ash. She wasn't quite sure why but she wanted to keep it to herself for a bit longer. She couldn't face the barrage of questions and judgements and the gossip which would then most likely do the rounds. Then she frowned as she realised that there hadn't been much communication with her friend group at all since she started working on Arran. She had been a bit disappointed with Lily's response when she told her about the new job in Brodick. Lily had pulled a face and asked her why on earth she would want to move to the back of beyond for a job. She had been quite dismissive which had hurt Bella more than she cared to admit. The other girls in the group, she now realised, tended to follow Lily's opinion on things and despite promises to visit, Bella now realised that it was a case of out of sight and out of mind. However, she wasn't going to feel sorry for herself. People had far bigger troubles to bear and perhaps it was time for her to let go and move on. Her mum always told her that people sometimes came into your life for a reason or a season, and that was okay. Which then made her think about Ben and the reason that they had reconnected again after years apart. She was glad she had taken Ash's advice and let the worry about Mabel go. The main thing was that she and Ben were friends. If that was all they could be then that was better than nothing. She also reminded herself that it was easy to romanticise a person who had been living on the opposite side of the world. The reality of him being here on the island and geographically *available* didn't then mean he was guaranteed to fall for her in the same way she had fallen for him. She had to remind herself not to read into anything anymore. She should have learned that lesson with the whole Luke fiasco.

CHAPTER FORTY-FOUR

Luke had left London first thing to drive to Scotland. Having his car with him on Arran would be so much easier. He was glad that he had never bought himself a flashy sports car during a midlife crisis. The last thing he needed was to draw attention to himself. His black hatchback was ideal for this journey, especially as so many people seemed to drive them these days. He could just blend in with everyone else. Being on the island had been a taster of what his life could be like and he had loved it. He couldn't wait to get back to Beach Cottage even if it was only going to be for a few more weeks. The mammoth journey would be worth it.

The journey gave him plenty of time to think, especially when he hit traffic near Birmingham, which had also allowed him a chance to press the record button on his phone as Rosie had suggested. He had managed to remember quite a lot, although when it came down to certain details, he did second-guess himself as he couldn't always remember exact timings and locations and was a bit worried he was confusing some of the escapades. He felt his jaw tighten. He knew there was someone that he *could* talk to, who could make this book a whole lot better. But for that to work he would need to push his male pride aside and Luke realised that until now he hadn't been ready to do that. But this *very* long drive north was giving him plenty of time to reflect. Luke had never been the type to hold a grudge but what had happened with Cindy and his brother had been a particularly hard one to forgive. He reached for his coffee in the cupholder and took a sip. Luke knew he needed to rise above it all if he was going to be able to move on. Hearing Linda's news, and then seeing her, had made him realise just how fragile life was. You just didn't know what lay ahead. He realised he no longer felt anxiety and panic grab at him in the way that he had when he first discovered their affair. For months he felt his stomach twist in anger and betrayal when he thought about them together. But he had to accept that if they wanted to be together then who was he to stand in their way. Not that he had done anyway as they were clearly very much *together*.

Then his thoughts drifted to Rosie. He could actually feel his shoulders dropping and a slow smile spread across his face as he thought about how much he had enjoyed getting to know her the past couple of weeks. Not only was she beautiful and great company, but she had been a tower of strength in helping him power through the book. Especially when she had been dealing with her own marriage woes. It felt like the two of them were kindred spirits and he had Bella to thank for bringing them together again. He couldn't wait to surprise her.

His phone rang, interrupting his thoughts.

'Hello,' he said, without checking the caller ID.

'Aw-right mate,' boomed a voice.

Luke's stomach sank. It was Warren from the golf tournament. *God*, he was the last person Luke wanted to talk to. 'Hi, Warren,' he said flatly. 'How's tricks?'

'Great, mate. Just great. What happened to you then? You pulled a bit of a vanishing trick when I last saw you.'

'What do you mean?' Luke wished he would cut to the chase and get to the point of his call.

'You disappeared when we were playing that game in Scotch land. You were meant to meet me in the bar after.'

Luke rolled his eyes. The man really was a prick.

'Great game of golf, eh?'

And the rest, thought Luke. The man really had no shame and didn't seem one bit bothered that he'd kicked off and caused a scene afterwards which was splashed across the tabloids. Again.

'Anyways, just phoning to see if you can make up a fourball with me and the lads. Mark Wahlberg was supposed to be joining us but has had to drop out. Filming stuff, you know?' His voice was then muffled as he spoke to someone else in the room.

Luke shook his head in disbelief. *Mark Wahlberg*. Yeah right. As if Mark Wahlberg would agree to do anything with this pillock. He laughed as he remembered the word that Rosie and Isobel used to describe Warren. They were right, the man was an utter gobshite.

'Sorry mate, you still there? That was Beckham on the other line.'

'Is that right?' *What a load of bollocks.*

'What do you think then? A week on Monday at Sunningdale?'

'Sorry, mate,' said Luke, who wasn't sorry in the slightest. 'I'm out of town for a while. No idea when I'll be back.' *Never, if I can help it and I will also be blocking your calls in future.*

'Aw, mate. That's a crying shame, that is. We could have done with you to liven up the banter. D'you know what I mean? Banter — you're my decanter.' Warren then cackled heartily down the line, clearly delighted at his ability to rhyme two words together.

Luke rolled his eyes again. He needed to end this call pronto. 'Here's an idea, *mate*. Why don't you try Ally McCoist? I've heard he likes a game of golf and I'm sure his banter will be much better than mine.'

'Ally McCoist?'

'Yes, you know, the football pundit?' said Luke tersely.

There was a silence.

'Sorry, mate, looks like I've hit a spot of bad reception, I can't hear you. Oops, it's gone all quiet. I can't hear you. What's that you're saying? Sorry, I really can't hear you. Bye then.' He ended the call and reminded himself to always check who was phoning before answering. Then he chuckled. He had no idea if Ally McCoist even played golf and hoped he hadn't thrown the guy under the bus. He had been too busy thinking about Rosie and Coisty that it was the first name to enter his head.

Two hours later, he pulled over to a service station to stretch his legs and fill up the car with petrol. As he waited in line for a coffee, he quickly tapped out a message on his phone then deleted it again. He and Rosie had exchanged a few texts since he'd been away. He had let her know he was thinking about her. *A lot.* Should he let her know he was on his way back? Nah, he would just surprise her. He had brought a bottle of champagne from his apartment and planned to stop and buy her some roses at a florist and sweep her off her feet.

When he got back into his car, ready for the next leg of the journey, he took a deep breath and flicked through his contacts until he found his brother's number. Then he hit dial.

* * *

Speaking to Fred had been the best thing he could have done. As well as passing the time on the long drive, it had helped him to have a frank conversation about how they could move on for the sake of their family and his boys. Fred had apologised profusely again and again and this time Luke had listened. Whereas previously he had ignored all of his calls. He hadn't wanted to listen to any explanations or excuses as to why he and Cindy had fallen for each other. It wasn't an easy discussion to have and Luke told Fred that he didn't need to know all the details about their affair. He just hoped that they were both happy and they could all now move on. Fred had been more than willing to help with the information that Luke needed for the book. As they chatted about the good old days and some of their escapades, it almost felt like they'd never fallen out. Then Luke remembered that they had. Although deep down he could forgive his brother he wasn't ever sure that he could forget. The concept of happy family get togethers wasn't one he could ever imagine. It was still early days but at least they were now talking again which was something.

When he arrived at Ardrossan Harbour several hours later to catch the ferry, he realised what all the text messages on his phone were. He'd had several alerts to let him know that the ferry had been delayed due to technical issues and wouldn't set sail for another couple of hours. But Luke just shrugged and joined the queue, turning off his ignition when he parked his car in the designated lane. The sky was streaked with white and pink clouds and the water was as still as a pond. He rubbed a hand over his face and yawned. Then he reached into the backseat and grabbed his laptop. In the meantime, he had plenty to keep him busy.

CHAPTER FORTY-FIVE

Bella woke up and felt a ripple of excitement when she remembered she would be seeing Ben. They had *so much* to catch up on properly rather than their snatched conversations on his breaks and before her shifts started.

He was waiting for her at the Little Rock café and waved as she walked towards him. 'Hey, how are you?'

'Good, thanks,' she said, suddenly feeling a bit nervous. 'Amazed that we finally have the day off together.'

'What do you want to do first?' his eyes lingered on hers.

'Order some food. I'm starving.'

Ben chuckled.

As he studied the menu, she glanced appreciatively over at him. His hair looked casually tousled and he wore a teal t-shirt with his signature shorts.

'Ready to order?' said a smiling waitress, who was clearly also appreciating Ben's good looks as her gaze lingered on him.

Bella felt herself prickle in annoyance. Then checked herself for getting possessive. *What had come over her?*

Ben grinned easily at everyone and was extremely charming. A bit like Luke.

'Have you met your mum's new neighbour?' she asked, in a bid to make conversation.

'Luke?' He shook his head. 'Not properly. Mum said he's been busy writing his book and is away in London for a bit. She said she would introduce him properly when he's back. He's an actor or something?'

'Erm, yes, though not someone obviously famous.' Bella studied his face for any signs of worry or concern. But there were none. She had to assume Rosie hadn't said anything yet and she would leave it for Ben to bring it up with her. The last thing she wanted to do was gossip and create any issues.

'Mum has invited me home for dinner tonight,' he said. 'And you're very welcome to come too. If you want to.'

Bella sighed. 'I'm on the early shift tomorrow and the last bus isn't very late. By the time I get there, I will probably have to leave again.'

'It's fine,' he said casually. 'You know, Mum, she is very laidback. She did say you may be working but to make sure I invited you.'

After a hearty breakfast of rolls with Lorne sausage and coffee, they walked the length of the beach and back before Bella suggested that she show him around the hotel. 'I can show you my place if you want,' she had suggested then worried that was too forward. Why would he want to see her little room?

'Sure,' he said.

The rest of the day had flown by and Bella had given Ben the full tour of the hotel, quickly showed him her room — grateful that there were no knickers lying on the floor — and then, not realising he was so close to her, she had spun round and collided with his chest and felt herself blush as she muttered an apology. He had smelt amazing, like fresh laundry mixed with a gentle scent of woody aftershave.

Both had paused and she wondered if he might kiss her. He was standing so very close to her. Then one of her housemates had arrived home, singing loudly, which had ruined the moment. She had managed to contain herself by quickly suggesting she take him to the spa to show him where she worked. Then she had given him a tour of the hotel grounds with its beautiful, manicured lawns and the benches which were tucked away in corners, surrounded by rose bushes.

Ben had stared in wonder at the setting. 'What an incredible spot,' he said, looking over at the patchwork of hills behind them. 'You know, sometimes we forget that the things we are searching for are right in front of us,' he said, looking at her thoughtfully.

Bella paused, wondering if he had just said what she thought he had. Or whether he was referring to his recent travels. There she went again, reading into things. 'Do you fancy a drink before you head back to your mum's?' she suggested quickly. 'I know a wee bar not far from here, which I think you will love.'

He raised an eyebrow and wiggled it suggestively. 'Sure, lead the way.'

When they were both settled with drinks and sitting on a bench at the beach bar, Ben sighed. 'This is the life, eh? I remember when you showed me pictures of this place; I said it looked like the type of bar I went to in Bali.'

The sky was blue and streaked with pink and white clouds and the water was perfectly still.

Bella took a swig of her beer, wondering if he was thinking about Mabel. 'Yes, I can imagine there are lots of fabulous spots over there. In fact, I saw some of your pictures on Instagram. With some of your friends . . .'

Ben nodded and raked a hand through his hair. 'Yes, we had a lot of good times there. Though I haven't posted any pictures recently?' He looked bemused.

'Oh, I noticed your friend Mabel had tagged you in them,' said Bella casually.

Ben pulled out his phone and quickly looked at his account. 'Ah, right, I'd forgotten about these. They were taken just after Easter. She must have forgotten to post them.' He paused and looked at Bella. 'These are from *way* back.'

Bella kept her response as casual as she could, even though the way Ben was looking at her made her in no doubt that him and Mabel were *not* together. She wanted to punch the air and shout *Ya beauty*. She cleared her throat. 'Oh, I see. And is Mabel still around?'

Ben shook his head vehemently. 'No, she moved on. Thank goodness. It was a bit awkward as she got very full on very quickly. The last I heard she was volunteering with orangutangs in the Borneo Rainforest.'

'Oh,' said Bella, slightly lost for words.

'Do you want to know something,' he said, taking a sip of his drink. 'It was a fun relationship to begin with but when I started texting you, I realised I didn't know much about Mabel in the way I did you.'

Bella realised she was holding her breath.

'I found myself wanting to know about your day and not hers.' He looked intently at her.

She sat back, trying her very best to look casual, although she was fizzing with excitement.

'Hopefully we will have plenty of time to spend together, Bella. Especially now I'm here for the summer at least.'

Bella blushed. 'Hopefully. Anyway,' she added quickly, 'your mum will love having you here for a bit. She is amazing, you know.'

'I know. She has been through a lot. But somehow, she is still as graceful and dignified as ever, despite what my dad did.' He paused. 'That was the thing I wanted to ask your advice on.'

'What?'

He lowered his voice. 'I've been going round and round in circles, wondering whether to tell her or not . . . but my dad's new partner is expecting a baby.'

Bella gasped. 'Oh.'

'I know. That was my reaction when he told me. But I knew he wouldn't have the balls to tell Mum. So, I did. I spoke to her yesterday.'

'Oh, Ben,' she whispered. 'I'm sorry. That can't have been easy.'

'It was actually easier than I thought. She took it fairly well.'

'She's one of the strongest women I know. You should be proud of her.'

Ben looked down at his feet for a moment and she saw him wiping away a tear. His voice was choked with emotion. 'I am. She's my superhero.'

'Oh, Ben . . .' she said, moving closer to him and clasping his hand in hers. They sat together in silence for a few moments. 'Your mum deserves to be happy.'

'I agree. I wonder if she will meet someone.'

Bella froze, not knowing how to reply.

'I hope she does,' he said. 'She is one in a million.'

And just like that, Bella let out a breath of relief. She had a feeling that Ben might be more accepting of Luke than Rosie was anticipating. 'How about you, Ben? Is it weird to think you will have a sibling?'

'Yup, it is. After wanting a brother or sister the whole time I was growing up, to then accepting that I would always be an only child . . . let's just say it will be weird to have a sibling who is twenty-four years younger than me. But it's not the baby's fault. I just need to try and be kind and accepting. At least there are a few months for me to get my head around it all.' There was a small crease of worry on his forehead but then he shrugged his shoulders and smiled at Bella.

She couldn't tear her gaze away from him. What an amazing thing to say. Was Ben too good to be true? She flicked her glance away from him for a moment then realised she could see a ferry in the distance. That was strange. She knew the last ferry from Ardrossan left at six o'clock. Surely it was well after that time. She looked back at Ben who was leaning towards her as though he was about to say something when she suddenly glanced at her watch. It was after nine. The ferry must be *very* late.

Ben then looked at his watch too. 'Shit,' he said, quickly finishing his beer. 'I didn't realise that was the time.' He jumped up off the bench. 'I'd better go if I'm going to catch the bus.'

Bella giggled as she pulled her shoes back on, which she had automatically kicked off when they'd walked on to the sand and picked up her bag. She grabbed his hand again. 'The bus stop isn't far. Come on. Let's go.' Ben clutched her hand tightly as they ran towards the road, panting for breath and laughing. They made it with seconds to spare and Ben kissed her tenderly on the cheek. 'Thank you for a lovely day,' he murmured and looked at her with longing. Bella had an urge to grab him and ask him to stay.

'Are you on or are you off mate?' said the cheery bus driver who was smiling in amusement.

Ben looked at Bella questioningly.

'He's staying here,' she said boldly.

The bus driver grinned, closed the doors and gave them a wee wave as he drove off.

Ben chewed his bottom lip as he looked at her. Then he cupped Bella's face in his hands and gently kissed her on the lips. She didn't hesitate to kiss him back.

CHAPTER FORTY-SIX

'Hi, love, how was your day?' asked Rosie, as Ben came clattering through the front door. He had texted her last night to apologise that he had lost track of time and that he was staying in Brodick and would be back at Creel Cottage later the following day to pick up some things.

'Everything about it was great,' he called from the hallway.

Rosie poked her head out the kitchen door and saw him kicking off his shoes and patting Coisty who was pawing him in excitement.

Rosie stood with her hands on her hips and smiled, waiting for him to elaborate.

'The company, the beach, the bar, everything,' said Ben, walking through and kissing Rosie on the cheek. 'Sorry I didn't make it last night. We lost track of time,' he said, blushing and sitting down at the kitchen table. Coisty immediately sat down on his feet. 'Bella is brilliant, isn't she?'

Rosie could tell Ben thought of her as more than a *mate* by the way his eyes were shining. 'Well, I suppose you have known her forever. But, yes, she is lovely and it's been great to spend a bit more time with her this summer. I'm very fond of her.' She ruffled his hair.

'How's your day been, Mum?'

'Oh, you know, it's been fine. I've just been pottering around and doing some gardening.' Rosie had actually spent most of yesterday cooking and baking so the cupboards and fridge were stocked for Ben. Then she'd had a very brief reunion with Luke as she had been expecting Ben to arrive. 'Are you hungry?' she asked, knowing full well what his answer would be.

He rubbed his stomach. 'I suppose I could eat something,' he said. 'I hope you didn't wait on me coming back before you ate?'

Rosie smiled. She knew, after many years of being on standby and waiting around, that it was best to eat when she was hungry. 'No, I didn't wait.'

Ben looked sheepish. 'Sorry, I feel bad now.'

'It's fine and there is no need,' she said. 'I'm used to living on my own remember, so you have nothing to feel bad about.' Rosie walked over to the stove where she had been keeping his penne with Bolognese sauce warm, knowing when he arrived he would want some lunch. She dished it up and took it over, placing it on the table in front of Ben. Then she got a little dish of parmesan cheese out the fridge.

'Oh, Mum, I have missed this so much,' he said, as he hungrily tucked into the bowl of pasta. Then he liberally added the cheese. 'It's delicious. I forgot what a great cook you are.' He ate another mouthful and chewed for a minute.

Rosie pulled out a chair opposite Ben and regarded him for a minute. 'I don't cook like that every day.'

'Do you get lonely being here in the cottage on your own?' he asked.

'Not with Coisty around. He doesn't leave my side,' said Rosie, looking at Ben guiltily and wondering when she should tell him about Luke.

'I know you like your own company and you've got your friends. I just hate the thought of you being bored or lonely.'

'No chance of that,' said Rosie cheerfully. 'I've had plenty to keep me busy this summer. I don't quite know how I find the time to work normally.' She could feel spots of colour appearing on both cheeks.

Ben nodded as he continued to eat. 'I guess you'll be back at school before long?'

'Next week,' replied Rosie. That was a bit of a thought. 'Anyway, it will be great to have you around for however long you plan to stay,' she said, changing the subject. 'And please don't worry about me. I am just fine. Even with your dad's latest announcement. *Honestly*,' she added reassuringly when Ben gave her a pointed stare, concern in his eyes.

'If you're sure . . . though I was expecting more of a shocked reaction,' he said. 'Those flowers are nice.' He pointed at the vase which was stuffed with roses.

'Thanks, dear,' she said, glancing at them. 'Life moves on, love. And your dad has made his choices. Now it's time for me to make mine and get on with my life.' She gulped and then ticked herself off for feeling guilty. She had nothing to feel bad about it other than keeping Ben in the dark. 'The thing is,' she said slowly as she watched Ben take the last forkful of pasta and put it in his mouth. 'I've actually got some news myself . . .'

Then there was a loud rap at the door. Coisty started to bark.

'Are you expecting someone?' said Ben, raising an eyebrow.

Rosie shook her head. 'Unless it's your dad?' Her heart sank at the thought. 'In fact, does he even know you're here and back in the country?'

Ben shook his head guiltily. 'No, I haven't yet let him know.'

Rosie stood up, she really hoped it wasn't Dermot. She could do without another showdown with him. *Surely Luke wouldn't just show up?* Ben was right behind her as she unlatched the door and opened it.

'Just me,' said Luke grinning.

'Luke,' she said, her voice sharper than she intended. 'How great to see you.' She looked pointedly over at Ben. 'And you'll never guess who else is here too,' she said, watching as realisation dawned on Luke's face that she wasn't alone. 'Ben. He has the day off work. He was meant to come last night but is here today instead.'

'Ben,' Luke said, stepping into the hallway and extending his hand. 'It's so good to finally meet you.' He energetically pumped Ben's hand and then bent down to pat Coisty who was in his element at someone else coming to the door tonight.

'Um, hello there,' said Ben, confused as he looked at Rosie.

'This is Luke, who has been living next door for the summer in Beach Cottage,' explained Rosie.

'Ah, okay,' said Ben, still clearly unsure as to why the next-door neighbour was so friendly with his mum. 'Nice to finally meet you.'

'I was just going to tell you all about Luke,' said Rosie with a small sigh. 'Then the door went.'

'My bad timing,' said Luke earnestly, and he looked at Rosie pointedly, as though to apologise for landing her in it with her son. 'I'll go next door and sort my stuff out and we can catch up later. Really great to meet you, Ben. Hopefully I'll see you again.' He nodded, and then beat a hasty retreat through the front door.

'Come on, let's go through here to the living room and I'll fill you in,' said Rosie.

Ben sat down on the sofa then swung his legs up and got comfortable. He didn't look as annoyed as Rosie expected him to, which was a positive sign. She took a moment to think and then started to tell him about the events of the summer which had brought Luke to Arran. Ben's eyes widened when she told him about the fling that she and Luke had had in Australia many years ago and how Bella had mistakenly assumed Luke was her father.

'Okay,' said Ben, clearly puzzled. 'I was not expecting you to say that at all. I had no idea he was a blast from the past.'

Rosie shook her head and gave him a wry smile. 'I don't think you would want to know what I got up to when I was your age.'

'That is very true.' He shrugged. 'And no wonder Bella was reluctant to tell me how the truth came out about Ash. She said she would save the story for another day. So she knows?'

Rosie nodded. 'Yes, and for that I feel bad. I didn't want her to keep it a secret from you but I felt I needed to tell you myself.'

'But what's the big deal, Mum? You're single and I'm assuming he is single too? Why not have a summer fling?'

Rosie breathed a huge sigh of relief as she realised that she had been worrying unnecessarily. 'I was just worried you'd be hurt. I know how upset you were about your dad and I separating.'

Ben leant forward and clutched his mum's hand. 'Mum, you're an adult and what you do is entirely up to you. Are you happy?'

Rosie smiled. '*Very*. It wasn't at all what I expected to have happened this summer.' Privately she hoped that it was perhaps more than just a summer fling but she would never voice those words aloud. She knew she just had to make the most of it while it lasted.

'Wow, no wonder you weren't too fussed about me staying in Brodick,' he said with a chuckle. 'I thought you would be really upset.'

Rosie didn't reply for a moment, trying to work out how she could diplomatically answer. 'Um, I am happy with whatever you want to do, dear. I'm sure there are more attractions in Brodick than there are here.' She looked at him knowingly.

Ben gave her an amused roll of his eyes. 'True. Any other secrets you want to tell me? It's certainly been quite eventful by the sounds of things?'

'No,' said Rosie, airily. 'Certainly not from me anyway. But watch this space. You just never know what might happen next.'

CHAPTER FORTY-SEVEN

Luke was up early the next morning and went for a run. Now he had been back to London he had returned a little more prepared than he had been when he had first arrived in Kildonan. It looked set to be another beautiful day and he couldn't help but smile as he looked at the sea which was shimmering with the rays of the sun. He had messaged Rosie last night to apologise for the surprise visit. He hoped that he hadn't made things awkward for her and her son.

When he got back to Beach Cottage, he briefly glanced to Creel Cottage but there was no sign of life, although Rosie's car was still there. He knew he would have to wait for her to get in touch with him when she wanted to. She had sent him a quick text last night telling him Ben was staying over. He had a quick shower and had just pulled on a fresh t-shirt and pair of jeans when he heard the doorbell. His heart skipped a beat. He hoped it would be Rosie. Luke opened the door. 'Oh hello,' he said, his face lighting up when he saw Rosie standing there. 'I am so happy to see you but so sorry for putting my foot in it yesterday.' He groaned.

'Good morning,' she said, grinning. 'I hope I've not woken you up but I thought you may like some scones. Fresh out the oven.'

'Fresh scones? Rosie, you are too good to be true.' She was wearing a floaty pink sundress and biting her bottom lip. 'That is so kind. Do you have time to come in? I could make you a coffee?'

Rosie glanced up and nodded. 'I would love that.'

It was warm in Luke's cottage and they walked to the kitchen where she put the scones on the worktop.

'About yesterday and my bad timing,' said Luke. 'Is everything okay with Ben?'

Rosie reached up and kissed him fully on the lips. 'Yes. I was just about to tell him about you when you arrived. It's all been a bit of a whirlwind these past few days.'

Luke reached over and brushed the hair from her eyes. 'In that case, I think we should talk,' he murmured, before kissing her back. 'Grab a seat and I'll make the coffee,' he said, reaching for a blue dish of butter on the counter. 'I'll let you sort the scones.'

'That's a deal,' she said.

Luke poured the coffee into two pottery mugs. 'Shall we go outside?'

Rosie followed him out onto the decking. 'Tell me how Linda was and how was London?' she said, taking a sip of coffee.

'She was much better than expected,' said Luke. 'In fact, she told me to get myself back to Arran as soon as possible to get the book finished. She also said she hadn't seen me looking so relaxed and happy for yonks.'

Rosie smiled shyly at him and he pulled his chair closer to her. He yawned again and clamped a hand over his mouth. 'Sorry. Being back in London has obviously sucked the energy from me. It was a bit of a culture shock. Anyway, how are you doing?' he asked, his eyebrows knitting together. 'Is everything okay with Ben? What brought him back?'

Rosie gave a small laugh. 'Mm, not sure where to even start. It has been quite the week since you left.'

He smiled lazily as he realised he could sit and listen to Rosie talk for ever. 'What's been happening?'

'Well, Ben came to tell me some news.'

Luke leant towards her his face etched with concern. 'And is everything okay?'

'Sorry, Luke,' she said dismissively. 'I feel bad as I was only meaning to drop the scones off. I didn't mean to come over and offload like this.'

'Not at all,' he said, taking a sip of coffee. 'I'm glad you're telling me Rosie. That's what I'm here for. Is everything alright with Ben?'

'Yes, bless him. He came to tell me the news that his dad's new woman is pregnant. My ex was supposed to tell me but, of course, didn't and poor Ben has had to do his dirty work. I think Ben thought I would be devastated. That's why he wanted to come home to see me.'

Luke clattered down his cup on the table. 'Wow. That would have been a bit of a shock.' He looked at her for a moment. 'Yet you don't look devastated,' said Luke gently. 'You look great. In fact, you look beautiful.'

She raised an eyebrow. 'Maybe I'm in denial. But I actually feel fine,' she said, catching her breath. 'Honestly, I just think good luck to them. I don't think he will know what has hit him when he's up in the night and having to change nappies . . . he did none of that when Ben was a baby. So I think he's in for a rude awakening.'

Luke chuckled. 'Still, it would have been nice if he had told you himself. But it sounds like you have moved on emotionally. It's not like you're hanging out for him to come back?'

'Not at all,' she said firmly. 'This summer has been good for me. It's helped me move on and that's all down to my friends.' She shrugged. 'Which includes you, Luke. Thank you.' She leaned across and kissed him. 'It's been nice having you here for the summer. Despite the circumstances . . .'

'I've enjoyed it too,' said Luke with an honest shrug. 'And thanks to you I have my book well and truly underway. And it's been good having some space from London. It's given me some perspective, too, about my marriage.' He paused. 'I called my brother on the drive up here.'

'You did?' said Rosie.

'Yes. It cleared the air. I decided if he and my ex are happy then that's all that matters and you have reminded me that I deserve to move on too.'

'Well,' said Rosie, reaching over to clink her coffee mug against Luke's. 'Here's to moving on from our exes.'

'Cheers,' he said with a wry smile. 'I really did . . . ' his voice faltered and he groaned. 'Sorry Rosie, I'm not so good at this. But I did really miss you when I was away.'

'You did?' she whispered.

Luke gazed at her. 'Yes.'

'Me too,' she said softly. 'I missed you too.'

'I know Ben is back and he should be your priority . . . but I hope we can pick up from where we left off? That's if you have some time?'

Rosie gave him a seductive look. 'I'm sure we'll be able to figure something out. I have a feeling Ben will have *other* plans while he is here rather than just hanging out with me.' She glanced at her watch and quickly drained the rest of her coffee. 'Speaking of which I will have to run. I said I would give him a lift round to Brodick. I won't be long though,' she said and gave him a wink.

He jumped to his feet. 'Thanks for bringing the scones over. Which were delicious by the way. Another one from your mum's recipe book?'

She nodded. 'You remembered about the recipe book? Very smooth,' she said teasingly. 'Let's catch up again soon. Maybe you could come over for dinner?'

He walked her to the door and kissed her on the cheek. 'I'd love that,' he said.

'How about tonight?'

He answered by gathering her in his arms and kissing her. Then when he waved her off, he walked back into the cottage grinning from ear to ear.

CHAPTER FORTY-EIGHT

It was Bella's birthday and her mum and Ash had come back to Arran for the weekend to celebrate. Her gran had already called her first thing to wish her a happy birthday. She and Bill were in Edinburgh for the weekend to see the *Ladyboys of Bangkok*.

'I'm sorry I'm not there with you today,' she said. 'Bill didn't realise the date when he booked the tickets. But I'll come and see you soon, I promise. Sounds like you are going to have a nice time though with your mum and Rosie and Ash. Though tell him he owes me a visit. I haven't seen the boy for years. And your mum said Ben is back too and you're both getting on like a house on fire? That will be nice. He always was a lovely lad, too.'

Bella shuddered to think what her mum had said about her and Ben. Though to be fair, her and Rosie had been fairly well behaved even though they knew she and Ben were spending a lot of time together. She got the impression that her mum hadn't yet told her gran the truth about Ash. Which was fine. She knew she would choose her moment.

'Thanks, Gran. Er, I take it you know what you're off to see then?'

'Aye, it's a cabaret show in a big top. There are wee tables that you sit at and you can get a glass of wine as well. You know how much I love a wee bit of cabaret music and nice glass of red. It should be a lovely afternoon.'

Bella winced. She wasn't sure her gran knew what she'd signed up for. Bella didn't want to throw Bill under the bus either. It was very possible that he didn't know what he had booked either despite the clue being in the title of the show. 'Well enjoy, Gran, and we'll definitely get together soon.'

'Bye, love. I'll let you know how it goes. Ciao for now.'

Bella groaned. *That* update would be interesting. Bella was meeting her mum and Ash at Meadowbank Guesthouse and they were going for brunch. They had plans to meet Rosie and Luke later. Given that it looked set to be a scorcher of a day, she couldn't wait. Ben had promised to call her as soon as he had finished work at the distillery. They hadn't seen each other properly since that night at the beach bar a few days ago. He had been working flat out since and they had only snatched hours here and there between their shifts. However, he had managed to tell her that he now knew about his mum and Luke and he was fine about it. Bella was so relieved. She'd hated knowing when he didn't. It didn't feel right at all. Bella quickly pulled on her shorts and a blue t-shirt and left her hair wavy over her shoulders. Then she sunk her feet into her sandals and grabbed a bag, stuffing a sweater and a brolly in, just in case. This was Scotland, after all, and you never could be too sure.

The sun was shining and she couldn't believe how still the water was as she made her way up the hill towards the guesthouse. Bella was almost tempted to go for a swim. Hopefully they would be able to go for a dip later on. Bella always loved the walk up here as it was so peaceful and had the most amazing view over the bay at Brodick. The name Meadowbank leant itself to a rustic and quaint building that needed lots doing to it. However, Becky's parents had turned their childhood home into an oasis of luxury and her aunt, Amy, had recently had the dilapidated barn in the grounds converted.

The cottage itself was actually quite a substantial blonde sandstone, with an elegant timber staircase leading to a wide hallway and six bedrooms, three of which were ensuite, and a family bathroom. The house was full of character and charm but they'd also added a modern twist. Each of the three guest rooms had white linen and thick duvets and the plumpest pillows with cosy throws in different colours to match the room names: yellow, orange and green. Outside, the garden, lush with colourful blooms and palm trees, thanks to its warming position in the Gulf Stream. Behind was the glen, which led on to a lovely meandering walk through trees and past rivers all the way to Lamlash. She could understand why Ash loved it so much.

As she approached the guesthouse, she spotted her mum and Ash sitting outside on a bench enjoying the sunshine. They were also dressed for the weather with their sunglasses perched on their heads.

'Hey, birthday girl,' said Ash, jumping up and hugging her. 'How are you now that you're a year older?'

'Positively ancient,' she said with a wide smile.

Isobel stepped forward and wrapped her arms around her. 'Happy birthday, darling.'

Bella grinned. 'Thank you, Mum. And thanks for both coming over to be here.'

'Wouldn't miss it for the world,' she said firmly.

Ash nodded in agreement. 'Any excuse to stay here too. It's just so idyllic.'

Isobel nodded. 'I agree. It feels like my birthday and not yours!'

Bella laughed.

'So, we do have gifts,' said Ash. 'But shall we go and find a nice place for breakfast? I'm not going to lie, I'm hungry this morning. It was such an effort having to miss Kirsty's breakfast, especially when I could smell it.'

Isobel hit him playfully. 'Och, away you go. It will do you good to give your digestive system a rest. You're always eating, Ash. It's good to have a bit of a fast. It's all the rage.'

He gave her a pointed stare.

'Let's go,' said Bella, linking arms between them. 'Does anyone want to hear my interesting piece of news?' she said, in a bid to distract them from one of their *discussions*. They had been known to go off at tangents when food became the topic.

They both stopped still in their tracks and stared at her.

'Oh, good gawd,' said Isobel. 'What more? I've had enough interesting news this summer to keep me going for life.'

'Oh, but I'm intrigued now,' said Ash, raising both his eyebrows. 'Do share.'

Bella chuckled as she continued walking towards the village centre. 'All in good time,' she said. 'All in good time. I'll wait until you're sitting down.' Suddenly, their pace quickened and within a few minutes they were sat in the Little Rock café overlooking the water with a prime window seat.

'Right, spill,' said Isobel tersely.

'Well, Gran was on the phone earlier and she was telling me about her plans tonight. Oh, and by the way, Ash, she said you'd better go and see her before you leave the country.'

He nodded. 'Yes, I will make sure that I do. Either before or after your mum tells her the news. Maybe after?'

Bella noticed her mum wince. 'Anyway, Mum, do you know where she's away to tonight?'

'She's off to see a cabaret show at the fringe in Edinburgh.'

'Turns out it's the *Ladyboys of Bangkok*.'

Ash, who had just taken a sip of water, spluttered.

Isobel grinned feebly and sank her head in her hands and Ash's eyes then twinkled with amusement.

Isobel pulled a face. 'It's maybe not a bad thing, you know. Hopefully by the time she has watched it, then *nothing* will surprise her. By the time we tell her about Ash being your dad, then she'll maybe just take it in her stride.'

'Mm, maybe,' said Bella doubtfully, then she stifled a giggle. Soon, the three of them were doubled over, laughing until tears ran down their faces.

* * *

Later that day, Bella was stretched out on a picnic blanket on the beach after sharing a delicious picnic provided by Rosie. Luke and Ash had offered to go and buy some little pots of the local dairy ice-cream and Coisty had trotted after them, hopeful that he might benefit from wherever they were going. Luke and Ash were getting on brilliantly and were like long-lost friends.

'Bit of a bromance going on there,' said Bella with a giggle as they walked off together.

'There certainly is,' said Rosie, fondly watching them go. 'I'm almost expecting them to announce they're off on a mini-break together.'

'You mean a manmoon?' said Isobel, chuckling. 'You were always so good at this.' She reached over and opened up a box of food which had been packed away when they all insisted they'd eaten enough. 'I mean, look at your beautifully cut sandwiches. And your homemade sausage rolls are to die for.'

'Yes, no offence, Mum, but your packed lunches were never the best. It was usually a squashed roll wrapped in tinfoil, with a bruised banana, which I never ate, and a wee carton of warm juice. Bleurgh.'

Isobel grinned. 'Well, you can't be good at everything, can you?' Then she turned to Rosie. 'How are things going then with lover boy?' She nodded towards Luke who was now far enough away not to hear.

Rosie's cheeks reddened. 'Very well,' she said coyly. 'What's even better though is that when I told Ben about it, he was fine and very chilled.'

Isobel smiled. 'That's a relief. What's going to happen when he leaves though? Are you going to do the long-distance thing?'

Rosie shrugged her shoulders. 'We've not yet had *that* chat. I've just decided to make the most of it while he is here. Life's too short to worry, right?'

Bella slumped back on the rug and checked her phone wondering if Ben might have texted her. She wished she could be more like Rosie with her relaxed attitude. There were no messages from him and she couldn't help feeling disappointed.

Then she reminded herself that he wasn't officially her boyfriend so she didn't really have any right to expect anything from him. The main thing to focus on was that she was here with some of her favourite people in the world who had made a huge effort to make her day special. Ash had given her some perfume and money for her travel fund, her mum had bought her the necklace to match her earrings from The Wee Trove and Rosie had gifted her a gorgeous blue handbag. And most importantly, they were together on a beautiful beach in the sunshine. What more could she want? If she saw Ben, that would be the icing on the cake. Bella lay back and dozed in the sunshine, enjoying listening to her mum and Rosie chatter and the sound of the waves gently lapping the shore. A wee while later she felt someone nudging her foot and her mum was whispering in her ear.

'Wake up, love. There's another birthday present just arrived.'

Bella sat up startled and saw a tall figure standing in front of her. She wondered if she was dreaming. The sun was high in the sky and she couldn't quite make out who it was. She rubbed her eyes and stood up.

'Happy birthday, Bella,' said Ben from behind a huge bouquet of flowers. 'Sorry I'm so late. It ended up being busier than expected.'

'Ben!' she said with a gasp. She could now feel herself blush especially as they had an audience on the sands next to them. She flicked her glance to where her mum and Rosie were. They were pretending to be absorbed with their ice-creams, which Luke and Ash must have returned with when she was dozing. Even Coisty was busy digging a huge hole in the sand and was otherwise engaged.

Ben handed her the flowers and then reached down and kissed her gently. His lips lingered for a moment on hers and he gazed at her.

Bella felt her legs turn to jelly. 'Thank you,' she managed to whisper. Then there was a bang. Coisty yelped and Bella jumped, leaning into Ben. He kissed her on the top of her head and held her tightly.

'Oops, sorry about that,' said her mum sheepishly. She then proceeded to fill up champagne flutes with the pale fizz.

A grinning Rosie appeared from behind with a pink cake which she must have kept hidden earlier. 'Happy birthday, Bella,' she said.

Bella felt overwhelmed as she took a step away from Ben and went towards Rosie to hug her. 'Thank you so much, Rosie. Thank you, everyone,' she said, then looking at her mum, Ash and Luke.

Isobel made sure everyone had a glass of something and Bella felt Ben's eyes on her as her mum cleared her throat. 'Here's to a birthday and a year to remember,' she said. 'And thanks to Rosie's secret journal for bringing us all here today.' She paused to allow the ripple of laughter to pass. 'You're wonderful, Bella, and we wish you every happiness. We love you. Happy birthday!' She raised her glass in the air.

Bella felt her eyes well up with tears of joy.

'Cheers,' chorused the group. 'Happy birthday, Bella!' As they started to sing 'Happy Birthday' to her, she felt Ben clasp her hand tightly. She saw Ash looking at her knowingly and he gave her a wink. He was right. Things did have a way of working out as they should. It had been the most memorable summer for so many reasons. It had been a summer of secrets on Arran. But the truths had been transformational. It was a summer she would never forget and today was a birthday she would always cherish.

EPILOGUE

One Year Later

It was a beautiful summer's evening and everyone had gathered together in the garden of Creel Cottage for a barbecue. Isobel glanced around and smiled as she saw the collection of smiling faces and listened to the hubbub of chatter and the peals of laughter from different corners. She had volunteered to be on bar duty and was busily topping up drinks while Ben, living up to the image of a stereotypical man, had insisted that he would keep an eye on the barbecue. Though, given the scent of burning sausages which now permeated the air, and the fact that Bella was standing next to him, it wasn't hard to work out that his attentions were elsewhere.

Rosie's garden looked even better than last year, with its new patio dotted with bright pots of shrubs. She caught a glimpse of Rosie who looked stunning this evening in a green dress. Her blonde hair had grown longer and she pinned it up, some wavy tendrils loose and framing her face. After last year's drama, she had finally come to an agreement with Dermot that she would be keeping Creel Cottage and he could have the Edinburgh flat. Dermot had been in no position to argue.

Isobel was glad he had finally seen sense as she had been extremely tempted to go and visit him in person and give him a piece of her mind.

Rosie was chatting to Bella, who looked lovely in denim shorts and a red vest. She seemed like a different daughter to the worried and anxious girl she had been at the start of last summer. Her hair was pulled back in high ponytail and her face was glowing. Isobel was pleased to see a few familiar faces including Ben's boss, James, who ran the distillery and was here with his girlfriend, Amy. Bella's friend from work, Becky, had come along with her twin brother, Tom, and their parents, Kirsty and Steve, who ran Meadowbank Guesthouse. Edie had even brought Maisie along and the pair were deep in conversation. Then, of course, there was her mother, who everyone seemed to know as Granny Margaret, who was holding court in the corner with her partner, Bill, and his daughter, Beth, and her partner, Callum, and Fergus from the outdoor centre with his fiancée, Amelia.

Earlier, Isobel had had a stern few words with her mother and Margaret had been sworn to secrecy about the details of Rosie's new neighbour.

'Don't you worry, hen,' she said. 'My lips are sealed. I know how to keep schtoom.'

Isobel begged to differ and had thrown her mum a *look*. Although to be fair, her mother had taken the news about Ash in her stride. She claimed she had always known he was Bella's dad. 'She's more like him than you. She's messy and you're tidy, and those waves in her hair don't come from you or me. Our hair is poker straight. And who do you think she inherited her sense of humour from? Aside from me,' she'd said drily.

Had it really been this time last summer that sparked the whole chain of events that brought them all together tonight? She glanced across the garden to Beach Cottage. She knew that Rosie had appreciated the fact that there hadn't been a high turnover of different guests this year although tonight, if she stood on her tip toes, she could see that there were four men standing in the garden. She hoped they would be over to join the party soon given that they were now the official new neighbours.

Luke had quietly bought the cottage as an "investment" when the owners had told him that they were planning to sell. He had been a regular customer this past year and they offered him first dibs on it before it went on the market. His book was now out and his agent, Linda, was doing really well with her treatment and was planning to take a trip to Kildonan later in the year to see what all the fuss was about. Arran was Luke's latest favourite golfing destination and he'd even encouraged Rosie to take the game back up. It was something Dermot had always hated and had unkindly teased her about. Isobel gave a wry smile as she thought about Dermot who had spent the last few months elbow deep in nappies, exhausted from limited sleep and, if what Rosie said was to be believed, was actually more miserable than ever. Ben, being the kind boy he was, had made the effort to see his dad for the sake of his new baby brother. Rosie admitted she almost felt sorry for Dermot. Needless to say, Isobel did not.

Tonight, they had all gathered to say farewell to Bella and Ben who were now off on their own adventure. Having worked on the island for the past year, they had saved enough to now go travelling. They were flying off to Singapore the following day and were then heading to Australia with a lengthy visit to see Ash.

Meanwhile, he had stepped up even more so this past year and was never off the phone to Isobel and, most importantly, Bella. He had insisted that she and Ben visit him while they could as he had his own news to share. He had been offered a position at a university in London and would be moving back to the UK before the end of the year.

Last year's trip to Arran had been full of secrets and she hoped that this year would be a summer of fresh starts.

'Hey there, Isobel,' said Luke, who had appeared in the garden with his sons Scottie and Ralph, over visiting Arran for the first time. They were both tall and good-looking like their father. However, it was the man lingering shyly behind Luke who really caught her eye. He was tall, with dark hair and twinkling brown eyes. He wore navy chinos and a pressed white shirt, which meant he could iron — always a plus in Isobel's eyes. *And* he looked like the type of guy who would be very comfortable on a yacht, manfully fiddling with the sails.

'Hi, boys,' said Isobel, beaming. 'Come on in and make yourself at home. Can I get you a beer?' she said, handing them all a bottle before they had a chance to answer. 'Will you do me a favour and go and see what Ben's doing with those sausages, though, before he turns any more to ash or slips them to Coisty. That's the dog, not the TV pundit.' She gestured towards the barbecue. Then she frowned as she tried to get a better view of Luke's friend. 'Hello, Luke's friend. I'm Isobel. Lovely to meet you.' She firmly nudged Luke to the side.

Luke laughed and gave her a wink. He put a hand on the small of the man's back and ushered him forward. 'This is my mate, John. He's been desperate to come to Arran for ages and finally we've made it happen.'

'Well, hello, John,' she said in the sultriest voice she could manage. 'You are rather lovely, aren't you?'

John blushed and Luke burst out laughing. 'This is Isobel who calls a spade a spade.'

'What?' said Isobel, feigning innocence.

'It's good to meet you,' he said, his voice smooth. 'I have heard a lot about you.'

'From this guy?' she said, gesturing to Luke with a shake of her head. 'I hope it's all good things he's been telling you.'

John nodded and smiled widely. He really did have lovely teeth. Not too white either. 'I'll give you a tenner later for that, Luke. Thanks. Anyway, come on in, John, and make yourself at home.' Isobel turned to reach for her own glass which she had set down on the makeshift bar. She felt in a bit of a tizz. It wasn't often members of the opposite sex had that effect on her. But John *was extremely* dishy. She fanned her face then turned round again. John and Luke had walked over to talk to Bella.

'Isn't this ace?' said Rosie in her ear. 'I mean, where would you rather be, Isobel? Here in the garden with everyone we love or lying on a packed beach in Spain.'

Isobel smiled. 'Indeed. And I know where I would rather be right now, especially with guests like him.' She jerked her thumb over to John.

Rosie giggled. 'What are you like, Isobel? But yes, he is very easy on the eye.'

'Hands off, he's mine,' she barked.

'He's one of Luke's best friends. Will I get him to put in a good word for you?' she said. 'Mind you, he hasn't taken his eyes off you since he arrived, so I think you're in.'

'What was that?' said Isobel, unable to take her eyes off John either.

Rosie laughed. 'Never mind.'

Isobel watched as Rosie wandered over to find Luke and she slipped her hand around his waist. She whispered something in his ear and Luke turned to Isobel and raised his glass in the air, throwing her a wink. Their romance had been a very slow burn process, starting twenty-five years ago in Sydney, and who knows what would happen in the future, but Isobel was delighted to see Rosie looking so happy again. She watched as Rosie clinked a spoon against her glass to make a toast.

'It's great to have you all here tonight,' said her friend, smiling at the small group. 'Thank you so much for coming and for supporting Bella and Ben with this next new adventure. Here's to a summer of fresh starts.'

John looked over at Isobel and smiled shyly. Then lifted his glass as though to say, 'Cheers.'

Isobel gave him a small nod, realising at this very moment, there was nowhere she would rather be. Bella was in a good place, Rosie was like her old self again and that made her happy too. Her mother was clearly very happy with Bill. Could it be that her time had finally come and she might be ready for some fun? Everything was as it should be in her world and reminded her how important the people in her life were and the way in which everyone was inextricably linked. Isobel may have been single for a long time, but she was now ready to put herself first. She was ready to go and *mingle*. She glanced up at John whose gaze was back on her, smiled and made her way towards him.

THE END

ACKNOWLEDGEMENTS

As always, I would like to thank the Choc Lit and Joffe Books team for their wonderful support and encouragement. I'd like to say a huge thanks to Becky Slorach for her input and invaluable advice. I have learned so much from working with you and look forward to what comes next! Thanks also to Jasper Joffe, Kate Ballard, Sarah Bauer, Sasha Alsberg, Tia Davis and proofreader Elane Retford.

Thank you to the very talented book cover designer — Jarmila Taka — for another wonderful cover! I am also hugely grateful to all the ARC reviewers for taking the time to add my books to their list.

I must also say a huge thanks to everyone who has read one of these books! When I wrote the first book set on Arran, I never imagined it would then become a series. It has been an absolute privilege to write every one of these books and I am so grateful for all the lovely feedback people have shared with me both in reviews and in private messages. Although many of the places that feature in this book are the product of my creative imagination, there are loads of places worth visiting on Arran. It will always hold such a special place in my heart, and I'm delighted and grateful that these books have resonated so much with readers. It has been a joy to write five books set there — thank you for supporting me to do so.

I had a lot of fun writing this book and taking a trip down memory lane and revisiting music from my youth! It reminded me of the importance of music and the way in which it can connect us with each other. It brought back a lot of happy memories of times with old and special friends including Nicola, Tricia and Heather. Thanks to my brother Alasdair for taking me to my first ever gig, Wet Wet Wet, at Glasgow Pavilion. And to my parents for encouraging my love of music over the years even though at times it was questionable! Most of all, thanks to Dougie for getting tickets to take me to see Luther Vandross in Glasgow even though it meant stepping well out of your comfort zone!

Once again, my friend Becks Armstrong, deserves a special mention as she gave me some really helpful insights which I will always appreciate. And thanks to Eleonor Kerr for some more musical inspiration.

A special thanks to Dougie, Claudia and Grace for all of your love and support as always. You are my world. And to my furry writing buddy, Molly, who has faithfully sat at my side throughout the series.

THANK YOU

I would like to thank you, the reader, for choosing to read *A Summer of Secrets on Arran*. I hope you enjoyed the story of Rosie and Luke as much as I loved writing it.

The island of Arran has a really special place in my heart, and I hope I have done it justice and inspired you to visit!

If you enjoyed *A Summer of Secrets on Arran*, then please do leave a review on the website where you bought the book. Every review really does help a new author like me.

You can find me on Twitter, Facebook and Instagram (details on the 'About the Author' page next).

Please do get in touch for all the latest news. I look forward to chatting with you.

Huge thanks again, Ellie x

ABOUT THE AUTHOR

Ellie Henderson is the author of the Scottish Romance series, which includes her debut romance, *A Summer Wedding on Arran*, *A Christmas Escape to Arran*, which was in the Amazon Top 100 for several weeks, and *A Christmas Wish on Arran*. *A Summer House on Arran* won the Gold Award in the Romance category of the 2025 Feathered Quill Book Awards.

She has been a writer in residence with Luminate and Erskine Care Homes and Women's Aid East and Midlothian. This work has twice been nominated in the Write to End Violence Against Women Awards. In 2022 she was appointed as the first storyteller-in-residence at the Fringe by the Sea festival in North Berwick, East Lothian.

She is also part of the Scottish Book Trust's Live Literature Author Directory.

You can find Ellie Henderson online:
Facebook: /EllieHendersonBooks
Instagram: @elliehbooks
Twitter: @EllieHbooks

THE CHOC LIT STORY

Established in 2009, Choc Lit is an independent, award-winning publisher dedicated to creating a delicious selection of quality women's fiction.

We have won 18 awards, including Publisher of the Year and the Romantic Novel of the Year, and have been shortlisted for countless others. In 2023, we were shortlisted for Publisher of the Year by the Romantic Novelists' Association.

All our novels are selected by genuine readers. We are proud to publish talented first-time authors, as well as established writers whose books we love introducing to a new generation of readers.

In 2023, we became a Joffe Books company. Best known for publishing a wide range of commercial fiction, Joffe Books has its roots in women's fiction. Today it is one of the largest independent publishers in the UK.

We love to hear from you, so please email us about absolutely anything bookish at choc-lit@joffebooks.com.

If you want to receive free books every Friday and hear about all our new releases, join our mailing list here: www.joffebooks.com/freebooks.